Jake stood there staring at Eve lying just beyond his reach.

He couldn't help but see all the *other* Eves he'd met over the course of the past twenty-four hours.

The battered bride, taking him by surprise in his van and then turning to him with terror and pleading in her eyes...

The sleeping beauty he'd had no choice but to undress—it had been like Pandora opening her box—and inside he'd found her lush femininity wrapped in creamy skin and all tied up in garters and lace...and her long, smooth legs in silky white stockings that he could *feel* wrapped around him....

Hoo boy, how was he supposed to put *that* mischief back in the box? Tell himself he hadn't seen it? Order himself not to remember?

Dear Reader,

What is there to say about a month with a new Nora Roberts title except "Hurry up and get to the store!" *Enchanted* is a mysterious, romantic and utterly irresistible follow-up to THE DONOVAN LEGACY trilogy, which appeared several years ago and is currently being reissued. It's the kind of story only Nora can tell—and boy, will you be glad she did!

The rest of our month is pretty special, too, so pick up a few more books to keep you warm. Try *The Admiral's Bride*, by Suzanne Brockmann, the latest TALL, DARK & DANGEROUS title. These navy SEAL heroes are fast staking claim to readers' hearts all over the world. Read about the last of THE SISTERS WASKOWITZ in Kathleen Creighton's *Eve's Wedding Knight*. You'll love it—and you'll join me in hoping we revisit these fascinating women—and their irresistible heroes—someday. *Rio Grande Wedding* is the latest from multiaward-winning Ruth Wind, a part of her MEN OF THE LAND miniseries, featuring the kind of Southwestern men no self-respecting heroine can resist. Take a look at Vickie Taylor's *Virgin Without a Memory*, a book *you'll* remember for a long time. And finally, welcome Harlequin Historical author Mary McBride to the contemporary romance lineup. *Just One Look* will demand more than just one look from you, and it will have you counting the days until she sets another story in the present day.

And, of course, mark your calendar and come back next month, when Silhouette Intimate Moments will once again bring you six of the most excitingly romantic novels you'll ever find.

Enjoy!

Leslie J. Wainger
Executive Senior Editor

Please address questions and book requests to:
Silhouette Reader Service
U.S.: 3010 Walden Ave., P.O. Box 1325, Buffalo, NY 14269
Canadian: P.O. Box 609, Fort Erie, Ont. L2A 5X3

EVE'S WEDDING KNIGHT

KATHLEEN CREIGHTON

Published by Silhouette Books

America's Publisher of Contemporary Romance

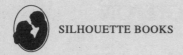 SILHOUETTE BOOKS

ISBN 0-373-07963-X

EVE'S WEDDING KNIGHT

Copyright © 1999 by Kathleen Modrovich

This edition published by arrangement with Harlequin Books S.A.

Visit us at www.romance.net

Printed in U.S.A.

Books by Kathleen Creighton

KATHLEEN CREIGHTON

has roots deep in the California soil but has relocated to South Carolina. As a child, she enjoyed listening to old-timers' tales, and her fascination with the past only deepened as she grew older. Today she says she is interested in everything—art, music, gardening, zoology, anthropology and history, but people are at the top of her list. She also has a lifelong passion for writing, and now combines her two loves in romance novels.

For Ildy,
who is in some ways Eve
and some ways not,
but all ways,
loved.

Prologue

Jake Redfield stood in the early morning fog and watched the uniformed sheriff's deputy stride toward him. Behind him on the banks of the river, other men, some wearing diving gear, were gathered around the shrouded body of a man.

"Fingerprints will have to confirm it," the deputy said as he drew near. "But it's Robey, all right. Everything matches."

"Did he have anything on him?" Redfield asked. *Like a computer disk, maybe?*

The deputy shook his head. "Wallet, several different IDs, a little cash, not much. Sorry…"

Redfield turned without a word and walked back to his car.

Chapter 1

It was true that Mirabella Waskowitz Starr's sister Eve had always been a maverick, and never much of one to stand on ceremony. So naturally it had come as a big surprise to everyone when she decided to get married, for the first time at the ripe age of forty-three, in a traditional church wedding with white satin and all the trimmings.

It was equally natural that Eve herself could see nothing contradictory in this.

"It's tradition," she told Mirabella in a superior tone. Mirabella had just finished buttoning the last of the long row of tiny satin-covered buttons that ran down the back of her sister's bridal gown from nape to coccyx, and was now gazing with exasperation at her reflection in the mirror. "I've never had anything against tradition. Traditions are what hold us together, as a family or as a society." Offsetting the oratorical tone, her lips turned up at the corners in a maddeningly demure smile as she set the pearl pillbox with veil attached at a more jaunty angle atop her short, straw-colored hair. "And I get to pick which traditions I choose to honor."

Mirabella replied with a snort, which caused Eve's eyes to widen as they met hers in the mirror. "Hey—why not? Some traditions are just plain silly. And some are downright insulting. That garter thing? There's just no way in hell I'm doing that. Like I'm going to let Sonny peel it off me in front of everybody while the band plays bumps and grinds, and then hurl it into a pack of rabid male animals like some damn trophy? Tell me you don't think that's a bunch of sexist—"

She turned from the mirror with a swish of her white satin skirts to ask, breathless as a teenager dressing for a dance, "How do I look?" But the sparkle in her eyes and the color in her cheeks said plainly enough that there wasn't anything Mirabella could tell her she didn't already know.

"Gorgeous," Mirabella dutifully supplied anyway. Not grudgingly. Not really.

Of course she thought her sister was beautiful—breathtakingly so. How could she not? Both her sisters—Evie, the oldest, and their baby sister, Summer, who'd just gotten married herself this past summer in a private civil ceremony, were drop-dead gorgeous in the classic tall, tan and blond California tradition. And at five feet one on a good day, Mirabella had had forty-plus years to get used to being the little round *O* between their two willowy letter *l*'s. On a *good* day. Which this, in her sixth month of pregnancy, definitely wasn't. In fact, in the loose-fitting floor-length royal blue gown Eve had chosen for her to wear as co-matron of honor, her greatest fear was that someone would mistake her for a mailbox.

It wasn't the dress or the pregnancy or her lack of stature that was making Mirabella grumpy and out of sorts on what should have been a joyous occasion. Those things had stopped having the ability to influence her happiness and well-being the day she'd fallen in love with Jimmy Joe Starr, the most wonderful man who'd ever been born, and who, miracle of miracles, loved and adored her exactly as she was.

She wished she felt certain her sister was going to be as lucky in her choice of mates. Not that she had anything against her soon-to-be brother-in-law. Nothing she could put a finger on anyway. Just a *feeling*.

Mirabella would admit to herself—and to no one else—that maybe she wasn't being entirely fair. For one thing, the man couldn't help but suffer by comparison to Riley Grogan, the wealthy and prominent—not to mention gorgeous—Charleston attorney Summer had stunned everyone by marrying barely two months ago, in August.

Mirabella hadn't quite forgiven Summer for going to Riley for help during that difficult and scary time, and for being afraid to reveal, even to the closest members of her family, what had been going on in her life. Finding out only afterward just what dire financial straits Summer's no-good compulsive gambler ex-husband, Hal Robey, had left her in when he'd deserted her and their two children had been bad enough. But then to discover how she and the kids had been harassed and threatened—even had their mobile home burned—by mob thugs trying to track down Hal and some stolen financial records, and how Riley had taken them all in, including that menagerie of theirs…

The best thing about it was, a person had only to look at Riley to see that he utterly adored Summer. And, amazingly, he seemed fond of her kids, as well—which really *did* make him a hero in Mirabella's book.

But this fiancé of Evie's… Well, that was another story.

"He's too *slick*," she'd said to Jimmy Joe, the husband she adored. "I don't trust him."

Naturally, Jimmy Joe, who seldom had a bad word to say about anybody, had hedged. "Aw, hell, honey, that's probably just the Las Vegas glitter that's rubbed off on him, is all. He's probably no different from anybody else, once you get to know him. Maybe we all just need to give him a chance."

As if she wouldn't! Just because she was opinionated didn't mean she was unreasonable.

And Jimmy Joe did have a point about Las Vegas, which was where Eve had met the man she was about to marry, while filming a documentary on the Strip's new megacasinos, one of which Sonny Cisneros happened to own. Mirabella wouldn't have thought it possible for anyone to sweep Eve Waskowitz off her feet, but apparently Sonny had managed it, and in short order. In fact, if Eve had gone along with the quickie Vegas ceremony Sonny had wanted, she'd have been married months ago. But before that could happen, Evie had come to Savannah with her production crew to film the arrival of Hurricane Angela and had fallen in love with that city's beautiful squares and historic old churches. Then and there she'd decided, in typical Evie fashion, that nothing else would do; she had to get married in one of them, with all the traditional bells and whistles. According to Evie, Sonny hadn't been at all happy about having to wait for an opening in the church's wedding calendar.

But then, Eve had always had a knack for getting things her way, and with such charm that few even noticed or would have minded if they had. It was just…Evie's way.

Mirabella sighed inwardly and reached up to free her sister's shoulder-length veil where it had snagged on the gown's pearl-and-lace-encrusted bodice. "I mean it," she said gruffly. "You look mah-velous." And couldn't resist adding with a sniff, "You ought to—I imagine the cost of this dress would make a sizable dent in the GNP of some Third World countries."

Deep inside where it didn't show, Eve winced. That was just so typically Mirabella. Why did it never seem to occur to people, even those closest to her, that when they said things like that to her it might actually *hurt?*

Though why should it occur to them, when she went to great lengths to make sure they didn't know?

Now, for example, all she said as she pirouetted back to the mirror for one final check, was, "If it makes you feel any better, all this lace-and-pearl handiwork was probably done in some Third World country sweatshop, so I'm contributing to their economy in my own little way." She glanced at the place on her left wrist that was customarily occupied by an ugly but practical sports-style watch. "What time is it? Do you know?"

"Quarter after," Mirabella said without having to check. "Still got forty-five minutes, so you might as well relax."

"Relax? I can't even sit down in this dress." She drew in a breath for which the dress's tight waist left little room, then abruptly exhaled and asked with a frown, "Where's Summer?"

"Downstairs in the choir room with the kids. Helen was threatening mutiny over her shoes—something about wearing Marvin the Martian sneakers with her flower girl outfit, I believe."

"God love her," Eve murmured in absentminded sympathy. "And Mom and Dad?"

"Probably still at the hotel. Dad's had some sort of bug, and Mom was going to make him take a nap so he'd be up for the reception. They'll be here, but at the last minute, if I know them. Troy and Charly are bringing them. Charly's resting, too."

"Ah." Yes… Charly she'd met at Bella's wedding. The maid of honor. She was the friend from Alabama, married now to Jimmy Joe's older brother, Troy. Also pregnant, about a month ahead of Bella, which would make her…seven months, or thereabouts.

It was getting hard to keep track of all the babies. The thought made her suddenly feel warm and shivery inside.

Sonny had promised her they'd start a family—soon. After they'd had some time together, just the two of them, getting to know one another, he'd said. She knew he was right. All the books said so. But at her age it was hard to be patient. When had she gotten to be forty-three? Had she left it until too late? She couldn't be too old…not yet. Not yet.

As always, when her thoughts wandered into those particular paths, her insides had gone warm and mushy, with pulses pumping in all her feminine places. Hormones, she thought, churned up, ready and eager to make a baby, just lacking one vital ingredient—a little guy with a tail and one missing chromosome.…

Not surprisingly, perhaps, she felt a sudden desire to see the man whose chromosomes she'd chosen to merge with hers. Of course, whether that would quiet her raging hormones or only stir them to greater excitement, she didn't know. Or care. When Evie wanted something, she generally wasted little time wondering about consequences. And right now what she wanted was Sonny—her *man*.…

A small, secretive smile played about her lips as she waltzed in her delicate satin pumps and rustling skirts to the dressing room's one small sofa and retrieved from the untidy pile of clothing, plastic garment bags and makeup and hair supplies the soft-sided portable drink cooler she'd brought with her from her River Street hotel. She was unzipping it when Mirabella came to peek around her arm.

"What's that? What—" Her sister interrupted herself with a small gasp, part scandalized, part envious. "Oh my God—is that what I think it is?"

Eve nodded. For a few moments there was silence as the sisters gazed at the champagne bottle she cradled reverently in her hands. Not just any champagne bottle. This one bore a legendary label and was worth approximately its weight in gold. Eve hefted it and made a smacking noise with her lips. "Bought it at a charity auction. I was saving it for my wedding night, but…" Her lips curved. "I don't feel like waiting that long."

One thing about Bella, she always had been quick on the

uptake. It took her about half a second to figure out it wasn't just the champagne her renegade sister didn't plan on waiting until the wedding night for. She choked and clapped a hand over her mouth and finally came out with "Evie, you can't."

Eve, rooting purposefully around in the pile on the sofa, glanced over her shoulder long enough to inquire, "Why not?"

"Why? *Why?* Because…you, you—"

But Eve had found what she was looking for and turned with a smile of triumph. "Ah—here we are. Now I'm all set." A small silver object hit the floor with a thunk and spun and wobbled to the toe of Mirabella's shoe. "Oops! Would you get that for me? I don't think I can bend over in this dress."

Her sister bent to retrieve the cork puller and handed it over. Her cheeks were flushed, but whether with exertion, embarrassment or anger Eve couldn't begin to guess. With Bella it was sometimes hard to tell the difference. "Are you out of your mind?" Mirabella said in a hoarse, scandalized whisper. "Tradition aside—do you know how long it took me to button you into that dress? And now you want to go and take it off again?" Her voice ended in a squeak of pure outrage.

"Who said anything about taking it off?" Eve said blithely, waving the glasses. Then something occurred to her and she thrust them at her sister. "Here, hold these for me, will you?"

"What are you—you're not going to open that *here?*"

Already wielding the cork puller with practiced ease, Eve looked at her in surprise. "Better here, don't you think, than wait until it's gotten all shook up?" She murmured a soft "Ah…" as the cork gave with an expensive-sounding *pop*. She held the bottle up to her nose, closed her eyes and inhaled a fragrance that instantly filled her mind with visions of Parisian cafés and the hot, dusty vineyards of Provence.

"There now—I'm all set." She turned, brandishing the champagne bottle by its foil-wrapped neck in one hand, the two wineglasses by their stems in the other. "Now, all I need's mah man. Where is he, dahling, do you know?"

That attempt at whimsy was lost on Mirabella, who had an unpredictable sense of humor at the best of times. She flushed furiously and bit out, "The men are supposed to be dressing in the parlor—and by the way, who *are* those guys, anyway? They look more like bodyguards than groomsmen. Anyway, that's across the garden. Follow the walkway that goes alongside the rectory—door's at the far end. And I swear, if you mess up that dress—"

Eve interrupted her sister's scolding with laughter; never had she felt so deliciously *wicked*. "Will you stop worrying about my dress? How do you suppose they got along in olden times, with all those corsets, laces and petticoats? Didn't you ever see the movie, *Tom Jones?*" She waltzed toward the door.

"Eve, you are *impossible!*"

"So I've been told!"

Her exit line was spoiled somewhat by the closed door and the fact that both her hands were full, but she shifted the champagne bottle to the crook of her arm and managed to get herself through the door without spilling or dropping anything. In the dim, empty hallway with the high stone walls of the church soaring around her, she paused to get her bearings.

Best if she bypassed the sanctuary, narthex and front entrance, she supposed. She could hear organ music coming from the sanctuary—the organist was practicing, it sounded like—and from somewhere nearby the sounds of muffled voices, the scuff of footsteps. She turned right, doing her best to tiptoe in her high-heeled shoes and voluminous skirts, laughter and mischief tickling her nose like an incipient sneeze. Even as a child, Eve had taken impish delight in being naughty.

Outside in the garden she paused again. Like most Southern gardens, this one was deeply shaded by huge live oaks and magnolia trees. In the springtime it would be a breathtaking riot of azaleas, rhododendrons and flowering dogwood, but now, in early autumn, it was an Eden of cool, quiet greens. On the other side, through the dark lace of foliage, she could see late-afternoon sun shimmering on the stone walls and leaded windows of the rectory. The air was warm, and alive with the songs of birds. In that pause, in that one brief moment, she thought how happy, how lucky she was and how right she'd been to have chosen this time and this place for her wedding.

It wasn't unusual for Eve to take such moments to reflect on her good fortune. She was a happy person by nature, and besides that, she'd witnessed enough of the world's misfortunes to know how richly she herself had been blessed. First with a safe, if somewhat boring and conventional childhood, followed by a relatively angst-free adolescence, thanks to parents who'd managed somehow to nurture without smothering, during which she'd been allowed—even encouraged—to dream big dreams. And thanks to a career she'd blundered into through roughly equal parts charm, talent, perseverance and luck, she'd had most of those dreams fulfilled. She'd wanted to travel the world, have marvelous adventures... explore oceans and mountaintops, fly an airplane, ride a camel! And she'd done all those things, plus so many more, she couldn't have listed them all if she tried. And now the icing on the cake: just when her biological clock had begun chiming its wake-up call, she'd met the perfect man.

Oh, yes...they were going to make beautiful babies, she and Sonny. How could they not? Not only was her fiancé tall, strong and healthy, handsome as all get-out and rich as Croesus—not that that mattered to Eve, since she'd done quite well in the financial department herself—but he was witty and loaded with charisma. Plus, he treated Eve the way she expected to be treated, which was very well indeed. And he wasn't too bad in the sack, either.

A warm little shiver of anticipation rippled through her as she hiked up the skirts of her bridal gown with one hand and hurried through the garden.

Really—how could she be so lucky? So far, life had been good to her—so good that when restless little doubts and vague uncertainties did creep into her thoughts, she instantly felt guilty and ungrateful, and banished them with almost superstitious assurances to whichever Fates might be listening that she *didn't mean it!* How could she, who had so much to be thankful for? How *dared* she still feel that there must be something…*more?* That something of vital importance was missing from her life—if only she could figure out what it was!

But…there were no such clouds upon her spirits now as she ran lightly down the shaded paths of the lovely old garden that separated the church from the rectory, a bride on her way to a wholly improper and deliciously naughty prenuptial tryst with her groom. She felt sexy and mischievous, and as full of effervescence as the champagne bottle she carried in her hand. Through the live oaks and banks of azaleas she flitted, the skirts of her gown lifting and floating like the wings of a giant butterfly, the promise of laughter on every breath.

The flash of movement on the video monitor caught Special FBI Agent Jake Redfield's attention.

"What's this?" he muttered aloud to himself as he leaned forward to adjust the zoom. A moment later he sat back with a flat "Ah!" of recognition, and although the blushing bride was not the party he was supposed to be watching, for a few moments he allowed himself to track her progress through the church gardens just for the sheer enjoyment of it.

Though it wasn't anything like enjoyment he felt when he thought about the likes of Sonny Cisneros with a woman like that. What was it, he wondered, that made a slimeball like Cisneros so damned attractive to women? Was it the money? The power? Except that this woman—Eve Waskowitz—didn't strike him as the type to be susceptible to any of those things. Or maybe he just didn't want to think so.

Watching her like this—though he was well aware that no one looking at him would ever guess it—made him feel like smiling. Reed slender she was, buoyant as a ballerina but without the dancer's studied grace. There was something artless about her, something wild and carefree, almost spritelike, that made it hard to believe she could be as old as he knew her to be. According to his information, about to turn forty-three. On All Saint's Day, which seemed fitting, in some obscure way.

But what in the hell was the lovely Miss Waskowitz, soon to be Mrs. Cisneros, doing flitting about in the church gardens little more than half an hour before she was scheduled to become the wife of one of the most powerful crime bosses west of the Mississippi? And as much as he'd have liked to indulge his curiosity in regards to that question, Jake doubted it had any relevance to the reason he was spending taxpayers' money sitting in front of a Savannah church in a surveillance van.

He was there for one reason, and that was to keep a watchful eye on Sonny Cisneros. If it was the last thing he ever did, he was going to bring the man and his organization down. Bring them down hard. Bring them down for good. It was more than just a job to him. His superiors knew it, too, and had threatened more than once to take him off the case. An agent who let a case get too personal was no help to the Bureau and a danger to himself—he knew that. The Bureau's patience and his time were both running out—he knew that, too.

He'd had high hopes for Hal Robey. The man had had something on the Cisneros syndicate; there was no doubt about that in Jake's mind at all. Something big enough to send Sonny's thugs after Robey in a very determined way, even to the point of threatening the man's ex-wife and two little kids. When Robey had died before he could hand over his information, Jake had figured he'd reached a dead end. But then, almost immediately thereafter to find out that Cisneros planned to marry Hal Robey's ex-wife's *sister*—no, no, coincidences like that didn't just happen. Not in the real world. Not in Jake's world. If Cisneros was still hanging around that family, there had to be a reason for it. There was something there. All Special Agent Redfield had to do was find out what it was.

At the intersection with the walkway that ran along the side of the rectory building, Eve paused once more. Several of the leaded casement windows were open, and she could hear the murmur of voices issuing forth on the warm autumn breezes. Her heart beat faster as she turned left, tiptoing now, making for the door at the far end.

The voices were directly overhead—men's voices. And was that…? Yes, it was her fiancé's voice. Sonny had such a loud, brassy voice, like a seventies Vegas playboy; she'd know it anywhere. But dammit all, he wasn't alone.

Her lips formed a little pout of disappointment. Why hadn't she foreseen the fact that the two "groomsmen" would be with him? Sergei and Ricky—and Mirabella was quite right, they were Sonny's bodyguards, and why not? Sonny was a wealthy man, and he'd made his money in a dangerous business—nothing illegal, though; Eve was certain of that. Although, to be honest, that little element of danger was part of why she'd been attracted to the casino owner in the first place. Anyway, it stood to reason that such a man would have enemies. That he would protect himself seemed to Eve to be only a matter of good sense.

But what was she going to do about this? She'd have to handle things so as not to embarrass Sonny in front of his men. He tended to be overly sensitive about that sort of macho nonsense, unfortunately. Okay, so nobody was perfect. Anyway, she couldn't just go slithering in, champagne at the ready and sex in her smile. This was going to take some thought....

As she stood there beneath the window, pondering her course of action, the murmur of conversation drifting out over her head began to separate into words and sentences. She paid no heed to the words at first, her mind being full of other things. Until all at once two of them—*just two*— exploded in her consciousness with the reverberating impact of a Chinese gong.

"...Hal Robey."

Hal Robey? Eve's sister Summer's ex-husband, now her *late* husband, the compulsive gambler Hal Robey? But how did Sonny Cisneros, multimillionaire hotel casino owner, know a weasel like Hal? And to speak of him with such venom in his voice?

So loudly and shockingly did those questions and their implications clamor in her mind that she missed the next few words. When her senses once more connected to her brain, she heard, "...dead, Mr. Cisneros." Sergei, with his Russian accent.

Then Rick, sounding like a character in a bad gangster movie. "Yeah, Mr. C—me and Serge, we both saw him go off that bridge. There's no way he coulda lived through that. No way. It was Robey's body they found—hadda be."

And Sonny again, his voice so low and tense, Eve felt herself stretching taller, up on her tiptoes, straining to hear. "The fact remains—the little bastard stole those computer files from me. If he had 'em on him when he went in that river, why weren't they on him when they found his body? Huh? Tell me that. If they had been on him, or in his car, the feds have got 'em and I'm in jail by now. And if he didn't? What'd he do with 'em, huh? I'll tell you what he did with 'em—he stashed 'em somewhere, that's what. Those damn files are sittin' somewhere like a ticking time bomb, just waiting for somebody to stumble over 'em. So where are they? Think about it...think about it....'' After a prolonged and unresponsive silence, there was a disgusted-sounding snort, and then, ''Okay, look—here's what I figure. The little weasel wasn't stupid. If he hid those files, he'd hide 'em someplace he'd be able to get back to without raising suspicions. Call it a gut feeling—I think he stashed 'em with his ex and his kids.''

Sergei's heavy voice interrupted. ''No, boss. Rick and me we searched every inch of that trailer before we torched it. They were not in there, I would swear to it.''

Eve heard a faint whimpering sound and realized to her horror it had come from her own throat.

But now, incredibly, impossibly, there was Sonny's voice again, edgy with annoyance. ''No, no, no—not then. Robey had the files with him when he came back to the States. Hey—he must have. He was ready to deal. And where does he go? Straight to his ex. And what does he do? He leaves a package—a present, he says. For his *kids*.'' He hissed a word so replete with disgust, it made Eve's stomach cringe, then muttered, ''You two choirboys...shoulda just done 'em both and taken the smokin' package while you had the chance.'' Only he didn't use the word ''smokin',' '' but one he'd promised Eve faithfully he'd never use in her presence.

Rick said, ''Don't look at me. I was out cold at the time.''

Sonny's laugh was derisive. ''Yeah—tripped over a cat and took a header down a flight of stairs. I'd been better off if I'da hired the Three Stooges.''

"Maybe it was only a present for his children," Sergei muttered, sounding sullen. "If it was the files in that package, why did she not turn it over to the feds?"

"Because she obviously doesn't have any idea what she's got." And Sonny's voice, though still soft, was pure, cold steel. "It's a damn computer disk—Robey coulda hidden it in just about anything. They just haven't found it yet, is all. It's just sittin' there in that damn fortress—a smokin' time bomb, is what it is." He sounded as if his teeth were grinding together. "Do you know what it's been like the last four months, waitin' for that thing to go off? Here—help me with these studs, will you?"

There was a moment's silence, then Ricky said, "Too bad Robey's ex had to go and marry that damned lawyer—that house of his is like Fort Knox! If it hadn't a'been for that hurricane knockin' out the power, we'd never have got in there."

Sonny snorted. "I figure I'll marry the sister, right? Then I can go in there as a member of the family—make some excuse to visit, you know?—so I can have all the time I need to look for the disk without anybody bein' the wiser. And what does the broad do? She goes and gets it in her head she has to get married in *Savannah,* for God's sake—in a blinkin' *church!*"

Someone—Sergei or Rick, she couldn't tell who—muttered something she couldn't hear. Then Sonny's voice came again, not loud, but tense and with a hard edge of fear. "I've got a *bomb* about to blow up in my face. If it does…if it does, I'm a dead man, you hear me? A goddamn *dead man.* I gotta find it, and I mean find it fast. Before—"

At that moment the two crystal champagne glasses slipped from Eve's nerveless fingers and dropped onto the stone walkway, where they shattered with a horrible, splintering crash.

Chapter 2

Eve never knew how she did it—it wasn't a conscious decision on her part—but the next thing she knew she was running. Running for her life, not even aware of her feet touching the ground.

But running where? She had no idea; hers was a purely instinctive, adrenaline-induced panic flight, like the gazelle's stampede, or the skyward leap of a flushed quail. And with as much real hope of escape.

OhGodohGodohGod…

They couldn't help but see her. All they had to do was look out the window! They would know who it was, know she'd heard. How could they not know? She had nowhere to go, no place to hide, and in that damned white dress she'd stand out like flashing neon. Why was she even bothering to run? They'd chase her down in a minute, and what would she say? What could she possibly say? *"Hey, guys, I didn't hear anything, I swear. I won't tell anybody, honest I won't!"* Yeah, sure.

OhGodohGodohGod...

Then she saw something at the end of the walkway, just past the rectory door. Something in the stone wall that extended between the sanctuary and rectory buildings and enclosed the garden, making of it a peaceful refuge, a world apart from the alley beyond. A gate. A wrought-iron gate that would be chained and padlocked after dark, but which now, in midafternoon with a wedding scheduled, stood open to allow access from the parking areas across the alley.

Hope surged within her as she made for it with a fresh burst of energy, catapulted through it and into the arched breezeway and the alley beyond.

There she halted, quivering with indecision. *Which way? Which way?* Any minute now, they'd be after her. Any minute!

Once again it was instinct that decided for her, pointing her toward the right, the shortest distance to the corner, to the street, to people and cars. *To witnesses.* But as she ran down the alley behind the rectory building, she heard the sound she'd dreaded: running footsteps. And there were no shouts, no alarms, just those rhythmic swishing sounds, like sandpaper on stone, all the more sinister for their stealth.

It was still much too far. She'd never make it to the street before they caught her. Not on this cobbled pavement. Never in a million years....

Just before the rectory wall ended, it jogged inward into a small alcove, with stone steps leading down to a basement entrance. Her heart gave a leap. Would the door be unlocked? What if it wasn't? She'd be trapped down there, cornered. No, no—she couldn't risk it.

No, but in the alcove there was also a trash bin!

Eve didn't have to think twice. The notion hadn't even taken shape in her mind before she had the heavy metal lid lifted up and was hauling herself over the side of the bin, champagne bottle, satin skirts and all. But—oh God—now she was caught on something! Her veil had caught on the edge of the Dumpster, and while she was trying to pull it loose, down came the lid on her head, with enough force to make her see stars.

As she huddled in the darkness, dizzy and a little nauseated from the conk on the head, she could hear her pursuers' footsteps out there in the alley, shuffling around in indecision. And while it was true that neither Sergei nor Rick had ever struck her as being overly endowed in the brains department, surely in another second it was going to occur to one of them that they should split up, one go one way, one go the other. Seconds—that was all she had before someone came running by her hiding place.

What an idiot she'd been! The bin was the first place they'd look! And here she was, like a rat in a trap. The Dumpster hadn't much trash in it; and oh, what she'd have given for a couple of cubic yards of nice, smelly garbage to burrow under!

Half-smothered by her own air-starved lungs, all she could do was listen...praying...rubbing the knot on her head... while a few yards away in the alley, footsteps scraped on cobblestones, coming closer...running hard. Any second now. Any second...

They were running...running...*right on by!*

Was it possible? Was the notion of a bride hiding in a Dumpster simply too ludicrous to occur to those two idiots?

She felt an impulse to laugh, but discovered instead that she was crying. And trembling. Yes, she was, shaking like a leaf and making little whimpering, gasping sounds, just one degree from a humiliating—not to mention dangerous—case of hysterics. Because she wasn't safe yet. Sonny's goons would be back. Of course they would. How could they let her go? They'd have to keep looking until they found her. Until...

The thought made her feel chilled and sick. But she

couldn't lose control now—had to keep her wits, keep calm. *Keep calm, Evie…don't lose it now….*

It was then that it occurred to her that at least part of the cold in the middle of her chest wasn't fear after all, but a bottle of unbelievably expensive vintage French champagne.

For a moment she felt as if the bubbles from the champagne were in her nose, tickling and prickling behind her eyes. She took several quick, shallow breaths, then lifted the open bottle to her lips and drank. She choked a little, spilled a little, coughed and drank some more. The wine prickled her throat and made her eyes water, but the panic seemed less imminent. She drank again, and felt a subtle warmth spread through her chest.

She leaned against a plastic bag filled with foam plastic cups—the trash from a choir practice coffee break, perhaps?—hugging the bottle of champagne against the pearl-encrusted bodice of her wedding dress while shudders coursed through her body. When she felt the urge to cry creeping back she drank champagne until it went away again.

She tried not to think, but her mind insisted on bringing up the question: *Evie, what are you going to do now?*

Mirabella was putting the finishing touches on her makeup when Summer opened the parlor door. "Ah, here you guys are." She came on into the room, closed the door behind her, then did a small double take and said, "Where's Evie?"

Choosing to ignore that for the moment, Mirabella countered instead with, "Who's minding the kids?"

"Riley volunteered to keep an eye on them. Thought I'd see if you needed any help. Guess not—you look fantastic."

"Yeah, right." Mirabella ground her teeth together as she glared at her reflection in the mirror. "I hate…this…dress."

"Really? Gosh," said Summer, "I didn't think they were so bad. I actually kinda like it."

"Why shouldn't you? It makes you look like a Greek goddess. I look like a mailbox."

"Oh, Bella, you do not. You look like a gorgeous pregnant woman. With stunning red hair. Who's gonna notice anything else?" Summer leaned over Mirabella's shoulder to examine her own face for nonexistent flaws. "Mom and Pop here yet?"

Mirabella shook her head and moved aside to give her sister the mirror. "Troy and Charly are bringing them. Do you think it's too early to get the flowers?"

"Probably," Summer murmured absently as she tweaked futilely at strands of sun-streaked blond hair that had already come loose from her French twist hairdo. "Where on earth *is* Evie? She go to the bathroom or something?"

"Not…exactly."

That was all it took; Summer knew their older sibling's penchant for mischief as well as she knew the not-too-subtle nuances of Mirabella's voice. She straightened up like a shot. "Oh no—don't tell me. Oh God, what's Evie up to now?"

Mirabella said darkly, "You do *not* want to know."

"Bella—"

Mirabella sighed. "All I can tell you is, she left here carrying an open bottle of champagne and two glasses."

Eve held the champagne bottle up in front of her face and squinted at it with one eye closed, trying without much success, in the meager light seeping under the lid of the trash bin, to gauge how much was left. And a damn fine wine it was, too, she thought regretfully. Meant for better things. But at least she hadn't wasted any of it on that sonofabitch Sonny Cisneros.

To her dismay, the thought was punctuated by a loud hiccup.

Hiccups! That was all she needed. Sonny's thugs were due back any minute. With that racket, even those two dimwits could hardly fail to find her. She sucked in a breath as deeply as the gown's tight, corsetlike bodice would allow, held it until she saw spots before her eyes, then released it in a rush.

Satisfied that the dangerous impulse had been vanquished, at least for the moment, she slid the wine bottle down along one hip and deliberately shifted her skirts to cover it. No more wine for you, Evie, she said to herself. Not until you've thought this mess through.

She had to *think*. Up until now she'd been operating on instinct, but now that the adrenaline was ebbing, it was occurring to her that, since her instincts apparently hadn't been all that reliable lately, especially where men were concerned, maybe she should try using reason and intelligence.

Okay. So she'd overheard some shocking, extraordinary things. What she had to do now was try and make sense of them.

First, the fact that seemed as incontrovertible as it was unbelievable: Sonny's goons—*her* Sonny!—were the very ones responsible for threatening Summer and her children and setting fire to their mobile home last June, apparently in an effort to flush Summer's ex-husband, Hal Robey, out of hiding. Why? Because Hal had stolen some files from Sonny, files containing something so incriminating they could send Sonny to jail.

Sonny? Jail? But according to Summer, the FBI was certain it was some big crime syndicate that had been looking for Hal. Syndicate…as in *The Mob*. So, if that was true, it had to mean Sonny—*her* Sonny—must be the mobster in question.

No! Impossible! Sure, Sonny owned a casino in Vegas, among other things; good grief, he owned resort hotels and businesses all over the world. But he was supposed to represent the *new* Las Vegas—a strictly legitimate businessman, good clean family entertainment, civic leadership, philanthropy. Sonny, her fiancé…a member of organized crime? No way—impossible!

"…Shoulda just done 'em both…"

She felt cold and clammy all over. Her stomach churned with nausea. Tossing aside her recent vow of temperance, she dragged the champagne bottle out from under her skirts and raised it to her lips with shaking hands. After several deep gulps she felt better—as well as could be expected, considering it had just become abundantly clear to her that the person in big, *big* trouble right now was Summer's big sister Evie.

The first thing on her agenda, she decided as she wiped wine from her mouth and chin with the back of her hand, was to get out of the trash bin. Yes, sir. She was a sitting duck in here. They wouldn't even have to dispose of the body. What she needed to do was get with some people, get to a phone, tell somebody. Like the police.

Yeah, and then what? Jeez, Louise, she had the Mob after her. Her future suddenly seemed very short. What was next for her—the Witness Protection Program?

Tears sprang to her eyes. Hoping to forestall them, she guzzled more wine. Then all at once she burped—loudly. *Oops.* Damn…she must be getting tipsy. Couldn't have that—had to keep her wits about her.

It seemed pretty quiet out there in the alley. Okeydokey, Eve thought, this is it. *Now or never.*

She floundered around for a few moments as she searched for solid footing amid the bags of garbage, but managed to achieve a more or less upright, if crouching position. Then cautiously pushed upward, lifting the lid with one hand while she peeked under the edge. *Aha*—the coast was clear. She lifted one leg, clad in a lacy white stocking, over the edge of the bin.

It had seemed a whole lot easier getting into the bin than

it did getting out. Something to do with adrenaline, probably. And possibly gravity…

That was her last thought before gravity took control of her exit from the Dumpster, as well. The next thing she knew she was flat on her back on the filthy cobblestones with half of her face on fire and her skirts hiked up in a bunch around her hips.

No doubt, she acknowledged as she groaned her way into a sitting position, it would have gone easier on her if she hadn't been holding on to the bottle of champagne. But no way was she letting anything happen to that bottle, nosiree. Not when it had cost her…she'd forgotten how many bucks. But lots. And she didn't intend to waste a drop of it just because she'd been stupid enough to marry a mobster. *Almost* marry a mobster.

Marry! Oh, Lord, she'd forgotten about that. Right this very minute there was a whole bunch of people sitting in there, in that church, who'd come to see her get married! Her family, her film crew, her friends. Sonny's friends and business associates, and—good heavens, were they all mobsters, too?

What was she going to do? She had to tell them something.

She had to find her sisters, that's what. Summer and Mirabella. They'd know what to do.

Yes. Get to the church, Evie. You'll be safe there.

Holding on to the side of the Dumpster, she managed to haul herself painfully to her feet. Oh, Jeez—her hands were scraped, too—and filthy. And she was bleeding! Tiny red polka dots spangled the sleeve and bodice of her wedding dress. Where had *that* come from? She touched her face and winced. She thought, What must I look like? Like I've been mugged, at least.

Never had she felt more stupid, more humiliated or more frightened. Please God, she thought, just let me get to my sisters before anybody sees me. Before Sonny finds me.

She'd almost forgotten about Sonny.

Back down the alley she crept, making almost no sound in her stockinged feet. Just before she reached the arched breezeway, she froze in a comical, teetering half crouch. Voices! Yes, definitely Sonny's voice. And Sergei and Rick's, too. Mumbling, so she couldn't make out what they were saying.

But then suddenly, and very distinctly, Sonny was saying, "Where's she gonna go? She's wearin' a wedding dress, for God's sake!" There was some more mumbling from one of the two stooges, then Sonny again. "I'm tellin' you, she's got no keys, no purse, nothin'. Her whole family's in there. I'm tellin' you, that's where she's gonna go. You two get those entrances covered. If any of her family even looks like they wanna leave, you tell me, and then you tail 'em, you got me? Now go!"

"What're you gonna do, boss?"

"Whadaya mean, what am I gonna do? I'm gonna go find the damn preacher, that's what. Hey—I don't know a thing, right? I'm here to get married, so I'm gonna go get married. What do I know?" He muttered angrily to himself under his breath, then said in a bitter tone, "My bride doesn't show up, I'm gonna look like a chump. In front of the whole world I'm gonna look like a blinkin' *chump....*" His voice faded, still mumbling, into the distance.

Eve slumped against the stone wall of the rectory and let out her breath. Boy, was Sonny ticked off. His ego was bruised. What could be worse for a man like Sonny than looking like a fool? He was never going to forgive her for this—never.

What was she saying? *Forgive her?* At the very least, it seemed to her, he was going to have to kill her. Or have her killed, more likely; murder didn't seem like the sort of thing Sonny Cisneros would actually indulge in himself.

But first he'd have to catch her.

Except...like Sonny had just said, where was she gonna go? Cut off from her family, with no purse, no car keys, no shoes, wearing a filthy dirty wedding dress, battered, bleeding and reeking of garbage?

For once in her life, Eve had no idea what to do.

This time, when, after a discreet knock, the parlor door opened a crack, it was the minister who poked his head through. Reverend Booker was a brisk, balding man with a no-nonsense manner more typical of a CEO than a man of God. Mirabella wholeheartedly approved of him.

"How're you ladies doin'?" he inquired now in his soft Savannah accent, after a quick, sweeping glance around the room.

"Fine!" stated Mirabella, before Summer could open her mouth and blurt out the obvious.

The obvious had not escaped Reverend Booker, who raised his eyebrows and said mildly, "It appears we are missin' a bride."

Again Mirabella jumped in and rolled right over her sister's stammering attempt at an explanation. "She just stepped out for a minute. She'll be right back."

"Well, okay, then." The minister looked at his watch, then double-checked it against the clock on the mantelpiece. "We're gonna want to have the bride and her party out front in the narthex at about ten minutes till. Miz Phillips is gonna meet you out there, get you all lined up and squared away, just like we did at rehearsal." Mrs. Phillips was the wedding coordinator, an almost frighteningly efficient woman of whom Mirabella also approved. "That's about it," said Reverend Booker cheerfully as he backed out of the room. "Now, I guess I'd bettah go and round up my groom."

Mirabella's stomach did a flip-flop and she threw Summer a look of appeal. How unbelievably embarrassing it would be if the minister, of all people, were to walk in on...whatever it was Evie was doing with her fiancé over there in the rectory!

But she was saved from having to think of an excuse to detain the man longer. No sooner had he finished his statement than his face brightened and he said, "I guess I don't have to."

And there was the groom himself, coming up behind Reverend Booker in the parlor doorway, smiling and showing every one of his pearly whites—caps, in Mirabella's opinion; like everything else about her sister's fiancé, those teeth were just too perfect to be real.

Swallowing whatever it was she was going to say, she instead gasped, "Sonny!" And dammit, she was going to blush; she could feel it coming on. How could she not? He could smile all he wanted to, like butter wouldn't melt in his mouth, as Granny Calhoun would say, but anybody could see the man was a lot more flushed and sweaty and disheveled than any decent groom ought to be—at least *before* the ceremony. He looked, in fact, like a man who'd just been doing…whatever he'd been doing with Evie over there in that rectory room. Mirabella gave a mental shudder and drew a curtain across the picture in her mind.

Sonny stuck his head past the minister's shoulder, looked around the room and then asked, "Where's my bride? Oh—" he snapped his fingers "—the groom's not supposed to see the bride in her wedding dress, right? So—she hiding, or something?"

Mirabella and Summer looked at each other. Summer opened her mouth, then closed it again. Mirabella moved a little closer to Sonny and muttered in a voice low enough she hoped the reverend wouldn't be able to hear, "Uh…you haven't seen her?"

Sonny laughed and held up both hands. "Hey—even I know it's bad luck for the groom to see the bride before the ceremony." As the reverend was hustling him out of the room he made a pretend pistol out of his hand and "fired" it at them.

After the door had closed behind the two men, Mirabella and Summer looked at each other again. Summer collapsed onto the sofa, unmindful of the piles of clothing and other debris, closed her eyes and groaned, "Oh, Evie..."

"He's lying," said Mirabella huffily. "Of course he is."

"Yeah..." After a moment Summer opened her eyes and met Mirabella's. "Then why isn't she back yet? Where is she?"

Mirabella snorted. "This is Evie, remember. God only knows. And doing what, I shudder to think!"

Eve had come up with a plan. There was only one way out of the mess she was in. She was going to have to hot-wire a car.

But not to steal it—oh, heavens no. She was only going to *borrow* it, just long enough to get away and get help. She planned to give it back to its owner as soon as she possibly could, she really did—along with a nice letter of apology and a check. Well, maybe not a check—cash would probably be more prudent, under the circumstances. So that would make it all right, wouldn't it? Sure it would. She didn't see how anybody could put her in jail for that, especially once they knew she'd really had no other choice.

But first she had to find a car to hot-wire.

Didn't anybody leave their cars unlocked anymore? She'd already been up and down the side street without success— and don't think it was easy, creeping around in broad daylight wearing a filthy wedding dress *and* lugging around a bottle of vintage champagne. Most of which, admittedly, was inside Evie.

What now? Did she dare venture out into the square? There was a no-parking zone directly in front of the church, she knew, but from where she lurked, well-camouflaged behind some sort of sports utility vehicle and a large magnolia tree, she could see cars parked along the square itself, including a van with an official-looking logo on the door. Some sort of utility company, probably; it had orange cones set out fore and aft. Working on the lines somewhere in the area, she assumed, although she'd been standing here for several minutes now, and hadn't seen any signs of work activity.

As she stood contemplating the van and its implications, her attention was diverted by a car—a late-model Jeep Cherokee—as it cruised slowly past the side street and her hiding place and eased to a stop in the passenger-loading zone at the foot of the church steps. Her heart gave a leap of hope as the driver's side door opened and a man got out. She knew him at once, both by his unmistakable military bearing and the way the late-afternoon sun glinted on his all-American-boy handsome dark blond head. It was Troy, Mirabella's ex-navy SEAL brother-in-law, and if anybody could help Eve out of the jam she was in, it seemed to her, an ex-SEAL looked like a good bet.

She moved cautiously toward the corner, still keeping under cover behind the parked cars, while Troy hurried around to open both passenger doors and bent solicitously to assist his very pregnant wife, Charly, from the car. Charly had practically become a fourth Waskowitz sister since she'd come out from California to be maid of honor at Mirabella's wedding and wound up falling in love and marrying Jimmy Joe's brother and best man.

Meanwhile, an older but still slim and youthful-looking woman was climbing out of the back seat unassisted, followed closely by a barrel-chested man with rusty gray hair—hair that had once been as red as Mirabella's. It was—oh God, it was her mom and dad, Pop and Ginger Waskowitz, come all the way from Pensacola to see their oldest daughter finally married, after they'd all but given up hope.

And seeing them, Eve gave a sharp little cry, which she

quickly smothered with her hand. Her emotions had sneaked up on her, taken her by surprise. It had been a very long time since she'd felt that particular relief and gladness—the un-adulterated joy a lost child knows when she spots her parents in the crowd.

But even as she surged forward to greet them, forgetting caution, a furtive movement caught at the fringes of her vi-sion and sent her shrinking back behind one of the ubiquitous magnolia trees that line the sidewalks all over Savannah. Up at the top of the steps near the arched main doors of the church, a man dressed in a tuxedo had stepped forward out of the shadows.

Sergei! And he was looking intently up and down the street, obviously looking for someone. Looking for *her!*

With a little whimper, Eve slumped to the ground and leaned her back against the door of a Volvo station wagon. *So near, and yet so far...* A weepy lump of self-pity began to swell at the back of her throat, so she hurriedly swallowed it down with champagne. And winced—evidently on top of everything else, she'd bumped her lip during her ungraceful exit from the Dumpster. It had been numb before, but now it was beginning to throb.

What was she going to do now? That van had been her best hope for a hiding place, it seemed to her, but with old eagle-eye Sergei up there watching the street, she'd never make it across to the square without being spotted. She'd have to wait until he went inside for the ceremony.

But wait...what ceremony? There wasn't going to be a ceremony. At some point that fact was going to be acknowl-edged and announced. As soon as that happened, Sonny and every single one of his "business associates" were going to come swarming out of that church with but one goal in mind—to find Evie!

She was running out of time. If she was ever going to make her escape, it had better be *now*.

It took some effort, but she managed to push herself into a crouching position from which to peer around the Volvo's front fender. And what she saw taking place now up on the church steps once again sent the roller coaster of her emotions rocketing into the stratosphere.

It seemed that Sergei had been summoned to perform his duties as usher. Although clearly not happy about being forced to abandon his vigil, judging from the way he kept twisting and turning and trying to look back over his shoulder, he had nevertheless been called upon by someone in authority—probably that dragon of a wedding coordinator—to escort the mother of the bride to her seat of honor.

Tradition to the rescue!

It was Eve's moment, and she wasted no time in taking advantage of it. In a flash she was out from behind the row of parked cars, sprinting barefooted down the middle of the side street to the corner, then across to the square. Crouched behind the car that was parked just behind the van, she took a moment to catch her breath while her mind careened wildly through the obstacle course of her options and possibilities. Which by this time, admittedly, could be classified as DWI.

Which probably explained why she arrived at the conclusion that the van was God's answer to her prayers. Such a nice big van, the kind with double doors that opened in the back. All she had to do, it seemed to her, was open those doors, get inside that van and close them up after her, and she'd be safe. The best part of it was, she wouldn't have to commit grand theft auto after all. Unless the doors were locked, and then maybe just a wee bit of breaking and entering... Hey—what was a little thing like a locked door to Evie Waskowitz? Piece a'cake.

First, though, just a little bit more champagne to bolster her courage...oops—all gone. *C'est la guerre.*

Her determination freshly primed, Eve tucked the empty bottle under her arm like a swagger stick, marched up to the rear of the van and took firm hold of the handle.

Chapter 3

Jake could not believe his eyes. What was this? What in the hell was going on?

First, Cisneros and a couple of his goons come running around the corner from the back alley, looking like kids with their pockets full of money and they'd just missed the ice cream truck. They look around all over the place for a while, up and down the street, then back they go.

A few minutes later, one of 'em takes up a position at the front door, and tuxedo or no, the guy looks more like a bouncer at a biker bar than an usher at a wedding. Now here comes the bride herself, creeping up and down the street, hiding behind parked cars, looking in all the windows, like, if he didn't know how crazy it was, he'd swear she's looking to boost one.

Then the minute Cisneros's goon turns his back, she's hot-footing it across the street, looking like she's got every intention of climbing into his van! What the hell was going on?

And what in the hell was he going to do about the woman out there right now, tugging and rattling his door handle? This wasn't exactly a situation covered in the procedure manuals—not that Jake normally paid much attention to things like that—and there wasn't anybody he could consult, as his partner, Burdell "Birdie" Poole, had gone for coffee about half an hour ago. Not that Jake would have heeded Birdie's advice in a situation like this anyway. This was strictly his call.

Something was about to fall into his lap—he could feel it. And Jake wasn't one to let such an opportunity pass him by.

He peeled off his headset and dropped it beside the bank of monitors, then rose to his feet and moved stealthily to the back door of the van. For a moment or two he listened to the ambiguously furtive sounds coming from the other side of the door. Then he took hold of the inside handle and gave it a turn.

He heard a little grunt of surprise and an exclamation of satisfaction as the door flew outward, and then had to dodge backward as the bride came lurching through the opening. An instant later, though, she froze, poised half-in and half-out of the van, resembling nothing so much, in her voluminous white skirts, as a large, extremely agitated swan.

"Yikes!" she exclaimed under her breath, and then, as her eyes traveled upward from the scuffed tips of Jake's cap-toe oxfords, along the nonexistent creases of his charcoal-gray cotton coveralls, added a chagrinned and breathy "Busted."

To his surprise, Jake found his customary dour demeanor being tested as it had not been in a very long time. Even maintaining a standard Bureau deadpan took every ounce of his will, as he responded with mild sarcasm, "Not at all. Would you like to come in? Do you need a hand?"

But she was already inside the van, straightening up and looking around—and he got a good clear look at her for the first time. My God, he thought, jolted in a way he'd no longer believed himself capable of. My God. What the hell was going on here?

Her face was scraped across one cheekbone and down the side of her face all the way to the jaw; she had a cut over one eye and another smaller one on the bridge of her nose; and either a very lopsided mouth or one helluva fat lip. He was about to say something, ask her what had happened to her, when he noticed the champagne bottle tucked under one arm. That and the bleary way she was looking around her seemed to him to offer one explanation—maybe even an obvious one—but somehow he didn't think it was the right one. Somehow it didn't fit.

She moved slowly past him, her mouth opening in silent awe as she took in the video monitors, the computer, the whole array of state-of-the-art electronic surveillance equipment. Then she rounded on him and exclaimed, "This is a surveillance van!" She leaned forward, eyes narrowed accusingly. "Who are you surveill-llin—watching? Hmm?" And she waited for his answer, breasts heaving and eyes shooting dark fire.

Even given her battered condition it was a potent combination, and possibly one reason why it took Jake a beat longer than it should have to become aware of the particular…aura she'd brought into the van with her. Once noticed, though, it was hard to ignore the unmistakable aroma of ripening garbage. And he saw now a few other things he'd missed in his preoccupation with the condition of her face: blood spatters, as well as a good many unidentifiable stains and smears on the white satin wedding dress, and something in her hair that looked very much like coffee grounds.

Though completely mystified as to what could possibly have happened that would explain the woman's condition, still he began to feel deep within himself the stirrings of a strange excitement. Treading carefully, he ventured,

"Ma'am, would you like to…sit down? I think you've had quite a bit to drink—"

"I've had a whole bottle of champagne to drink," she readily acknowledged, looking mysteriously pleased with herself, and the almost feline satisfaction in her smile sparked unexpected responses in the bottom of Jake's belly. Then, before he could even wonder about that, she was stern and serious again. "However, I am *drunk,* not *unconscious.* This is—these are—video monitors. I'm a TV producer. You think I don't know a video monitor when I see one? Listen, buster—"

She gave a soft gasp, then, and crouched down for a closer look at the monitor in question, which at the moment was displaying a fairly wide-angle shot of the front of the church, where a number of people were just emerging through the high-arched, ornately carved double door entrance. Jake reached past her to the remote controls. The grim little knot of men surrounding Sonny Cisneros grew larger. Jake zoomed in tighter still, until Sonny's face all but filled the screen, until he seemed to be looking right into the camera, right into the eyes of the woman who watched on the monitor screen with the frozen fascination of a bird in the thrall of a snake.

Without taking her eyes from the screen, she took a step backward, then another. Which was as far as she could go before her back was smack up against Jake's chest. He could feel the moist heat of her body, hear the rapid, rhythmic whisper of her breathing. Her blond hair, short and tousled as a small boy's, was just about on a level with his lips, and even through the overriding stench of champagne and garbage he caught a mouth-watering whiff of strawberries. He didn't think about putting his hands on her shoulders—didn't even know he had until he felt the crusty texture of lace and pearls beneath his palms. He snatched them away just as she turned, her face chalk-white behind her scrapes and bruises, her eyes enormous and the dark slate-blue of rain clouds.

"Why're you spying on my wedding?" she demanded in a slurred, airless voice. Her hand clutched at the front of Jake's uniform, gathering in a handful of it. "Who are you? Who're you watching—Sonny? *Are you?* Tell me, damn you!" Her breath caught and her hand tightened, twisting in the cotton fabric. "Who—are—you? It's important—I need…to know!"

She was close to losing it. Jake held up his hand—one finger—in front of her taut, battered face, with that simple gesture capturing her attention and pulling her eyes to his. Once he had them, he held them with the sheer force of his will and—tricks he'd learned in interrogation training—focused all his energy into bringing her into *his* plane…*his* sphere…*his* calm.

Only when her breathing had slowed and quieted, unconsciously timing itself to his rhythms, did he answer her. "FBI, ma'am. Special Agent Jake Redfield—"

He hadn't expected her to burst into tears.

Although it was hard to be sure that's what she was doing, at first. She kept sobbing, "Thank God, thank God."

And then she got the hiccups.

Mirabella was pacing furiously on the white runner down the center aisle of the church sanctuary, where the entire Waskowitz family had gathered in stunned indecision.

"I can't believe she did this," she kept muttering, while fear jumped and fluttered beneath her rib cage. "I can *not* believe it. This is too much—even for Eve. Just too much. This time she's gone too far."

"I can't believe it, either," Summer retorted from the front pew, where she was attempting to console the disappointed flower girl, her five-year-old daughter Helen. "That's the whole *point.* She wouldn't do this. She *wouldn't.*"

"Oh, yeah, right," Mirabella snorted, hoping to convince herself as much as anyone. "Have you forgotten about high school graduation?"

"That was different! We all knew she thought the whole thing was pointless and stupid! But this was her *wedding*. She was happy about it. Excited. Why would she—" She choked off something that sounded dangerously like a sob, which prompted her nine-year-old son, David, standing in the pew behind her, to throw his arms around her neck in mute and helpless sympathy.

"*Why?* Why does Eve do *anything?*" Mirabella raged, waving her arms. She was gently corralled by her husband, Jimmy Joe, probably the only person there who understood that the angrier she sounded, the more frightened it meant she was.

"Something's happened to her," Pop Waskowitz rumbled. "Had to." Beside him, his wife, Ginger, silently squeezed his hand.

Across the aisle, Charly cleared her throat and said in her dry Alabama drawl, "Anybody thinkin' about callin' the police?"

Her husband, Troy, leaning against the end of the pew at her elbow, shook his head. "That's probably a little premature. What're you gonna tell 'em? I doubt she's the first bride who ever got cold feet and decided not to show up for her own wedding."

"Sonny and his friends are out looking for her," Ginger Waskowitz offered in a hopeful tone. "Maybe we should wait and see…" Her voice trailed off.

"When's the last time anybody saw her?" Troy's eyes went from person to person, asking each one the question.

Summer met Mirabella's eyes and opened her mouth, then snapped it shut again at her sharp sound of warning.

Which, of course, Jimmy Joe didn't miss. "Marybell?" he prompted gently, as all eyes turned her way.

Mirabella fought it for a second or two, drew a reluctant breath and muttered, "Okay, this is really embarrassing. The last I saw her, she had a bottle of champagne and a couple of glasses and was going to the rectory to find Sonny."

"But," Summer quickly put in, "according to him, she never got there. He hasn't seen her, either."

That revelation was met with stunned silence, except for the rhythmic sound of footsteps. All heads turned to follow the elegant figure coming toward them down the long center aisle.

"One of Sonny's men found this on the walk beside the rectory," Summer's husband, Riley, said quietly, showing them what he held, nested in the folds of a pristine white handkerchief. Shards of broken crystal. "Could be champagne glasses."

Someone—Ginger—uttered a small, stricken cry. Her husband, who had once been a chief of police, rose slowly to his feet as Riley carefully rewrapped the glass shards, then put a hand on Summer's shoulder and gave it a gentle squeeze.

"I've put in a call to Jake Redfield," Riley said in a low voice, meant for his wife's ears. "He wasn't there—out on assignment, they said. I left my beeper number." Summer swallowed, nodded gratefully and put her hand over his.

"Jake Redfield?" Mirabella said sharply. "Where have I heard that? I know I've—who's Jake Redfield?"

Summer and her husband exchanged a look. "Someone we know," she said in a shaken voice, "with the FBI."

"Oh, God," her mother whispered.

Jake was on the phone to his Bureau office, which happened to be located only a few blocks away from the church in downtown Savannah. He, however, was going in the opposite direction, heading southwest on Abercorn as fast as he could go without risking official attention, a course of action he knew was not apt to make either his partner or his superiors happy. He was, in fact, at that very moment holding the phone some distance from his ear in an attempt to lessen the impact of the irate voice on the other end. But Jake had a considerable amount of experience in getting yelled at and had a pretty good ear for when he was nearing the limits of someone's patience. Right now he was confident he was nowhere near the red zone.

"Get her in here," the distant voice of his supervisor, Don Coffee, was bellowing in tinny impotence. "Right now! You hear me, Agent Redfield? *Now*."

Jake waited for a break, then calmly drawled, "That's… not a good idea, Don. At the moment she's in no shape to talk to anybody. I'm gonna need to get her cleaned up and—" he flicked a glance in his rearview mirror and wryly offered "—calmed down," as a euphemism for "sobered up." "I'll bring her in as soon as she's up to it. Hey—do me a favor, would you? When you hear from Birdie, tell him I'm sorry I had to leave him stranded. Tell him something came up. Tell him—" Then he had to hold the instrument away from his ear again.

"Redfield! Where are you taking her? Dammit, Red—"

"Someplace safe," Jake growled, and broke the connection. In the ensuing quiet he heard a distinct hiccup from the interior of the van, and then a musical little ripple of sound he realized must be laughter.

"Someplace…*safe*," his passenger murmured with mocking solemnity as her head with its tousled cap of sun-shot hair pushed past his shoulder and into his line of vision. She gave that delightful giggle again, followed by another hiccup.

"Hey!" Jake barked as he threw out his arm just in time to bar her way to the front passenger seat, "where do you think you're going? Get back inside and keep down out of sight."

At that order she sort of reared back in surprise, and he

watched in the mirror as she stuck out her lopsided lower lip, then winced and gave it an exploratory poke with her finger, while a frown darkened her eyes. But only briefly—so briefly, it was like the shadow of a bird flying between him and the sun. The pout became a quirky, fat-lip smile, and she muttered, "Okeydokey," and sank to the floor of the van right where she was, all but disappearing into the billowy cloud of her skirts.

"Oh, Lord," Jake sighed under his breath. But his mind retained the image of her lower lip, and he felt a sensation at the back of his jaws like the feeling he got walking past a bakery on a cool early morning.

A sharp hiccup and some exasperated swearing brought him back to the here and now.

"I can't...stop *hiccuping*," she said in a disgruntled voice. "An' you know why? I can't...get a deep breath. This dress is...too *tight,* that's why. I really, really wish I could get out of this...stoo-*oop*id dress. Hey!" Jake felt a tug on his arm and glanced down at fingers tipped with virginal pink nail polish, several of the nails chipped and broken now. "How'm I gonna get out of this...dress, hmm? It has a million little buttons down the back. Who's gonna help me unbutton 'em—*you?*"

"If necessary," he grunted, keeping his eyes on the road.

"Ha," she said, and then was silent for a moment. Thinking about it? he wondered. That mouth-watering feeling was back—with a vengeance.

But when her voice came again it was low and whispery with regret, and it appeared she'd stopped hiccuping. "Boy, I sure messed up, didn't I? Messed up my dress, too. Damn thing cost a fortune. And you know what? It's all wasted. Whssht—down the drain. But—" she heaved a little sigh "—I guess it's a good thing I found out...when I did. Otherwise, I'd be married to a mobster right now..."

A shiver rippled down Jake's spine. The stirring of excitement he'd felt before became a stiff breeze. "And what was it you found out?" he asked softly.

But the only answer he got was a murmur and some rustling sounds. Casting a quick glance over his shoulder, he discovered that the battered bride had curled herself down in the nest of her skirts and was softly snoring—passed out with her head uncomfortably pillowed on her pearl-encrusted arms.

Patience, he told himself, willing his heart to resume its normal rhythm. *Patience... She's here, she's safe and she's yours. Whatever it is, you'll find out in due time.*

But it was hard—damned hard. How many months had it been since he'd allowed himself to believe that victory might actually be within his grasp? How many nights since he'd slept without having nightmares about the goal that had already cost him five years out of his life, a good bit of his professional reputation and the wife he'd adored?

Not since last summer when he'd watched Hal Robey's body being pulled from that hurricane-swollen river near Charleston had he felt this close to the end. *So close.* But now...*now.*

He had that sensation at the back of his jaws again, but it wasn't craving for food or hunger for a beautiful woman that made his mouth water. It was the blood lust of the hunter, closing in for the kill....

Once he'd made sure he wasn't being followed, Jake headed straight out to Abercorn. The traffic near the mall on a Saturday afternoon was brutal, but once past that he could turn off onto the back road that skirted the outer boundaries of the hospital parking lots, and from there it was a matter of minutes before he was pulling into his own driveway.

The town house apartment he'd rented when he'd transferred—temporarily, he devoutly hoped—to Savannah was in a neighborhood of brick Colonial-style apartment buildings arranged along wooded, curving dead-end streets. On weekdays it was peaceful enough, with the children in school and most of their parents at work, but at that hour on a beautiful October Saturday it was a hive of suburban activity. Children slalomed through the streets on skateboards, in-line skates and bicycles; minivans zipped in and out, disgorging noisy teenagers, pizza deliverers, housewives bearing armloads of grocery bags and armies of children wearing soccer uniforms. Stereo speakers thumped, dogs barked and engines revved at the whim of men happily up to their elbows in car parts and motor oil.

And how, Jake wondered, was he going to sneak an unconscious bride past all that?

It was, in fact, easier than he'd expected. The fact that the van he was driving bore the insignia of a utility company helped; no one would think twice about such a van backing in between the buildings, so as to have easy access to the rear of the apartment. And Jake's was on the end, so he was able to park close to the door.

After glancing at his still-unconscious passenger, he felt reasonably safe in leaving the van unlocked while he let himself into the apartment. There he gave the ground floor a habitual and cursory once-over, then went upstairs and into the only one of the two bedrooms that had furniture in it. He was trying to decide which would be the least conspicuous method of transporting a body: rolling it into a rug, zipping it into a garment bag or just draping a sheet over it, when he heard something that made alarm impulses go whistling through his nerves, lifting the fine hairs on his arms and the back of his neck.

Stealthy movements…swishing noises.

One hand on his weapon, he crept down the carpeted stairs, bending nearly double in order to peek around the corner into the living room while still out of the intruder's range of vision. An instant later he hissed out an exasperated breath and proceeded down the remaining steps at a more sedate pace while his heart banged without apology against his ribs.

The "intruder" was standing in the middle of the room, looking around her with a small, confused frown on her face, the champagne bottle clasped to her bosom.

When she saw Jake, she said, "Oh, hi..." in a vague, breathy voice. Then, as the frown deepened into distress, "Would you mind if I used your rest room?"

Jake muttered, "Upstairs," as he dodged past her to the door she'd left standing wide open.

After satisfying himself with a quick look around that his mystery guest's arrival had gone unnoticed in the neighborhood in spite of his dangerous lapse, he went out to the van to button down and lock up. Though that only took him a few minutes, by the time he got back inside, the bride had vanished. The apartment seemed empty and silent. Way too silent. There wasn't a sound—no footsteps, no running water...nothing.

Jake took the stairs two at a time, swearing under his breath. Too late. As he'd feared, the bride in all her blood-stained finery, still reeking of garbage, still cradling the champagne bottle, lay sprawled facedown across his bed, the black-grimed soles of her lace-stockinged feet peeking out of the froth of her skirts like the tar baby's footprints.

Muttering a disgusted "Aw, man..." he went over to her and gingerly touched her shoulder. He really had hoped to get the woman cleaned up a little bit before she conked out in his bed. "Hey—Miss Waskowitz...Eve...ma'am?" But the only answer he got was a determined snore. "Come on now, ma'am," he said firmly, "at least let's get you out of those clothes. Upsy-daisy..."

No dice.

With an exhalation that was more groan than sigh, he sat down on the bed beside her. *Damn...* All those buttons. She was right; they went all the way down her back. *All* the way.

Given a choice between peeling an unconscious woman out of her wedding dress and having that smell all over his bed, plus the remains of whatever it was she'd been wallowing in, Jake had no trouble coming up with the answer to that question.

"O-kay," he muttered, "if that's the way it's gonna be...." He leaned across her and gently eased the champagne bottle out from under her arm. When he got a good look at the label he did a double take, then whistled softly. No wonder she'd been cradling the thing like it was the crown jewels. Probably cost almost as much. He set the bottle carefully on the floor and went back to the problem of the buttons. No sweat, he thought. Just start at the top and work your way down....

It was nowhere near that easy. The neckline began high on the back of her neck, then looped across her shoulders and breasts in a series of scallops designed to show off a triple-strand pearl choker of what sure did look to Jake like the real deal. He decided to leave the pearls where they were and just concentrate on the buttons—*concentrate* being the operative word. It was hard, damned hard not to think about the intimacy of what he was doing. Hard not to let his fingertips feel the cool, wet kiss of her sweat-damp hair.... Hard to avoid the velvety warm brush of her skin. Hard to hold himself aloof from the beckoning warmth of her body, and to keep his head clear with her sweet woman's scent enveloping him like an opium cloud....

By the time he'd gotten as far as her waist, he'd worked up a good sweat. The problem was, he couldn't seem to convince himself that what he was doing was just a routine procedure for a highly trained federal law-enforcement agent. In his Special Forces training he'd learned how to kill a man with his bare hands inside three seconds and in total silence, and was confident he could do so with ice water in his veins. As a hostage negotiator he'd talked down men wired with enough explosives to demolish a high-rise, without breaking a sweat. So why couldn't he undress a woman without his heart pounding like a runaway freight train?

It didn't help that she had the most beautiful back he'd ever seen. And so far, he'd gotten the dress apart almost to her waist, and that was *all* he'd uncovered—lots and lots of that smooth-as-satin skin, sweet little bumps and ripples of spine, muscles delicately hinted at rather than bluntly defined. What was she wearing *under* that dress? *Nothing?*

He was relieved when he encountered lace a couple of buttons farther on. Well, he *was*. After all, he reminded himself, he was going to want to interrogate the lady. It would be nice if he could look her in the eye while he was doing it.

Once he had the buttons dealt with, he rolled her carefully onto her back. He was breathing easier now, figuring the worst was over. There were a few more buttons on each sleeve at the wrists, but once those were taken care of, all he had to do was peel the top over her shoulders and ease it on down…down her arms, carefully over her breasts… And all the while she went on sleeping soundly as a child, lips slightly parted, a fine dew of moisture clumping the hair on her forehead—

He avoided looking at her battered face, concentrating instead on getting the tight sleeves over her limp hands. And then it was easy to pull the dress past her hips and—

His heart stopped. He felt like a Chinese gong, and he'd just been rung.

What the hell was she *wearing?* He wasn't much of an expert on feminine undergarments, so he wasn't absolutely certain that what he was looking at was a teddy. Whatever it was, it seemed to consist entirely of some kind of stretchy lace that hugged her body like a second skin, only to end abruptly at the top of the curve of her hips. Below that, elastic garters snaked down over a tiny lace triangle, arrowed the length of smooth golden thighs to connect with the tops of the lacy white stockings.

All Jake could think, when his mind started working again, was, *All this for a creep like Cisneros?* What a waste.

He'd peeled back the covers and was just about to roll her between the sheets when he remembered those grimy black feet. So instead of tucking her in, he went to the closet and got the blanket he'd taken off his bed and stowed there, being a warm-blooded sleeper himself. When he got back with it, he found that his sleeping beauty had rolled away from him onto her side and pulled her knees up, the way little kids do when they sleep. Except she sure didn't look anything like a kid, especially from where he was standing. He got that blanket over her just as fast as he could.

Once he'd done that, the cop part of him was able to resume functioning. He stood there looking down at the woman asleep on his bed, snoring softly with her ungrazed cheek pillowed on one hand like a child. Eve Waskowitz...who by this time should have been married to the man Jake hated most in this world.

Lady, he thought, what happened to you in that church garden today? *What in the hell happened?*

He sat down on the edge of the bed and carefully lifted the bottom edge of the blanket, then put his hand under one slender, lace-stockinged ankle and tilted the bottom of her foot toward the light. The stocking was torn and worn through, almost nonexistent in places. And under all the dirt and grime, he could see that the ball of her foot and the delicate pads of her toes were scraped and bruised.

And he thought, Lady, where in the world have you been? What happened to make you run in fear for your life from the man you were about to pledge to love, honor and obey until death do you part? What happened to your face? Did *he* do that to you?

His belly burned at the thought. But the lady's only response was an inarticulate murmur, and Jake knew that was all the answer he was going to get, for a while, anyway. With a silent sigh, willing himself to patience, willing the trip-hammer beat of his heart to resume its normal rhythms, he lowered the foot into place beside its mate and tucked the blanket around them both.

He rose and walked out of his bedroom, and was about to start down the stairs when he changed his mind. Instead, he went across the hall to the bathroom, took his bathrobe from its hook behind the door, carried it into the bedroom and laid it across the foot of the bed.

Then he went downstairs, poured himself a cup of cold coffee and settled down to wait

Chapter 4

Eve felt no sense of surprise or unease when she opened her eyes; she was accustomed to waking in unfamiliar places. As far as she was concerned, there were two items of greater importance to her at that moment than figuring out where in the world she was. Number one, she was thirsty; her mouth felt like the bottom of a birdcage. And second—okay, maybe even first—she really, *really* needed to go to the bathroom.

The first alarms went off when she threw back the blanket that covered her and found that she was dressed like a page from a Victoria's Secret catalog. "What the hell?" she muttered aloud.

Sitting up, she shifted her feet around and lowered them to the floor, where they encountered something soft and slithery. It was when she leaned over to peer at the pile of white satin under her lace-stockinged feet that the bells really cut loose—a cacophony of bells, a pounding of drums, a whole anvil chorus. In an attempt to shut out the din, she moaned and put her hands over her ears—which was when she discovered that the clanging was coming from inside her own head.

She waited, breathing slowly and shallowly until the pounding had subsided, then rose with caution. Someone had thoughtfully left a bathrobe on the foot of the bed, she observed. The same person who had peeled her out of the expensive pile of white satin she was standing on? She just wished she could remember who that someone was. The last thing she did remember was being in some sort of surveillance van.... Good Lord, had it been the FBI...? And a video monitor... Sonny's face...

"Oh, God..." She was overcome, all at once, with cold and pain and nausea. She groped for the bathrobe and shrugged it on, drew it tightly around herself, hoping to draw from it the warmth and comfort that would dispel the horror that had just enveloped her. Because she remembered it all— *everything*.

She just did manage to find the bathroom in time.

When she heaved herself up off the bathroom floor a short time later, she still felt wobbly in the legs, but considerably less queasy. "Well, Evie," she softly scolded herself, "you've really gotten yourself into it this time, haven't you?"

She tried her best to avoid the mirror above the sink as she leaned over the basin and turned on the tap, letting the cool water run through her fingers, frowning at the dirt and stickiness, the scraped and broken nails. A shame, she thought. How often did she pamper herself with a real manicure, colored polish, the works? And for what? *For what?*

Disgusted with herself, she splashed water on her face. The unexpected sting of it made her straighten up like a shot. She whispered a shocked oath, then leaned closer to stare at her reflection in the mirror. "Jeez," she muttered, "I look like I've been mugged." Her gaze shifted, taking it all in—the cuts in her eyebrow, on the bridge of her nose, the scraped cheekbone, the fat lip—before she finally forced herself to meet her own accusing eyes. *Yeah, and it's probably the least of what could happen to you. You got yourself into this. Now it's time to face the music. What're you gonna do about it?*

She drew the terry-cloth robe closer around herself and belted it tightly, picking up as she did a scent that was strange to her yet somehow familiar—a mixture of soap and after-shave, fabric softener and male—definitely a man's scent. And definitely one she didn't know. She remembered a tall man, though, with a long, rather patrician face and melancholy eyes. *Jake.* That was his name—Special Agent Jake…Something.

Pulling in one more deep breath, both for comfort and for courage, Eve turned off the light and left the bathroom. It was time to hobble downstairs and face this Agent Jake Something of the FBI, the man who'd brought her here, to his home, undressed her to her undies and covered her with a blanket while she slept. And very thoughtfully left her his bathrobe.

Jake had been waiting for her, sitting stiffly on the rented brown tweed sofa in the living room with a cup of cold coffee on the table in front of him and an album from his collection of blues LP's playing on the old-fashioned turntable on the floor under the window. He'd shed the coveralls for a comfortable pair of slacks and a polo shirt, and had a copy of a John D. MacDonald paperback—a Travis McGee—open on his lap. He'd been reading the same paragraph over and over since he'd first heard signs of life coming from his bedroom upstairs.

Now, as the scuff of footsteps sounded on the carpeted stairs, he closed the book and placed it on the coffee table, then peeled off his drugstore reading glasses and hitched forward on the cushions. He was ready. More than ready. In a way he felt as if he'd been waiting for this woman all his life.

His heartbeat quickened as he watched her slender legs in their white lace stockings come slowly into view. He told himself it had nothing to do with memories of what those stockings were attached to, the way those golden thighs had curved into hips cleft only with a tiny scrap of lace. The tension, the dry-mouthed anticipation, he insisted, were solely for what she could tell him about the man he'd spent five years of his life trying to bring down. They had no connection whatsoever with the fact that she was a beautiful, sensuous woman wearing a white lace teddy under his favorite bathrobe.

She waited until she'd finished navigating the stairs before she spoke, and then only a husky "Hi" as she came toward him with the careful, slightly canted gait of someone walking barefoot on pebbles while balancing a jar on her head.

"There's coffee," Jake offered, with a gesture toward his own chilled dregs.

She shook her head, flinched and whispered, "Water, if you have it," as she groped with one hand for the back of the sofa.

He got up and headed for the kitchen, inquiring over his shoulder, "Can I get you a couple aspirin, while I'm at it?"

She gave a single huff of laughter—breathy, chagrinned, and a little surprised. "Yeah, okay...maybe...sure." Then, for a few moments, gave herself up to the complex task of sitting down on the sofa. That accomplished, she looked over at him and frowned. "What time is it? How long've I been...?"

"Asleep?" Jake glanced at his watch. "It's a little after eleven. You've been out about six hours." He went into the kitchen, filled a plain white mug with water from the faucet, snagged the bottle of aspirin from the top of the refrigerator and went back out to the living room. "There you go," he said as he placed the mug and aspirin bottle on the coffee table. Outwardly calm, he felt deep inside the shaky nervousness of adolescence. "It's tap water—that's all I've got."

She shrugged and reached for the mug. When she made no move to pick up the aspirin, he opened the bottle and shook two tablets onto the tabletop. Wordlessly she held up three fingers. He shook out one more, then picked them up and held them out to her, watched as she took them from him and placed them on her tongue, avoiding contact with her swollen lower lip. He tried not to watch the way the pearl choker rippled against her throat as she swallowed; it was too short a distance from there to the deep, shadowed V of his bathrobe and the secrets hidden therein.

Cradling the mug in both hands, she cleared her throat and nodded toward the window. "Is that Billie Holiday?"

Jake arched an eyebrow. "Yeah, it is. You like blues?"

One shoulder lifted as she eased them both back against the cushions. "I did a piece on blues musicians couple years back...great stuff—fascinating. Don't really have much time to listen to music myself, unfortunately." A frown briefly pulled her eyebrows together, drawing lines that were almost a caricature of distress above eyes dark with pain. "It's nice...but would you mind turning it down...a little?"

Since the record player was already turned down about as low as it would go, Jake switched it off. Then, since his witness was occupying the only piece of furniture in the room designed for sitting, he leaned his backside against the windowsill, folded his arms on his chest and waited.

After a moment of the silence, the witness opened one eye and ventured, "FBI, right? And your name is...Jake?" She waited for his nod, then smiled her skewed smile, showing an unexpected dimple, like a little girl much pleased with herself. She sat up and placed the mug on the coffee table with an air of getting down to business. "I suppose you'd like an explanation."

"Whenever you're ready," Jake murmured.

She acknowledged his politeness with an ironic snort, waited a moment, then angled a look at him and said, "Well, for starters, I did *not* get mugged, no matter what I look like. I got this face falling out of, or maybe into—it's sort of a blur—a Dumpster." She held up a hand, though he wouldn't have dreamed of interrupting. "I do *not* make a habit of getting falling-down drunk. I'm not even very much of a drinker at all. I seriously do not know what got into me. I didn't even realize I'd drunk the whole bottle—I *did* drink the whole bottle, didn't I?" She sighed and closed her eyes. "What a waste. Do you know what that was? There probably aren't more than a few hundred bottles of that vintage left in existence, and I just…oh, hell."

She covered her eyes briefly with one hand, and when they met Jake's again they held a different kind of pain, the kind aspirin doesn't have much effect on. "I just kept drinking it. It seemed like the only way I could keep from coming completely unglued. After what I'd heard… I didn't know what to do."

Jake cleared his throat. In spite of the fact that his stomach was tying itself in knots and his jaws were tight as steel traps, his voice when he spoke was almost gentle, issued from a layer of calm that was like a thin film of oil on roiling waters. "What exactly was it you heard?"

She regarded him thoughtfully for a moment. Then her mouth quirked sideways in her droll little half smile. "Why do I have a feeling you already know this? But…I just found out the man I was going to marry is a very bad man."

Jake held himself still, except for a single nod.

Her smile vanished. "I, however, had no idea. You have to believe that. I had no idea he—or anyway, his men—were the ones who burned down my sister's mobile home and threatened her and her kids. I think he would even have had her killed.…" Her face blanched dangerously and a look of panic crossed her face.

"And how," said Jake softly, giving her a moment to regain control, "did you find this out?"

"I heard him say so." Equilibrium restored, she rose and began to pace. "It was an accident! Pure chance. Just think—I could be married to him right now. If I hadn't had this crazy idea—" She stopped and put her hands to the sides of her head, her face, trapped between them, a horror-stricken mask. "Oh, God. To think...I've actually *slept* with—oh Lord, I feel sick..."

"Would you like a moment?" Jake asked, pleased that his voice could sound so calm—merely solicitous, nothing more. Because this time it was he who needed that moment, those few heartbeats of concentration in which to find his pathway, his solid footing once again. Because to his astonishment, somewhere in the part of him that was most primitively and essentially male, a clarion call had sounded, roused to battle readiness by her words and the images evoked by them. It seemed half a lifetime of training had failed to make him immune to gut-churning passions and primal imperatives after all.

Outwardly relaxed, he watched her through half-closed eyes, watched her shoulders shrink inside his robe as she fought her own inner battle against shame and self-revulsion, while he fought to block out the images his mind had formed...of this woman and Sonny Cisneros, writhing together in tumbled sheets. He told himself the brassy tang in the back of his throat had nothing to do with the woman, that it was his hatred of Cisneros that cloaked those images in a bloodred fog of rage.

"I'm okay," she said, though the tightness in her voice betrayed that for the lie it was. Jake knew that "okay" was something Eve Waskowitz was not likely to be for a while, no matter how hard she might try to convince herself otherwise. She was an intelligent woman, and quick-witted; and for all her charm and buoyant agelessness, not a bit naive.

Not one of the nuances of her situation or their significance had escaped her; her agile mind had followed each possible consequence to its unpalatable conclusion, and it was what she had seen there that gave her eyes that dark and hunted look.

Because he understood gentleness from him would only confirm her certainties, he chose a businesslike tone. "Tell me what happened, everything you remember. From the beginning."

Eve stared at the top of the kitchen table from between the hands that framed and supported her face. "I *have* told you everything three times." Her voice was soft, exhausted and hopeless. "That's all—there just isn't anything else."

"I know. It's okay." Jake muttered the soothing words while his mind hurled itself against the cul de sac to which her story had led him with the helpless fury of a trapped eagle.

With his back to her, he braced his hands on the edge of the sink and leaned his weight on them while he stared out the window at the black-lace pattern of thinning woods silhouetted against the floodlit silver of the hospital parking lot beyond. The distant wail of a siren grew louder, then abruptly ceased.

"It's not enough," he said in a voice thick with disappointment. "Not to take to the U.S. Attorney. A statement overheard and uncorroborated—a good attorney would have it buried before it ever got to court. You know that, don't you?"

He heard the careful clearing of her throat, and then, in a flat voice he imagined must be totally alien to someone so naturally effervescent, "Unfortunately, it's more than enough for Sonny—just the fact that I heard it. He can't let me go. You do know that? Plus, I humiliated him—publicly." She laughed, utterly without humor. "*Nobody* gets away with that."

Jake let out a slow and silent breath as he turned to look at her. Though only a few feet away, she seemed somehow to have retreated to a great distance and at the same time grown smaller, not as though she'd shrunk, but more as if she'd consolidated herself—gone inside the walls of privacy and pulled them close around her. It wasn't the first time he'd seen it happen. It seemed to be in the direst circumstances that people felt most constrained from seeking help. It was the instinct of the doomed animal to go it alone.

"Sonny won't let this go," she went on, in a voice close to breaking. "He won't stop—and he'll stop at nothing—until he finds me. What scares me is, if he can't find me, he'll go after my family. Like he went after Summer and the children...to get Hal. He'd have killed them, if he'd thought it would serve his purpose. The children, too—without even blinking—"

"We're not gonna let that happen," Jake said flatly. But it was an automatic response. An angry pulse tapped against his belt buckle, while beyond the windows yet another siren sliced through the night. It's Saturday, he thought. The hospital would be a busy place, the terminus of the night's sweepings, the usual debris from the bars, back alleys and... *Back alleys...*

His heartbeat quickened. "Tell me again," he said slowly, "what happened after you dropped the champagne glasses."

She shrugged. "I ran like hell—I told you that. And I hid in the Dumpster—"

He held up a hand, stopping her. "How far were you from the alley? How sure are you that they *saw* you running?"

"Well, they had to know it was me," she said with a snort.

"But—" and he was forming words carefully, reining in his hope with the ruthlessness of long practice "—*how* did they know? You ran like hell, you say—in what? Your high-heeled shoes?'' His gaze shifted to the feet she'd tucked back under her chair, feet still clad in the tattered remains of white lace stockings. He heard a gasp, and looking once more at her face, found that she'd touched the fingertips of one hand to her swollen lip.

''My shoes. I think…I must have left them there. I heard the glasses shatter on the walk, and the next thing I knew I was running. I never even—but how could I have run like that in heels? I *must* have left them. So…that could have been how they knew it was me. Not that it makes a whole lot of difference.…''

''Maybe it does…maybe it does.'' The pulse was beating in his throat, now, so that he had to breathe carefully around it. ''Think about it. Sonny and his men are talking. They can't be looking out the window at that time, or they'd see you coming and shut up before you got there. They hear glass breaking. What do they do? What most people do—they freeze. For a second or two. Even if they react instantly, it takes a couple of seconds to get to the window. You're already running. *Maybe* they catch a glimpse of you disappearing through the gate—maybe not. They run out, see the shoes and broken glasses. Meanwhile, you dive into the Dumpster. Your veil gets caught, the lid falls and hits you on the head—''

''Boy, did it ever. I've got a bump, even. And I actually saw stars—'' Her voice broke off as Jake grabbed her arm and all but lifted her out of the chair. ''What?''

''Come on—'' and his voice was like a growl, low and intense ''—go get your dress. Put it on—don't bother with the buttons. We're getting out of here. No, wait—''

''Where are we going?'' He'd frightened her; she was breathless and pale, tense as wire.

''Let me have those pearls—hurry up—come on, take 'em off.''

Her eyes held his, bright with questions, as she nevertheless lifted her hands to the back of her neck. After a moment she gave up her own attempt at the choker's clasp and simply turned her back to him.

"I have an idea, but we have to move fast." Jake frowned at his fingers as they slipped under the slightly curling ends of her short-cropped hair, dipped into the humid warmth inside the collar of his robe, found the clasp and opened it. When, without thinking, he rubbed his thumb over the tiny red mark the metal had left on her skin, he felt her shiver.

She turned again to face him, the fingers of one hand absently rubbing the place where the choker had been, and he knew the questions that must be quivering on her lips. But he had no time for questions then. Already he was opening a drawer, taking out a box of zippable plastic bags, pulling one out and dropping the pearls inside, while his mind rocketed on like a missile leaving its own noise behind.

He growled, "The rock, too—your engagement ring—come on, come on," motioning impatiently when she looked confused. But she took off the diamond ring and gave it to him. Trusting him. And a part of him acknowledged that trust and was warmed by it as he dropped the ring into the bag with the pearls, returned it to the box it had come out of and the box to the drawer.

It was that warmth, and his fear of softening, that made his voice harsh when he spoke to her. "Go—get the dress on and meet me back here. Dammit, *move*—it's been six hours already."

But this time she stood where she was, hands clutching the lapels of the bathrobe. "Are you going to tell me where we're going?" As softly as she spoke, Jake recognized the danger in her tone, as well as in the slight elevation of her chin. Trust him she might, but not blindly; it wasn't in her nature.

He frowned, but let go of his impatience with a breath.

"To the hospital. But I need to make a call first." The receiver was already in his hand.

"The...*hospital?* But I'm not—I don't need—"

Jake punched a button, then leveled a look at her, this time asking her for the trust she'd given so freely a few minutes before. "I think we might have a way out of this, but we have to hurry. I'll explain on the way. *Go.*"

And he turned his back to her, already growling instructions into the phone. Eve waited for a moment, waiting for the spark of rebellion within her to mushroom into full-blown insurrection. When it didn't happen, she gave a mental shrug and went. It wasn't in her nature to take orders without a full and detailed explanation. But the man was...the FBI. And she had, after all, pretty much committed herself to his protection when she'd crawled into his surveillance van. Probably the least she ought to do was trust him.

Upstairs, she made use once more of the bathroom, then crossed into Jake's small, spartan bedroom, unbelting the robe as she went. She shivered a little as she abandoned the warm terry cloth and its comforting masculine smells for the cold satin wedding gown and the sour odors of garbage and stale champagne. Though that seemed somehow weirdly appropriate to her, now. Once beautiful, the dress now seemed spoiled—in more ways than one. It felt contaminated...slimy against her skin.

She suppressed a shudder as she pulled the stiff, pearl-and-lace-encrusted bodice up and plunged her arms into the narrow sleeves. Then, holding up the top with one hand and the skirts with the other, she made her way carefully down the stairs.

She met Jake coming from the kitchen, the cordless phone still in his hand. "Can you help me—" she began, but he anticipated her request and brusquely waved it aside.

"Never mind the buttons—the dress is just for the witnesses, anyway."

"What?" She looked at him blankly.

"In case anybody's asked how you came in—to the emergency room, *capish?* They'll remember a woman in a wedding dress."

She breathed a silent "Oh" as he guided her past him, his manner almost deferential, not touching her, just a slight gesture toward her elbow. She felt the tension in him, the energy radiating from his body like heat from a stove. The exposed skin of her back felt it, too, and shivered as if something—the barest of touches—had skimmed across its surface.

When they were in the van, Jake said in the low but sharp-edged murmur of a man intent on his mission, "Okay, here's the story." They were heading slowly out of the cul-de-sac, quiet at that hour except for the thumping of someone's stereo. Eve turned her head to look at him and caught the grim shape of his profile, frozen in the cold illumination of a yard lamp. Feeling her eyes on him, he returned her glance, his eyes flicking to her throat and then to the hand with which she held the top of her dress in place just above her breasts. "You *were* mugged—robbed." He hesitated for Eve's bark of surprise, then shifted his gaze back through the windshield. "The assailant conked you on the head, took your necklace and engagement ring, then dumped you into the trash bin. You regained consciousness, crawled out of the bin and wandered off in a state of confusion. You apparently found your way into my unlocked van, where you once again lost consciousness. I only just found you and called the local police." He glanced her way again, briefly. "An officer will meet us at the hospital to take your statement."

Eve could think of nothing to say. At his first words her heartbeat had kicked into high gear, spurred by excitement, reaction…hope. Was it possible? Could this man really accomplish such miracles? Could Sonny be outwitted, his suspicions allayed, her life salvaged so easily? Even allowing for the resources of the FBI, it seemed too much to believe.

Almost as if he'd heard her thoughts, Jake went on in a flat, policeman's drone that was somehow the more convincing for being utterly devoid of emotional intensity. "The police have been apprised of the situation and have promised cooperation. Medical personnel will be brought into the picture only on an as-needed basis, but—" and he flicked her a sardonic glance "—I don't think it's going to be necessary to tell them much. You look pretty convincing. In any case, you will be provided with all necessary verification and evidence of your injuries—"

"Injuries?" said Eve faintly.

"You suffered a concussion. Consequently, you have no memory of the attack, or of events immediately preceding or following the incident. Your family and, uh, loved ones will be notified as soon as you are able to identify yourself. You will probably be kept in the hospital for observation, however, as is customary with any potentially serious head injury."

Her own eyes were fixed without focus on the windshield, but she felt his head turn toward her, and as they idled at a signal light, the long and weighty burden of his scrutiny. The light changed and as they moved forward again he added, "That gives you a day or two, if you need it."

She nodded. Words screamed inside her mind, trapped behind the hand she'd clamped across her mouth; emotions tumbled futilely inside her, trapped simply by their own enormity. She sat trembling—ironically, now that her predicament seemed all but solved, on the verge of tears—feeling Jake's glance brush her intermittently, like the sweep of a searchlight.

Finally, as the van turned off the main street and jolted through the hospital's emergency entrance, driven to panic by the knowledge that the opportunity was about to slip by her, she blurted it out, and all of her horror, fear and despair was there in her voice for him to hear. And she felt more naked; the exposure was more intimate to her, than even the knowledge that he'd undressed her.

"What am I going to do?" she cried, in the rapid, breathless voice of a frightened child. "I can't go back to Sonny—I can't! If I don't, he'll know something's wrong. But how can I go back to…being *with* him, knowing…what I know?"

"Well," said Jake without much evidence of sympathy, "I guess you'd better hope you're one hell of an actress."

An incredulous gust of laughter blew away her tears. "The man was—is—my fiancé. You *do* realize what that means? He's going to expect me to sleep with him. Can you imagine what that would be like? Nobody's *that* good an actress!"

"Oh, I don't know," Jake said in a curiously acidic tone. But he checked himself, and his gaze slid past her to the side window as he jerked the van to a stop beside the E.R.'s double automatic doors. When he spoke again, it was in an altogether different voice—crisp, quiet, full of authority.

"Speaking of acting, it's showtime. Slump down and put your head back—you're supposed to be half-conscious, remember? One thing at a time. Right now let's worry about saving your life. You can figure out what to do with it later."

Eve muttered, "That's easy for *you* to say." But she did as he'd told her and slid down in the seat, closed her eyes and let her head flop to one side. She felt the driver's side door of the van open and then slam shut. A moment later the door on her side opened, letting in a gust of damp October night.

"What are you doing?" she demanded in a squeaking whisper as an arm insinuated itself between her bare back and the seat cushion. A hand pushed roughly under her knees.

"Dammit, what do you think I'm doing?" His voice was so low, its vibrations were felt rather than heard, so near her ear, the breath that carried it was a gauzy stirring of warmth on her skin. "You're barely conscious—what are you gonna do, *walk* in?"

"Oh…God." That was all she could manage. Eve was not a small and dainty woman—five foot nine in her stockinged feet, at least; she hadn't been carried since she was six years old.

"Holy…" Jake's blasphemy hissed past her ear, raising goose bumps all over her body and contributing dangerously to her giddy impulse to giggle. "What do you want me to do, drop you? Put your head down on my shoulder, dammit. And relax—my God, would you just please *trust me?*"

Relax…trust me… With few or no other options open to her, what else could she do? She closed her eyes and buried her face in the FBI man's warm, masculine shoulder and thought of carnival rides…roller coasters. For all her daredevil nature, she had never liked roller coasters—something to do with the surrendering of control. She hated being strapped in, powerless to do anything but go along for the ride. Like now, at this moment. She felt frightened, helpless. The sensation of motion, of being carried through space, made her queasy.

But…with her face pressed in the hollow of Jake's neck and shoulder, as she breathed in his warmth, felt the rasp of his beard against her temple, the beating of his heart against her breasts, a certain scent began to invade her nostrils…a scent somehow familiar to her. She'd smelled it just this evening, in Jake's bathrobe. It was the smell of safety, and she inhaled it like a drug, pulled it deep inside herself. While around her footsteps hurried and voices questioned and strangers' hands took control of her fate, she wrapped it around her panicked soul like a security blanket. When Jake's arms relinquished her to the cold and sterile efficiency of a gurney, she felt bereft.

"You okay?" she heard a deep voice murmur.

She opened her eyes and found Jake's gazing down into hers, darkly brooding and only inches away. She looked into them for a long time before she nodded. "Showtime," she whispered.

Like it or not, she was *on* the roller coaster. Nothing to do now but buckle herself in for the ride.

Chapter 5

The Waskowitz family's vigil was taking place in Pop and Ginger's hotel room in downtown Savannah. Everybody was there except for Charly, who, under her obstetrician's strict orders to stay off her feet, had gone to her own room down the hall to lie down, taking the three older children—Summer's two and Mirabella and Jimmy Joe's eleven-year-old J.J.—with her. Their baby, Amy Jo, was also sound asleep, snuggled up next to her daddy on one of the two double beds with her thumb in her mouth and her bottom in the air.

Everyone else was wide-awake. However, only Mirabella was up and pacing, so when the phone rang, although everyone jumped reflexively, she was the one who got to it first.

She snatched it rather rudely from under her mother's hand, barked a breathless "H'lo?" into the mouthpiece, then listened for about three seconds in frozen stillness. Then she thrust the instrument at her sister, stalked angrily into the bathroom and shut the door. Whereupon she burst into tears.

When she ventured forth a few minutes later, tear-blotchy

but belligerent still, Summer was sitting tense and roused on the bed with the phone pressed to her ear and one hand upraised in a futile effort to fend off the barrage of questions and instructions being lobbed at her from all sides. Her side of the conversation consisted of nods and an occasional "Uh-huh."

While Summer was hanging up amidst a chorus of protests and raising both hands in a plea for patience, Jimmy Joe eased away from Amy and got up off the bed. He came over to Mirabella and gathered her into his arms.

"Hey, darlin'," he murmured gruffly to the top of her head. "She's in the hospital, but she's gonna be okay."

"That part I got," said Mirabella in a testy voice.

Summer, who was on her feet now, along with everyone else, cleared her throat. "She was too groggy to say very much, but I talked to the police officer who was there—I guess to take her statement." She flicked a sympathetic glance toward her mother, who had made a small, stricken noise. "It looks like—they think she was mugged." Somebody—one of the men—made an outraged growling sound. Quickly Summer went on. "Somebody hit her and knocked her unconscious, took her diamond ring and her pearl necklace, then dumped her in a trash bin in the alley. Behind the church, you know? Later on—it must have been while we were all inside the church waiting for her—they think she crawled out of the bin and somehow wandered off in confusion. Anyway, she apparently crawled into a utility company van and passed out. The guy just found her and took her to the emergency room, which happens to be close to where he lives—somewhere south of here, near the airport?" She made the last of it a question.

It was Riley who answered her. "I know where it is." He had the keys to his Mercedes in his hand, already taking charge, as seemed to be Riley's way—something to do with being such a successful lawyer, Mirabella supposed; he was used to telling people what to do. "Pop, you and Ginger come with us. Jimmy Joe, you want to follow me, or shall I give you directions? Troy—okay if we leave the kids here with you and Charly?"

Troy said sure, and to go on ahead.

"Wait." Summer, who'd been shaking her head and trying in vain to get someone's attention, now succeeded in breaking into the bustle of departure without noticeably altering it. "Do you think we should go running over there now? She sounded really out of it. She said they were doing tests and things, getting her stitched up and cleaned up. They probably aren't even going to let us in to see her, and even if they do, she'll probably be too groggy to notice. Maybe we should wait till morning."

There was a slight break, a brief cessation of sound and motion while that option was considered, and then universally rejected. Ginger simply shook her head and began buttoning the coat Pop had settled on her shoulders; others resumed interrupted searches for jackets, purses, car and hotel room keys. "Don't worry about the kids," Troy sang out.

The exodus was well underway when it was again halted by a word. This time it was Ginger who said, "Wait!" and turned in the doorway to cast a concerned look upon her husband, her daughters and sons-in-law, all crushed in around her. "Shouldn't we call Sonny?"

There was another silence, broken by Mirabella's snort. Summer elbowed her hard in the ribs, so it was Pop who answered, in his brusque way, "Hon, I imagine she's already done that."

"But," his wife argued, "Summer said she was out of it, and they were running all those tests. What if she didn't? It would be terrible, wouldn't it? To let him go on thinking…"

Mirabella heaved an ungracious sigh. "All right—anybody have his number?" Everybody looked at everybody else.

"Evie's probably got it in her purse," said Summer. "It

was with her things we brought from the church. It's all still in the car. You don't want us to look for it now, do you?''

Ginger gave in with a shrug as she moved on through the doorway. ''We can call from the hospital, once we've seen Evie.''

In the hallway, Riley and Jimmy Joe took the lead, setting a brisk pace which Mirabella, short-legged and pregnant, didn't even try to keep. Summer lagged behind with her, and as soon as they were out of hearing range of their parents and spouses, caught at her hand and hissed, ''What's the matter with you? I know you don't like Sonny, but the man is practically a member of the family. You don't have to love him just because Evie does, but you don't have to act like he's some kind of evil villain. What have you got against him anyway?''

''I don't *know,*'' moaned Mirabella, so dejectedly that Summer half turned, stopping her there in the middle of the hallway.

''Bella?''

Mirabella couldn't look at her sister's face. How could she explain to a face so full of compassion, love and finally, *finally* happiness, that whenever she looked at Sonny Cisneros she felt a sick feeling in the pit of her stomach? That when he spoke to her she got the shivers? That all she wanted for their sister was the same kind of love and joy they had each already been blessed with, dammit, and she knew— somehow she just *knew*—that this wasn't going to be it! That in some vague, formless way, she was frightened. She could not explain, because it made no sense even to her.

And because Mirabella's temper had a tendency to rise in direct proportion to her levels of fear and frustration, she lashed back at her sister with a furious ''I don't *know!* I'm worried for Evie. Something's not right. It's just not *right.*''

To her great surprise and even greater unease, Summer didn't say a word as they walked on together toward the elevator, holding hands as they had when they were very small children, and afraid of the monsters in the dark.

"How do I look?" Eve asked in a low voice.

"Like hell," Jake replied in his federal agent's monotone.

She was incomprehensibly annoyed that he didn't bother to look at her when he said it, his edgy frown trained instead on the hustle and bustle in the corridor outside the treatment room curtain, and the uniformed police officer pacing nearby. But she muttered a dry "Thanks—I think" as she shifted her eyes and their silent question first to the doctor standing with folded arms at the foot of her bed, then to the intern at her elbow.

Their answering smiles seemed tentative, for which Eve could hardly blame them. Supposedly this was a routine mugging, but there were undercurrents.... A bride in her wedding dress? And the guy who'd brought her in—who was he? Definitely not the groom, supposedly just a Good Samaritan, but she'd asked—begged—for them to let him stay.... Obviously they weren't being let in on the whole story.

"You'll do fine." The doctor, prematurely balding, impossibly young and trying hard to hide his baby face behind a wispy goatee, came around the bed and leaned close to inspect the bandage wrapped around her head. "Linda does good work. Shouldn't be any scarring, but you might have a little bit of a black eye, here. Hard to say. And," he added in a warning tone, "once the Novocain wears off, that lip is going to be a little uncomfortable. Now—that bump on the head... Since you were unconscious for a pretty considerable amount of time, we're gonna want to admit you for a day or two, okay? Just to be on the safe side. And we're gonna want to get some X rays, probably a CAT scan." He started to say something to the intern, then said, "Oops," in response to something he'd evidently heard over the loudspeaker, and instead nodded abruptly to her and went out. Beyond the curtain Eve could hear running footsteps, the swish of opening doors, voices calling incomprehensible instructions in tensely efficient tones.

The intern, a stocky woman—also impossibly young—with wiry, cinnamon-colored hair, freckles and a wicked glint in her green eyes, winked at Eve as she rolled back her stool and stood up, taking her tray of instruments with her. "Don't worry, hon, you're gonna be fine. Right now you look like you just went a couple rounds with Mike Tyson, but that'll pass. Your poor mama might have a heart attack when she sees you, though."

Eve's eyes flicked to Jake's somber face. "Is she here?" And suddenly, for reasons she couldn't begin to fathom, she was dangerously close to tears.

"She sure is," the intern answered cheerfully. "Your whole family, it looks like. They're out there in the waiting room."

"Can I...see them?"

"Don't see why not—looks like it's gonna be a little while before we can get those X rays. Just had an MVA come in—multiple victims. I'll go tell 'em they can come in for a few minutes."

"Thanks..." Eve felt unnervingly trembly. She caught a breath and held it, trying to steady her voice. "Is Sonny—"

The intern's eyes were bright and curious. "Sonny—is that your husband? Uh...fiancé? I don't believe he's here yet, but I'll let you know the minute he gets here, okay?" Eve nodded; her throat had locked up tight. "I'll send your family right on in," the intern said, and was on her way out when Eve stopped her with a hoarse sound that was meant to be "Wait!" The intern paused and looked at her, eyebrows raised.

"Could I just have a few minutes?" Eve whispered. Her eyes slipped away, found Jake and then came back to the woman again. "I'd like to...you know, say goodbye to him.

He's been with me through all of this...." And inexplicably, now she *was* crying.

The intern's freckled face held nothing but compassion. "Sure, hon," she said gently. "He can just let the desk know when he leaves, and they can have somebody send your folks on in. How'll that be?"

Eve murmured, "Thank you," and the woman went away.

Seconds ticked by. Then Jake came slowly toward her, hands in his pockets, brows lowered, darkening his somber gaze to a frown. "Helluva performance," he said dryly. "And you were worried about being a good enough actor?"

Eve just looked at him. She felt as if something heavy had come and sat on her chest.

He gazed down at her, and she glared back at him, furious with herself for crying in front of him, indefinably hurt that he'd so cynically dismissed her tears, and completely bewildered by the contradiction.

"What about it? Ready to take a test drive?"

She made a swipe at her cheeks and looked away. He came closer, bracing his hands on the bed as he leaned down and looked into her eyes. His voice was soft and very near; she had to stop breathing in order to hear it. "You have to be ready for this. I know this is just your family, but it's as important to convince them of what happened as it is Cisneros."

"I know," Eve muttered, "I know...."

"You've got to believe this. Live it."

"I *know.*" One more tear surprised her by escaping over the barrier of her lower lashes and sneaking away like a thief down her unmarked cheek. She slapped at it furiously. "I know what I'm supposed to do. Don't worry about me. I said I'm ready."

Jake's eyes had shifted dispassionately, first to watch the tear's progress, then to travel over her face, touching briefly on each of her injuries. It struck Eve that there was something oddly intimate, almost proprietary about the scrutiny. As he straightened, he brushed the tear's track with an index finger, and she felt a flash of something almost like disappointment. A sense of something glimpsed but not quite realized.

He paused to look down at her once more. "The tears—it's a nice touch. You've been through a trauma. You'd be expected to show some emotion."

And Eve, furious, surprised herself by thinking, What about you, Mr. Jake Something—Mr. Iceman? Do you *ever* show emotion?

Already turning to leave her, he paused as if she'd spoken the words aloud. He looked at her for a moment, then away, as if there was something more he ought to say to her if he could only remember what it was.

What about telling me it's going to be all right? Eve thought. What about a big ol' thumb's-up? A "Break a leg" and a smile for luck? Hey, Mr. FBI—are you even genetically capable of smiling?

She touched the strips of butterfly bandage that crisscrossed the bridge of her nose. "Where're you gonna be?"

"Don't worry, I'll be watching you. Out of sight, but I'll be watching." His gaze was heavy-lidded, veiled.

It occurred to Eve that his lashes were unusually long and thick, that his eyes slanted down slightly at the corners, and she wondered if that was what gave him that melancholy look. Maybe, she grudgingly thought…but only partly.

"Hey, Jake—" It had also occurred to her that she knew almost nothing about him—not even his last name. How old he was. Whether he had a wife…children. The town house he lived in was definitely a bachelor's quarters, and probably temporary at that, the only personal items anywhere in evidence being the old-fashioned turntable, the crate of LP's and the cardboard box she'd spotted under the coffee table, containing an assortment of paperbacks. A lonely existence, she thought. But did he have a home somewhere? A wife and a dog, a lawn waiting to be mowed?

He was waiting now, one hand on the curtain, for her to finish it. But with all she would have liked to ask him, she limited herself to a smile, lopsided and apologetic—a peace offering he wouldn't even know she owed him—and a lightly curious "When do you sleep?"

There was no answering smile, not even one of irony. No chuckle, not even the dryest snort, heavy with sarcasm. Instead he replied, very softly, "When Sonny Cisneros is behind bars."

Then he slipped out of the room like a shadow, leaving her with the chilled feeling that he'd meant it literally.

Sonny...behind bars. Sonny—the man she'd planned to marry, the man she'd...well, if not exactly wildly loved, at least chosen to be the father of her children—was a vicious criminal.

There was no one to distract her now—no doctors and nurses with their needles and bandages and slightly off-color banter, no dour FBI man with his somber warnings and instructions, nothing to keep the reality of that from crashing in on her. For the first time since waking half-naked in a strange man's bed with her soiled wedding gown on the floor beside her, she was alone, just her and her thoughts. And since there was no one to see, instead of pushing her thoughts away in instinctive, gut-level defensive panic, she gave them the okay to come and stay in her mind, and let the full horror of them seep into her soul.

Fear and loathing enveloped her, like the nightmare terrors of long-ago childhood when the miasma of nameless evil rising from under her bed, seeping in from under doors and out of closets and cupboards would send her, shivering with fear, to seek comfort in one of her sisters' beds. What a time of sheltered innocence that had been, when terror could be banished by a warm body, the smell of baby shampoo and a sleepy "Evie's havin' a bad dream?"

"Eve? Oh, Evie…oh my God—"

"Mom…? Oh, Momma, I'm so sorry…." All right, so she was forty-three years old. And yes, she'd been on her own, a world traveler and successful filmmaker, for years and years. But she had just come from that childhood nightmare, had been longing for a time when all it took to banish terror was to be gathered into those familiar arms. Perhaps she could be forgiven—and was most definitely not acting—when she burst noisily into tears.

And then her mother was bending over to kiss her and oh, so carefully touching her bandages, then tenderly cupping her cheek and whispering, "Shh…it's all right, sweetheart… you're all right, that's all that counts," and enveloping her in the familiar scents of Jergens lotion and talcum powder that in a way held more comfort than either the words or the touch.

Beyond her mother's shoulder, through a shimmer of tears, she saw her father's face hovering, flushed red and set in a mask of grief and anger. She could only imagine the frustration he must be feeling, that he, her father and a police officer, had yet been unable to protect his little girl from harm.

"Pop?" she squeaked, reaching for him with one hand as her mother moved aside to make room, "it's okay…I'm okay."

And her father was squeezing her hand, brusquely kissing it and then turning away, grumbling and harrumphing in the garbled and gravelly voice he used to camouflage fierce emotions, about talking to the officer in charge, and what was being done to ensure that the low-life scum that had done this to his little girl was found and brought to justice. And all the while wiping at his eyes and furtively blowing his nose on his familiar white pocket handkerchief, as if he seriously thought no one would notice.

Her sisters were there, too, crowded into that curtained space, and so were their husbands—Riley, the newest member of the family, and Jimmy Joe, hanging back a little as if they understood their purpose was mostly to provide backup—their faces, too, wearing the dark, set look of male outrage.

Eve murmured an abashed "Hi, guys. Some wedding, huh?" and gave her sisters a wry shrug and touched her lip in a way that said she'd smile if only she could. When they didn't say anything back, she gave a careful, whispering laugh and said, "Come on, I know what you were thinking. You were thinking, Boy, Evie's really done it this time! Right? Am I right? You know you were...." Summer and Mirabella both laughed then, but in a funny way that had more than a little of tears in it.

And then they were moving up, one on either side of her to form a protective phalanx around her just as they had when they were children and still believed that the three of them together were invincible, impregnable to any threat from near or far, grown-ups, other children or things that go bump in the night.

There was Mirabella, white as a sheet, puffed up like a little red bird spoiling for a fight, brushing and fussing at the bedclothes as if any imperfections in them were a personal affront. And Summer, the vet, forehead furrowed, sky-blue eyes misty with compassion, her strong, long-boned hands already resting on Eve's shoulder, gently stroking her arm, touching her hair, as if just their touch could make things better.

My family, Eve thought. And whether it was lack of sleep, the residual effects of too much champagne or simply a reaction to all the stresses and traumas of the past twenty-four hours, suddenly the love she felt for them seemed almost too much to bear. I don't want to leave them! she thought, terrified both of dying and of the separation from those she loved so much that would be like a kind of dying.

If this charade didn't work, if she couldn't convince Sonny she posed no threat to him, he would kill her. It was as simple as that. Or, to prevent that certainty, the FBI could whisk her away into some sort of Witness Protection Program, cutting her off forever from all those she loved. But even then there was no guarantee Sonny wouldn't then turn on her family as a way to force her to come back! Eve was accustomed to taking risks, but never before had she been asked to risk so much. Her life? Even that seemed insignificant. What was really at stake was all there with her in that cubicle—the love…the people…her family.

It has to work, she thought. It has to.

And right on the heels of that thought came another. *I have to stop Sonny. Put an end to him. I have to put him away. No matter what it takes. I must. It's the only way.…*

The only way she or any of the people she loved would ever be safe again.

With that realization neon bright in her mind, she heard a new commotion, voices raised in the corridor outside the exam room. One voice in particular.

"Hey, what're you talkin' about—*family?* I'm tellin' you I *am* family. If this hadn't happened, she'd be my wife right now!"

Sonny. Oh God, she thought, I'm not ready! I can't do this! *Jake…where are you?*

Beyond the curtain there were murmurs, low and adamant, and Sonny's voice rolling over them. Jimmy Joe and Riley were already moving to form a protective blockade, if need be, looking over at Eve to see if that was what she wanted. And it was—oh, it *was.* But how would she explain? Sonny was her fiancé, the man she supposedly loved enough that a few hours ago she'd been ready to pledge to honor and obey him until death—

Her heart skipped. She drew a catching breath, then nodded. But her eyes darted among the faces gathered around her like a panic-stricken mouse looking for a hiding place—Bella's and Pop's, so much alike, both gray and stormy; Summer's more like Mom's, sky-blue but clouded with compassion and worry.

And what about Evie's eyes? What do they show?

She thought, He'll look into them and know. How could she hide what she felt for him now—the fear, the loathing?

But the curtain was pulling back...and he was there. Sonny Cisneros, her fiancé—multimillionaire, loud and gregarious, bigger-than-life Sonny Cisneros—broad-shouldered and powerful looking in his expensive suit, no tie, expensive shirt open at the neck, showing gold chains and a thick nest of hair. He moved toward her like an emperor through a throng, sparing quick handshakes for the brothers-in-law, a little longer one for Pop, a one-armed hug for Mom...and then he was beside her bed, looming above her, bending over her... Reaching out to touch the bandage on her head, oh, so gently. Saying, with what sounded like a genuine break in his voice, "Evie...baby—look at you."

Eve drew a shuddering breath, held it and heard herself squeak, "I'm sorry, Sonny, I'm sorry!" And once more and, please God, for the last time that night, burst into tears.

"Hey, what you got to be sorry for?" Sonny crooned, leaning close, brushing her forehead with his fingertips. His breath smelled like Scotch and breath mints. Eve's stomach heaved, and she fought to control it. "You're the one got beat up. Hey—they catch the miserable slimeball that did this, I'm gonna kill 'im with my bare hands."

"He took my engagement ring...the pearls you gave me—"

"Hey, what's a pearl? Oyster poop, that's all. I'll buy you all the pearls you want. I'll get you another ring, too. A rock is a rock. Important thing is, you're gonna be okay. This is never gonna happen to you again, I promise you. I'm gonna make sure of that.''

"Honey—'' Eve's mother was patting her shoulder ''—I think we should go now—leave you two alone. Don't you think so, Pop?'' She squeezed Eve's hand and rubbed her arm as she moved away from her side, pausing to smile tearily at her past Sonny's broad shoulder as she grabbed at Summer and made shooing motions at Mirabella. "Come, girls— we can come back tomorrow.''

"They're going to keep me here a couple of days,'' Eve said, sniffling. "I guess they'll be admitting me soon—I'm just waiting for X rays.''

"We'll be back tomorrow,'' her mother assured her, "after you've had time to get some rest.'' And she was herding everyone out of the exam room amidst foot-shufflings and hand-squeezings and awkward little pats on whatever part of her sheet-shrouded anatomy was closest. Eve caught a glimpse of her sisters' faces, set and pale, clinging to hers until the last second, until the curtain swished back and she was alone…with Sonny.

It was strange. She could feel her heart pounding, feel her body trembling, feel the sticky dryness of fear in her throat— and yet there was a part of herself that felt detached from all that, as if she were sitting somewhere apart from the scene but watching events with a critical eye—the director, per- haps, judging her own performance. *Fear… Okay, the fear is real, so go with that. Make it work for you.…*

"Sonny, the wedding, our beautiful wedding…all our plans—''

"Shh… Hey, what'd I tell you? It's not your fault.''

"I don't know what happened. The last thing I remember, I'd opened the champagne—I had this bottle I'd been saving, you know?—and I was going to find you. There was a little time before the ceremony, and I thought we could…'' Sick- ness rose suddenly in her throat. Sonny was leaning down, his face blocking out the light as he pressed his lips to her undamaged cheek, then to the top of her head. The smell of his hair spray and aftershave almost made her gag.

"Shh...it's okay, baby. We'll make up for it, I promise you. As soon as you're outa here—"

"It must have been so awful for you...." Shaking like a leaf, she felt herself lift her arms and twine them around his neck....

In a windowless room not far away, Jake watched the scene on a hospital security monitor. He had a knot the size of a baseball in his gut, but his face betrayed only a slight frown of concentration, nothing that would have given him away even if the other two people in the room had been looking at him—which they weren't. Like his, their eyes were glued to the monitor.

"Scared to death," Jake's partner, Burdell "Birdie" Poole, muttered into his knuckles. He had one arm folded across his barrel chest, the other bent at the elbow, the hand fisted and pressed against his mouth, and as he spoke leaned slightly away from the screen, as if by distancing himself from it physically he could disconnect emotionally, as well. Birdie looked, with his buzz haircut, slightly harassed look and gradually expanding waistline, like the family man he was. He kept a picture of his patient wife, Marjorie—a saint, in Jake's opinion, and probably the only genuinely happy cop's wife he knew—and their four chubby children on his desk and carried snapshots of them in his wallet. When it came to women and kids he had a soft spot a mile wide. And a pit bull toughness when it came to the bad asses of the world that made Jake glad they were on the same side.

Now Birdie exhaled through his nostrils. "She's shakin' like a leaf—you can see it from here. She's gonna blow it...."

"Maybe not...maybe not." His supervisor, Don Coffee, was leaning toward the bank of monitors, his weight on one forearm while the fingers of the other hand beat an erratic tattoo on the countertop, eyes riveted on the screen. Without turning his head, he said, ''Redfield, you know the man—is he buying it?''

Jake snorted. The fact was, he did know Sonny Cisneros—just well enough to know there was no way in hell to know what the man was thinking. The guy was a sociopath—a man without a conscience. He played by nobody's rules except his own.

Aloud, he said, ''Why wouldn't he buy it? Sure she's shaking—she gets beat up and thrown into a Dumpster on the way to her own wedding, leaves the guy standing at the altar, no explanation, and now she's facing him for the first time? Hell, be strange if she *wasn't* shaking.'' He knew his voice sounded like a junkyard dog's growl, but didn't make any effort to clear it or ease the tension in his jaws. The two men in the room with him were used to him tightening up whenever Cisneros's name came into the conversation.

Right now, though, there was a lot more going on inside him than just the usual teeth-clenching edginess. There was that brassy tang at the back of his throat, for one thing—he wanted this to work so badly, he could taste it. And something else—that knot in his belly, which was something he didn't remember feeling before. Cold—no, not cold…white-hot, as if it would burn right through him. He'd felt it back in his apartment, when his witness had put it into words—the fact that she'd slept with Cisneros.

What the hell was the matter with him? Of course she'd slept with the man—she was marrying him, wasn't she? But whenever the thought came into his mind, he felt the knot…the cold fire in his belly. Right now, watching the two of them together, seeing that blond, bandaged head next to Cisneros's and those slender arms twined around his thick neck, those big, dark-blue eyes closed…he felt the fire eating its way through his guts…into his chest…all but eating him alive. He knew he should probably stop watching for the sake of his own mental health, if nothing else, but he didn't. For some reason he couldn't take his eyes from the screen.

"You really think she could pull this off?" Coffee asked, swiveling to look at him. "It's a hell of a risk—you know that, don't you? Are you sure she'll even agree to go along with it? What we'd be asking her to do would be dangerous even for a trained agent. She's a civilian and she's vulnerable—"

"She'll go along with it." Jake's eyes burned in their sockets as he watched Cisneros pull back from the bed, watched his hand, winking with gold and diamonds, slide lingeringly across the woman's breasts. He felt her shrinking in the depths of his soul. "She's tougher than she looks," he growled.

Cisneros was leaving, finally. Jake watched as he moved to the curtains...watched Eve give him a wan and teary smile...blow him a kiss. And then she was alone, and he saw her body shudder with revulsion, and her eyes, wide-open and staring, now, darken with rage until they looked like two holes burned into marble.

"She'll go along with it," Jake said softly, his heart quickening within him.

"Seems to me she's between a rock and a hard place," Birdie said. "She's got to go back to the guy—how'll it look if she doesn't? But can you imagine what it's gonna be like for her, knowing what she knows?" He shook his head.

"That's why she'll do it," Jake said. "Because she's got no choice."

"I think you're jumping to conclusions, Bell," Summer said in an undertone as she and Mirabella hurried across the hospital parking lot, once again bringing up the rear. The night was moving along toward the wee hours and the low-country fog was already coming in, swirling around the light posts and settling like crystal dust onto the hoods and windshields of parked cars. "Of course she'd be upset—"

"*Not* upset—afraid. You saw her face." Mirabella's voice was low-pitched, as well, but staccato with impotent fury. "I'm telling you, she's scared of him. Scared to death. We have to do something. We can't just let her—"

Her sister's hand clutched her arm, stopping her in her tracks. "You can't mean you think *he* did that to her. Bella, that's just ridiculous. On their *wedding day?* And even if he did, Evie would never put up with such a thing—never. She'd have him in jail so fast, it'd make your head swim!"

Mirabella grudgingly conceded, "Maybe not. But something's not right, I can feel it. You saw her face, Sumz. She didn't want us to leave her alone with him. I just wish I knew what the hell's going on. If she's in some kind of trouble—"

"If Evie was in trouble, she'd tell us," Summer said in a shaky voice. She was hugging herself against the dampness and chill, but shivering anyway. Her face looked pinched and unhappy. "I'm sure she would. We're her family, after all."

"Would she?" said Mirabella, her tone softly accusing. "*You* didn't."

Chapter 6

Eve opened her eyes in the hospital's perpetual twilight and knew at once that she wasn't alone. From her curled-on-her side position she let her eyes roam as far as they would, but saw only the stark walls, the bedside cabinet and visitor's chair, the graying rectangle of a window.

And yet she'd definitely heard something...someone...the stealthy brush of cloth on cloth...the whisper of an exhalation. The nurse, perhaps, coming to check on her yet again? But no, there'd been no footsteps, no sounds of an opening or closing door, no subtle swirls and eddys of air currents stirred by a passing body. Her mother, then, or one of her sisters, unable to stay away, come to sit quietly and wait for her to awaken? The thought made her feel deliciously warm and loved, and at the same time near to weeping.

She turned carefully onto her back and stretched her legs beneath the thin hospital covers, and the dark shape slumped in a chair near the door stirred to instant alertness.

Her heart gave an odd bump. "Jake?" she said on a rising note of surprised laughter. "Is that you?"

The FBI man leaned forward from the waist, arms extended above his head, stretching out stiffness. "Yeah, it's me." His voice sounded as if he'd stifled a yawn.

"What on earth are you doing here? When did you come back?" She felt the strangest all-over prickling, the tiniest shower of shivers, almost like goose bumps. It was the most pleasant feeling she'd had in quite a while actually, and it was hard to keep the smile out of her voice, even as she supplied the answer with its grim reminder, "Are you my bodyguard?"

His eyes regarded her from deep in their shadowed sockets. "You could call it that. Keeping an eye on my star witness."

"I take it you don't trust Sonny's 'All is forgiven' act?"

She heard a noise that she might have taken for a laugh, except she remembered that Agent Jake Something wasn't capable of laughter. "Just taking no chances."

"How long have you been here?" Now that she thought about it, the idea that he'd watched her sleep was disconcerting; she wasn't sure whether to be pleased or appalled.

His shoulders casually rose and fell. "Couple hours. I got tired of lurking in the hallway. When the nurse wasn't looking, I ducked in here. Hope you don't mind."

To cover the ambiguity of her emotions, she gave a dry snort.

She sat up and twisted half around and began lifting up bedclothes and pillows as she added sardonically, "By the way—Sonny plans to assign me a bodyguard. Isn't that nice? Dammit, where in the—"

"What're you looking for?" He rose, a silent, fluid motion that diminished the space between him and her bed by half.

Her heart gave another of those strange little bumps. To distract herself from that she pretended an irritability she didn't feel. "Isn't there supposed to be some sort of button to push when you want to crank this thing up?"

He pointed. "That it?"

"Where?—oh yeah, there it is." And he was close enough to her to evoke memories of how warm his body had felt as he'd carried her into the E.R., and the comforting smell of his bathrobe. Somehow those memories made the space between them seem emptier and the air chillier by comparison. A shiver wafted through her as she added a breathless "Thanks."

"Where are you going?" He'd perked up like a watchdog catching a whiff of an unauthorized scent when she threw back the covers and swung her bare legs over the side of the bed.

She raised her eyebrows at him, feeling with her feet for the floor. "To the bathroom. You want to check it out first?"

He frowned, ignoring the sarcasm. "Shouldn't you, uh…you sure you should be out of bed?"

Amusement rippled through her, but she kept her tone lightly sardonic. "You're really getting caught up in this, aren't you? Might I remind you that I was not *really* attacked, and do not *actually* have a concussion? Except for a minor bump I got when I dropped a Dumpster lid on my own head, and some scrapes and bruises that were the result of my falling out of said Dumpster flat on my, uh, face, I am perfectly fine." Poised to hop down off the bed, she paused and made a twirling motion with one finger. "Turn around, please."

Now it was Jake's eyebrows that arched, then almost comically pulled together in the middle of his forehead as his mouth formed a silent "Oh" of comprehension. Eve thought his discomfiture amusing, even rather sweet, until she heard what he'd muttered under his breath as he turned.

"I beg your pardon?" she demanded, halting with one hand clutching her hospital gown together behind her.

"Nothing I haven't already seen, and packaged a whole lot prettier," he repeated, his voice only slightly more audible and with a strange little burr in it that caused an answering vibration deep in her own chest.

So he'd actually noticed? And was that…amusement? Mr. Deadpan? *No way…*

"Mention that fact again and you're dead meat, buddy." And as she pulled the wide, heavy bathroom door closed behind her, she heard a sound that sent a jolt of wonder through her. *I heard that! That was a chuckle—definitely.*

Jake had it under firm control, though, by the time Eve emerged from the bathroom. He'd gone to stand by the window and was waiting for her, arms folded on his chest, one ankle crossing the other. He waited until she'd settled herself in bed with the covers chastely arranged across her middle, then said without stirring, "Lady, you pull that in the wrong place, the wrong time, you wind up dead."

She lifted a hand to touch the bandage around her head, closed her eyes and let a breath out loudly. Impatience tightened his chest and thickened in his throat, but he kept his voice low and even. "I mean it. In undercover ops, you get in the role and you stay there. Every second, every minute, twenty-four hours a day, seven days a week—you live it, breathe it, think it, *feel* it. Believe it. Or sooner or later you're gonna make a mistake. *Capish?*"

"Yeah." She sighed and leaned her head back against the pillow. "I'm sorry." But then her smile flicked on again, like one of those trick birthday candles you can't blow out. "Undercover ops—how exciting. Like something in a TV script."

It was only when her eyes slid past him, reflecting the graying darkness beyond the window glass, that he saw the smile and the remark for the valiant subterfuge they were. Saw that the smoke screen of banter and easy flirtation had cleared out and left her face-to-face with the reality of her situation. And the odd thing was, he was sorry; without her smile in it, the room already seemed colder.

Difficult as it was, he clamped down hard on the sympathy he felt for her, clenching his teeth together so that his voice came as a growl. "You're gonna have to think it, feel it, believe it if you're gonna make Cisneros believe it."

Still staring at the window, she mumbled, "When he touches me, I feel like I'm going to throw up."

Unexpectedly, it was anger, not sympathy, that flared inside him. He made a disbelieving sound and shook his head.

"What?" Her eyes were on him, defiant and wary.

The spark of resentment within him glowed hotter, brighter. It's none of your business, Redfield, he reminded himself. It's got nothing to do with you. Keep your distance. But he knew he wasn't going to. For some reason he couldn't figure the woman out, and he had to know. Just this one thing. He had to.

With deceptive quietness he said, "Just like that? Yesterday you were going to marry the guy. Before this happened, you were ready to jump his bones, wedding dress and all. Today he makes your stomach turn?"

She stared hard at him for a few moments, then shrugged and looked away. "I guess that's just the way I am," she said distantly, leaving him more frustrated than before.

Jeez—*women.* He thought, Are you all like that? Is it just something you women can do—change your feelings with the snap of your fingers? One day you can pledge to love and cherish a guy forever, and the next day it's gone—over, finished, kaput?

But of course he wouldn't ask her that; it wasn't his place, or his business. And at the same time, something in him wasn't ready to let it go. After a pause he said casually, "I'm curious. How did you ever hook up with a guy like Sonny, anyway?"

He could see that she wanted to hang on to her pique a while longer. And she tried; leaning back against her pillows and heaving a put-upon sigh, she looked at the ceiling and began with pointed reluctance, "How did I hook up with Sonny....?" But it took about that long for her natural gregariousness to take over, and she broke it off, laughing softly. "It's funny, really, the way it happened. See, I'd been in Brazil, on a shoot. We were doing a documentary about this tribe, in the rain forest, that had just been discovered in the last fifty years, and now they're being threatened with extinction because their habitat is being destroyed for lumber and farmland. Can you believe that?" Her eyes sparked with passion and her voice grew husky. "I mean, we spend billions of dollars trying to protect the habitat of some obscure species of bird or rat or tree frog, and here's a race of human beings who, if they were animals would be on every endangered species list there is." She stopped, and he could see her working at reining herself in.

"So, anyway, I was back in L.A. doing postproduction on the project—this was last spring—and I got a call from my boss, that's the head of the production company I work for, saying she wants me to put the Amazon project on the back burner, because they want me to go to Las Vegas, of all places. They've got this big new project in the works, a four-parter for one of the cable networks on *The New Las Vegas*. *Huge* amounts of money involved. I pretty much hit the ceiling. I mean, the Brazil project meant a lot to me. Plus, I'd just spent six months sweltering in the Amazon jungle, getting slowly eaten to death, and just when we're getting started with the actual *work*—the fun stuff, I mean. See—" And she broke off to hitch herself forward, talking with her whole body now, all traces of reluctance and resentment forgotten, enthusiasm shining in her face in spite of her battered features. "Making a documentary's not like doing a movie or TV show, where you have a script and a shooting schedule to follow. The camera work is just your raw material. I mean, those cinematographers are amazing, especially when it comes to shooting wildlife, but the actual film is made in postproduction—the editing, music, voice-overs. That's where the real creativity comes in. That's where..." Once again she throttled back, letting out a breath of exasperation.

"Anyway, I threw a class-A hissy-fit, but to no avail. Basically, I was not given a choice—the Vegas people had specifically asked for me. They'd seen my work. I was who they wanted, or no deal. All very flattering, I suppose. And like I said, *lots* of money involved. Which is the bottom line, right? I thought about walking, I was so mad—I really did. But then I'd have had to leave my Brazil project behind, and I wasn't about to do that. So off I went to Vegas, but I was still fuming, and let me tell you, I made sure everybody knew it!

"Anyway, we get to the hotel, right?—this huge casino, 'Shangri-La'—Sonny's casino—and we're all booked into these luxury suites, like royalty. I walk into my room, and I nearly fainted. I mean, it's *filled* with orchids and all sorts of tropical plants and birds in cages, and baskets of fruit, and there's even a recording of rain forest sounds playing on the stereo. And in the middle of it all, I find a note that says, 'Let me make it up to you.' And it's signed, 'Sonny Cisneros.'" She stopped with a small shrug and an off-center smile that said, *What was I gonna do?*

Jake said dryly, "So naturally you fell in love with him."

She didn't answer; she was staring out the window again. After a moment she shifted as if the bed had sand in it. "I'm trying hard to be honest with myself about it, but hindsight doesn't make it easy." There was another pause, and when she went on it was as if she were measuring each word before delivering it. "I know he dazzled me. Las Vegas is an easy place to be dazzled in, believe me. Nothing is real—it's all this great big fantasy. It was just...so easy to buy into the fantasy of falling in love...." She sat silently, her slumped shoulders giving her a forlorn look. "Actually, it probably had more to do with—" She broke it off to slide him a sideways look and a wry smile. "Are you sure you want to hear this?"

"Yeah," he said evenly, "I do."

"I mean, you just asked me how I got hooked up with Sonny. You probably don't want to hear my whole life story."

"I said I did—this part of it, anyway." He rather imagined this woman's life story would take a long time to tell and probably be well worth the time spent, but he didn't say so. "Go on—it had more to do with…?"

"Timing," she said on an exhalation, and gave him another of her off-center smiles. "The infamous biological clock. Lately it seems like all I do is go to weddings and christenings—other people's. First, my sister Mirabella has a baby and gets married—yes, in that order—after we'd all given up hope. Then her best friend, Charly, comes out from California to be her maid of honor, meets the best man and *she's* a goner. So off I go to the rain forest where I'm surrounded by burgeoning nature for a solid six months, and when I come out, *everybody's* pregnant. And it just occurred to me that I was in my forties, had never even been in love—" her smile broadened and her eyes gleamed, and Jake inexplicably felt that peculiar sensation of thirst at the back of his throat "—although I've been in lust a few times. And in love with the *idea* of being in love, I suppose. But never really in love. And I realized that if it was ever going to happen to me, it had better happen pretty damn soon, or what was the point? I guess I just wanted it badly enough that I convinced myself the fantasy was real."

He had nothing to say to that, and left unanswered and hanging in the silence, the words took on a greater poignancy than perhaps she'd meant them to have. Jake didn't know for sure; he couldn't know, because he couldn't allow himself to look at her. He didn't want to see her vulnerability just then. Afraid that if he did, he might let himself start to care.

He was leaning against the wall at the edge of the window, gazing along his shoulder at the uninspiring view of a well-lighted but almost empty parking lot, shrouded now in fog, when she suddenly said, "Hey, Jake."

He shifted his gaze back to her without changing his stance, and found that she was regarding him with her head slightly tilted and a bright, inquisitive gleam in the eye on the undamaged side of her face. He noticed that her eyes, although blue, were actually quite dark, and that her short, blond hair had gotten caught up in the bandage that was wrapped around her head so that it formed a comical little rooster tail. She made him think of a bird, one of the ones that used to come to the feeder his wife, Sharon, had kept in the backyard of their house in Virginia, way back when he'd still been in training at Quantico. A little gray bird with a yellowish topknot, big black eyes and a cheeky disposition—a titmouse, that was it. She reminded him of a titmouse.

"Yeah?" he prompted. And why was it that whenever he was in her company he kept having to fight an urge to smile?

"What about you? Are you married?"

He jerked his eyes away from her and looked down at his feet, while his arms folded of their own volition into a defensive position across his chest. The question had caught him off guard, but at least it had neatly disposed of the smile impulse. "Nah—" he said with a shrug and what he hoped was finality, "guess I don't have what it takes."

"Ever been?"

Cheeky—he should have known she wouldn't leave it there. What surprised him more than the question was the fact that he found himself answering it. "Yeah, I was married. Once."

Her head tilted even more, and her eyes regarded him with a directness that was almost hypnotic. "What happened?"

"She woke up one morning and told me she didn't want

to be married to me anymore. That she deserved a chance to be happy. I agreed with her. So we got a divorce.''

"Just like that? One day you were happy and clueless, the next day over, finished, kaput?"

He grunted, half in surprise, half in acknowledgment of the hit she wasn't even aware of—an unspoken *touché*—and said sardonically, ''Well, I doubt if it was that simple.''

"How long were you married?"

"Fifteen years." Eve whistled. He glanced at her, but saw only sympathy in her eyes—and that mesmerizing inquisitiveness. He shrugged and added, ''We got married right out of college. But I'd known her since high school.''

"Any kids?"

He shook his head. And though she hadn't asked, he found himself explaining as if she had. ''She...couldn't.''

There was the sound of a softly indrawn breath. ''That must have been hard.''

He hated sympathy. He held her eyes for several seconds, waiting for a rush of resentment that never came, and finally said, ''It was, for her.''

"Not you?"

He shrugged. ''I was pretty wrapped up in my job.''

"And...she had—?"

Again he paused, then said slowly, ''Oh, yeah, she worked. In an office. Nothing she was very excited about. Nothing you could call a career.''

"So," Eve murmured, "she just had...you. And you had—"

"My job." He shifted restlessly and said with a sardonic snort, ''And thank you, Dr. Brothers, for pointing that out.''

Her lips parted and a look of dismay darkened her eyes, and he realized too late that there'd been nothing but compassion in them before. The knowledge added to the burden of his guilt and made him feel even lousier than he already did—not angry, certainly not with her, not resentful, just…bad. As if a blanket of melancholy had settled around his shoulders.

"I didn't mean—" she began.

But he stopped her there, shaking off the mood of intro-spection and silencing her with the same swift motion. Swearing with sibilant vehemence under his breath, he dove into the bathroom and pulled the door closed just as the outer door clicked open to admit a hideously cheerful voice trilling, "Well, are we wide-awake already this morning?"

And there he lurked—feeling about as foolish as he ever had in his life and asking himself whether this was any way for an experienced agent of federal law enforcement to be spending his time, for what seemed like hours. It was, in fact, by his own watch, scarcely five minutes before there came a soft knock on the bathroom door. After a barely respectable pause, it opened, and there stood Eve in her short hospital gown, rooster tail waving jauntily above her bandages, one finger to her lips.

"You can come out now," she said in a hoarse and ex-aggerated whisper. "The big bad nursie is all gone."

Damnation, how was it possible, annoyed as he was with her, that he could still feel that bumpy, deep-down urge to *laugh?*

He limited himself instead to the small satisfaction of ex-plaining to her, in his driest, most professional manner, about the realities of hospital gossip. "How would it look," he said coldly, "if it got back to your…fiancé…through hospital per-sonnel that a man was keeping company with you in your room?"

As he was saying that, he watched her face, fascinated by the conflict so clearly written there. He could see part of her wanted to joke about it—laugh it off—but that part of her knew he was right.

She waited until he'd finished, then cocked her head like that cheeky little bird she reminded him of, and in a light but quiet voice—a compromise, he thought—inquired, ''Are you always so depressingly suspicious and pessimistic?''

In a voice just as quiet, he shot back, ''Are you always so annoyingly cheery and optimistic?''

Then for a few moments tension crackled in the quietness while their eyes waged their silent tug-of-war. But while Jake recognized the battle of wills, darned if he could figure out what the stakes were. If it was a matter of dominion, or authority—some kind of control thing—she had to know she was outmatched. Maybe in her own world she was the one that got to call the shots, but she was in his world now, and in that world she was vulnerable and clueless as a newborn baby. She wasn't a stupid woman, she had to know that. So why was she standing there bandaged and bruised and barely decent in that hospital gown, toe-to-toe with a federal agent in full battle armor?

It made no more sense to him than did the way he felt when she leveled those indigo-blue eyes at him and finally answered his question in a low, almost toneless voice. ''No, only when things look *really* hopeless.''

Outmatched she may have been, but he felt in no way victorious.

Instead, he found himself remembering what she'd said, about the idea of Cisneros touching her making her feel sick. They'd talked quite a bit since then, exchanged a few tidbits of personal history, even shared a secret or two. But nothing had been said that would change the fact that sometime soon Eve Waskowitz was going to have to find a way to resume convincingly the role of loving fiancé to a man she now abhorred. He suddenly realized that what he was looking at was a terrified woman. And that what she was doing was simply whistling in the dark.

He felt his belly clench, and something flare white-hot inside him and then go cold and still.

Hopeless? Not if he had anything to say about it.

"What'd the nurse want?" he asked gruffly.

Eve shrugged and turned, clutching her gown together where it mattered most, but giving him an unnerving glimpse of the back he remembered from when he'd undressed her in his bedroom—the creamy smooth skin, the delicate indentations of spine.

"Just routine stuff. They keep a pretty close eye on you, I guess, when you've been bumped on the head. She also said breakfast will be here soon, and she wanted to know if I wanted to 'freshen up' before visitors start arriving. Which I do," she added pointedly as she sat on the edge of the bed and leveled a look at him. Her eyes were shadowed and dark, impossible to read, and for the first time he thought she looked her age. "I'm sure you'd like some breakfast yourself—a cup of coffee, at least. Better make your escape while you can."

"Yeah, I will...." But he went on staring at her, his mind spinning furiously, hating to leave it like that. Hating to leave *her,* it shocked him to realize. Hating to leave her with that look of hopelessness in her eyes, and the thought of her and Cisneros in bed together twisting a knot in his belly.

He lifted a hand, palm out, and said with a voice full of gravel, "Listen—it's not hopeless. Okay? I'm workin' on it. Just...do me a favor, huh? Remember to act *injured?*" Her only reply was a very small snort.

He opened the door a crack, looked up and down the corridor, waited for his moment, then slipped through the door and closed it gently behind him. As he made his way, scowling, through the awakening hospital, bustling with the routines of morning, with the clank of breakfast trays and the ding of elevators and the swish of footsteps and voices on the intercom, he wondered when his first priority had changed from nailing the bad guy to keeping Eve Waskowitz out of the bad guy's bed.

* * *

Eve's day progressed in predictable hospital fashion. People popped in and out of her room on various errands, most of them involving indignities to her person. Out of sheer boredom, she dozed until the arrival of breakfast, an excitement relative in its anticipation to Christmas morning. Shortly after that, her mother and sisters arrived, bringing with them her small overnighter. She was so glad to see them, it was hard to remember to act feeble and wan.

"I'm not sure what's in here," Summer said as she laid the overnight case on the foot of Eve's bed. "I think it's mostly makeup and toiletries. I wanted to bring you something to wear—a nightgown, but it all looked like...you know—honeymoon stuff."

"Sweetheart, are you in pain?" her mother asked anxiously.

"A bit," Eve lied in a faint voice. "My head, mostly."

Her mother's cool hand touched her cheek. "Oh, honey, I'm so sorry."

"What does the doctor say?" Mirabella demanded, showing her concern in her own pushy way. "Have you seen him yet this morning? Do they know how bad the concussion is? How much longer are they going to keep you here?"

"I don't know," Eve said. "A doctor stopped by earlier this morning, just long enough to read my chart and huddle with the nurse for a few minutes. He seemed very busy...." Remembering Jake's parting words, *I'm workin' on it,* she added in a vague tone she hoped would cover all bases, "I think they're still doing tests...looking at X rays—stuff like that. They have to be sure...."

"Of course," Summer murmured, stroking her arm. Mirabella subsided, looking not in the least satisfied.

"So—where are the menfolk this morning?" Eve asked brightly, just as her mother was saying, "Have you heard from Sonny this morning?" Before either could answer the other, the phone on the bedside table trilled. Eve stared at it in surprise.

"Well. That's probably Sonny now," her mother said.

"Oh—yeah," said Eve, with what she hoped was a smile. She picked up the phone and ventured a tentative "Hello?"

"Get rid of them," Jake's voice growled in her ear. "Sorry to break up the family gathering, but we need to talk. *Now.*"

Chapter 7

Eve's mind was spinning like a bogged-down wheel, going absolutely nowhere. "Uh…" was all she could think to say.

"Did you hear what I said?" Jake growled again. "There's some things we need to go over before your fiancé gets there. It's important. *Capish?*"

Smile, she thought. Let them think it's Sonny. "Can't you come now? I mean, why…"

There was an impatient exhalation. "Look—your sister Summer knows me. We met during that business with her ex-husband last summer. If she sees me, she's gonna know something's going on. Is that what you want? You want your family in on this?"

"God, no." *Smile, dammit. Remember to smile.* "Okay, then, I guess I'll see you in a little bit. Yeah…bye for now, *darling.* Mmm-hmm…me, too…" She made sickening kissy sounds into the phone, taking great pleasure in imagining Jake's face as she did so, and hung up on the ambiguous hiss of his exhalation.

"That was Sonny," she announced, and smiled widely for the benefit of the three pairs of eyes that had been trying their best to watch her avidly without appearing to do so at all. "He's coming over in a little while. Hey, guys—I really hate to ask it, but I'd kind of like to, you know...clean up a little bit before he gets here? Would you mind terribly...?"

"Of course not, dear," said her mother, patting her shoulder. "We'll go, and let you get yourself spruced up."

Mirabella exchanged a look with Summer and complained, "We just got here."

"And we can come back later." Her mother leaned over to plant a kiss on the undamaged portion of Eve's forehead. "There's a nice mall just up the road. We can kill a few hours there. Anything we can get for you, honey? Some pj's, maybe?"

Eve made an attempt to hitch herself up on her pillows and tried to look pitiful. "Maybe you could pick me up something casual to wear...everyday stuff, you know? Something that buttons in front, so I don't have to pull it on over my head?"

There was a brief knock on the door, and a nurse stuck her head in. After smiles and a cheery "Well, hi, there!" for the visitors, she turned the smile on Eve. "Miz Waskowitz, your doctor's here to see you."

My doctor? Eve had never been sick a day in her life—not counting the occasional tropical bug or spider- or snake-bite—and except for her gynecologist out in California, did not have a doctor. However, before she could think of an appropriately noncommittal response, the door opened wider and a man she'd never seen before slipped past the nurse and into the room.

He was tall and thin and looked very fit, with hair that Eve suspected was prematurely silver, although it might have been his jovial manner that made him seem ageless. He seemed to bound into the room, rather like an overly friendly greyhound, with that slightly stooped-over gait very tall people often use in an effort to seem less so. Tucking the large brown envelope he'd brought with him under one arm, he beamed at her and said in a thick Georgia accent, "Hello there, Miss Eve. Well now—you don't look s'bad."

"Uh…hi. Mom, everybody—this is…my doctor. Dr.—"

"Dr. Shepherd—good to meet you." He lunged forward to pump all three hands with immense enthusiasm, and added in the polite Southern way, since it was apparent they were about to, "Don't rush off."

"Yeah, Mom, maybe you guys should stick around." But her voice was faint and breathless, and went unnoticed in the flurry of polite assurances and hasty goodbyes.

Eve kept her smile rigidly in place until the door had closed behind her mother and sisters. Then she filled her lungs with air and whispered, "Okay, you've got about two seconds to prove to me you are who you say you are and tell me who sent you, before I start screaming bloody murder. One…two…"

Instead of answering, Dr. Shepherd held up a hand, asking for—demanding—silence. Moving with surprising quickness for one so angular, he went to the door and opened it a crack, looked through, then opened it a little wider. As if he'd been waiting for a signal, Jake stepped into the room.

Eve let out the breath she'd been holding, in one great gust. "Okay, you want to tell me what in the hell's going on? Who the devil *is* this? First you spend the night guarding my room 'just in case,' so I'm seeing bogeymen under the bed, and then you send some strange guy in here without warning me? For all I know, he's some kind of hit man, for God's sake!"

From mild pique, the anger level in her voice had escalated with each sentence until the last three words were delivered in a splutter of full-blown outrage. Most of her annoyance, she acknowledged, was due to the absurd little surge of joy she'd experienced at her first glimpse of the FBI man's glowering face. A ray of sunshine he definitely wasn't, and she couldn't imagine why she should be so happy to see him. The only reason she *could* imagine was so ludicrous and unlikely, it didn't even bear acknowledging, must less thinking about.

Obviously unimpressed with her diatribe, Jake barked right back at her. "Waskowitz, do me a favor—shut up a minute and listen. Cisneros is probably on his way here as we speak, so no telling how much time we have. This—" he nodded at the silver-haired man, who thrust his jaw toward her and grinned toothily, rather in the manner of FDR "—is Dr. Matthew Shepherd. He is in fact an M.D., but he also consults for the Bureau. We think we may have come up with a solution to your problem. Matt?"

At his cue, the doctor lunged forward, opening the brown envelope as he did so, and extracted several X-ray films, which he laid across the foot of Eve's bed.

"Are those mine?" she asked as she raised herself up and hitched forward to get a better look.

"In…a manner of speaking." Dr. Shepherd took a pair of rimless glasses from his jacket pocket, put them on and peered through them down his long, bony nose at the films. After a moment his gaze vaulted the tops of the glasses to twinkle conspiratorially at her. "Actually, they are about to *become* your X rays. See this here?" He was once more bent over the films, pointing with a long, elegant finger.

Eve nodded and dutifully said, "Uh-huh," though she hadn't seen anything but fuzzy shades of gray. "What does it mean?"

Dr. Shepherd straightened, whipped off his glasses and beamed at her. "What that means, young lady, is that for the foreseeable future, you are gonna have to keep your upper spinal column as immobile as possible. That means wearing an orthopedic device to limit movement, sleeping in a specially designed bed…ahem…alone—'' Eve's sharp intake of breath barely interrupted him. "In addition to which, I would recommend a program of extensive physical therapy…."

Eve was barely listening. Her eyes had slipped past the doctor to find Jake's, and she clung to their steady and bottomless gaze as he added, without inflection, "Which gives us a reason to keep you here in the area, as well as cover in case you need to get in touch with us—or vice versa. If you need us, you'd just call your doctor. Or, say, if we need to contact you, your doctor's office would call you—maybe change the date or time of an appointment, for instance."

"My God," Eve whispered, "it takes care of everything."

Jake grunted. "It buys you some time. What you do with it's gonna be up to you."

"I understand. Jake…I don't know how to thank you."

Something black and angry slashed across his face, gone so quickly, she couldn't be certain she'd seen it at all. Because in the next instant he'd disappeared soundlessly into the bathroom as the outer doorknob turned and the door cracked open to admit the croaking sound of a naturally boisterous voice trying its best to whisper.

"He's in there with her now? Yeah…that's good. Sure, you bet I wanna talk to him. Okay…thanks, sweetie—you're a doll."

Yeah, Sonny, and it's a good thing you're such a flirt, Eve thought. Because even while he was stopping to sweet-talk the nurse, she barely had time to flop back against the pillows and arrange an appropriately pain-wracked expression.

Meanwhile, for the second time that day, Jake found himself reduced to the indignity of skulking in the bathroom like an illicit lover. The space was so small, he couldn't even pace to release his nervous energy, which he could feel building up inside him like pressure in a steam locomotive. Through the barrier of the door he could hear the muffled murmur of voices, mostly the doctor's, explaining his patient's "condition" and outlining the plan for her "treatment." That was punctuated intermittently by Cisneros's questions in his Vegas big shot's bark, loud and brassy, like something out of an old Rat Pack movie. Every time he heard it, Jake had to remind himself to unclench his teeth.

What was it about the man that got to him so? When had Cisneros stopped being just another case and become his own personal crusade? He thought about it while he waited, having nothing better to do. But the fact was, he knew it hadn't been one big moment of truth, but rather a lot of little straws—too many things he knew about Cisneros but couldn't find a way to prove, too many investigations that led nowhere, too many cases evaporating before they could even get to trial. Too many witnesses turning up missing, or suffering memory lapses following a tragic "accident" involving a loved one. Little straws…the last one the hit-and-run death of a key witness's wife and seven-year-old daughter as they walked to school, just three blocks from their house.

The day that happened, Jake had cut out early and gone home to find his wife on her way out the door with her suitcases. "I deserve to be happy," was all she'd said when he'd pressed her for reasons. She hadn't wanted to talk about it; plainly, she'd meant to be gone before he got home.

It didn't matter—he knew the reason. And he knew the fault was all his. For too long, all his time, energy and passion had been focused on getting Cisneros; he'd had nothing left over for his wife. What he'd told Eve—that it had happened overnight—had been a lie. The simple truth was, Sharon's love for him had died a long, slow death by starvation. And it was a whole lot easier to blame Sonny Cisneros than his own shortcomings as a husband.

He swore inaudibly and closed his eyes, wrenching himself out of the past and back to the present. Which for the first time in a long while was looking like it might just give him a future to look forward to. After Hal Robey had drowned in that hurricane last summer, he'd been ready to pack it in. He'd actually looked into it—leaving the Bureau—but something had held him back, kept him from taking that final step. And now, by God, it looked as if he was being given another shot. He had a witness, and this one he wasn't going to lose. He'd be careful, take it slow and easy…one step at a time.

He still had to convince Eve to go along with the program, but he was confident she would. Of course she would; she knew what the stakes were as well as he did—better than he did. It was her life that was on the line, after all, though the risks, if they were careful and she did what she was supposed to do, should be minimal. Minimal, he told himself. At worst, they'd get nothing concrete enough to take to court, she'd bide her time and break off the relationship, and that would be that. But if things went the way he hoped…at last, Sonny Cisneros was going *down.*

The tap on the bathroom door sent a shot of adrenaline through his system.

It was Shepherd. The moment Jake opened the door Matt said tersely, ''He's gone. I told him we needed to run more tests, get her fitted with the collar before she can be released tomorrow morning.''

''He'll be here with the limo to pick me up,'' Eve put in. Beyond Shepherd, Jake could see her sitting upright against the pillows, one eye purpling and bloodshot, the other glittering like moonlit water. In spite of the bandages she had a pugnacious look—a beat-up prizefighter on an adrenaline high.

Jake flashed her a sharp glance, then said to Shepherd, ''Where? He's not taking her back to Vegas—''

Eve shook her head, then caught herself. ''Oops—gotta remember not to do that, don't I?''

''The collar'll help you remember,'' Dr. Shepherd said cheerfully.

"I hope so. Anyway, no—actually, Sonny's being really sweet about this—he says he figured I'd want to be close to my doctor and my family, so he's made arrangements for us to stay at this new resort he's building on Hilton Head. That's not far from Summer and Riley's place—"

"Really," said Jake thoughtfully.

"And just a hop and a skip from my brand-new office here in Savannah." Dr. Shepherd aimed his FDR grin at Eve and began gathering up the scattered X rays. "Well—I've got things to attend to, looks like. I'm gonna leave you two to work out details between you. Jake, I'll have that collar ready by this evening, if you want to—"

"Yeah—fine." Jake silenced him with a surreptitious hand gesture and the smallest twitch of his head toward Eve.

"Right—see y'all later." With a wave and a wink, Shepherd tucked the X rays under his arm and bounded from the room.

The silence he left behind was thick as cobwebs. Jake felt it settle around him as he turned, so that he seemed to be moving through a sticky, gauzy curtain of his own guilt.

"What was that all about?" Eve demanded, not quite suspicious, just wary, watching him with her head cocked to one side, and that bright-eyed, titmouse look about her again.

"What was what?" he countered, about as convincing as a cookie thief with crumbs on his chin.

"That." She mimicked his little warning head jerk, then grimaced. "Oh, shoot—I've got to quit doing things like that."

"Like the doc said, that's what the collar's for," Jake said sourly. "To keep you from doing things like that."

"Uh-huh... He said he'd have the collar ready by this evening. He said that to *you,* Jake. He said he'd have the collar ready for *you.* What have you got to do with my neck brace?"

She sure didn't miss much. Which, he reminded himself, was exactly what was going to make her one helluva witness.

Instead of answering her, he walked over to the window where he stood for a few minutes looking out at the parking lot, slowly filling up now, with Sunday-afternoon visitors. Then he turned, leaned against the wall and folded his arms.

It was a small room; he could almost have reached out and touched her, and yet he felt that she was far, far away from him. Which was, of course, the way he wanted it. Detachment, that's what he had to have if he was going to make this work. Keep a professional distance, keep the operation and its goal in front of him at all times. Care about her safety—that went without saying. But beyond that—stay away.

But as he stood there staring at the Eve lying just beyond his arm's reach in her hospital bed, he couldn't keep himself from seeing instead all the *other* Eves he'd met over the course of the last twenty-four hours, the Eves from which he hadn't managed to keep that critical distance.

The battered bride, reeking of garbage and tanked on vintage champagne, taking him by surprise in his van and then turning to him with terror and pleading in her eyes...

The sleeping beauty he'd had no choice but to undress...and it had been like Pandora opening her box, revealing every adolescent male's fantasy.... Lush femininity wrapped in creamy skin and all tied up in garters and lace... Long, smooth legs in silky white stockings that he could *feel* wrapped around him—hoo boy, and how was he supposed to put *that* mischief back in the box? Tell himself he hadn't seen it? Order himself not to remember?

Oh, and for God's sake, don't remember the brave but doomed princess who'd stood with her head trustingly bowed, like Anne Boleyn baring her neck to the headsman, while he relieved her of her jewelry. And why was it he could still feel that mouth-watering sensation he'd gotten when he'd thought—just for an instant—of putting his mouth on the little red mark the clasp had made on her skin?

Why was it he could still feel the weight of her body in his arms, the warm, moist pool of her breath against his shoulder as he'd carried her into the hospital? The shivers of suppressed laughter—mostly nerves, he knew, but dangerously contagious nonetheless—that had made him think of tumbling her into something soft and near and romping with her there with the mindless abandon of puppies and children and very new lovers.

And finally, the one image that had brought him back to her room last night and kept him company through the hours of his vigil while she slept...one solitary tear slipping down her cheek, leaving its trail of silver....

"There's something else, isn't there?" Her voice was quiet, not accusing, just accepting. Waiting.

Jake shook his head, not in answer to the question, but to chase the images of those other Eves from his mind. And he frowned, not at her, but as a means to force himself to concentrate on the Eve that faced him now with her bruises and bandages and a bright, intelligent gaze. Finally he took a breath, let it out slowly and said, "That time I just bought you—I said it's up to you what you do with it?"

She nodded, her face grave. "I understood what you were saying. I have to find a way to break up with Sonny without making him suspicious." She looked away before she swallowed. "It's not going to be easy."

"How would you feel," Jake said carefully, "about doing something...a little bit more...preemptive than that?"

Her eyes came back to him. "What do you mean?"

"I mean, how would you feel about helping us nail your...fiancé?" He said it warily, not certain about her reaction. Regardless of what she'd told him about her feelings and how she'd gotten involved with Cisneros, the guy had been her lover. Breaking off a relationship was one thing;

taking somebody she'd been intimate with and putting him in prison for life was another.

She wasted no time in dispelling his doubts as she exhaled in an explosive little gasp of surprise. "Help you—you mean like...*spy?* On *Sonny?*"

Jake drew a hand over his face, muffling his swearing. "Jeez, Waskowitz," he finally muttered. "Spy? You think I'd go to this much trouble to save your ass and then get you killed? No. All we want you to do is plant some listening devices—"

"Bugs!" she cried gleefully.

He snorted. "Okay, we'd like you to bug Sonny's private space—bedroom, office, car—anywhere he's likely to do business—"

"What about his telephone?"

"That's...tricky."

"You could show me how." She was sitting up straight in bed, as eagerly predatory and bright-eyed over the idea of those bugs as a little banty hen who'd just scratched up a whole nest of the six-legged kind. "And—oh, God, now I get it—you're going to hide the bugs in my collar! That's what Dr. Shepherd meant when he said he'd have it ready for you. That is so cool."

"You don't miss a trick, do you?" said Jake dryly.

Eve shrugged. "It's a no-brainer. That was my question, remember? What's with the collar? So it's obvious." She gave herself kind of a shivery little hug, then looked past him toward the window as she said pensively, "I guess great minds do think alike. I was going—I was *planning*—to see if I could find anything out about Sonny's...business—" Jake's breath expired like a pressure valve letting go, but she raised her voice and rushed on before he could interrupt. "All right, I know—but the thing is, I'm not sure I can. What if I can't?—I don't know if I'm a good enough actress to break up with Sonny without making him suspicious. I'd always be afraid…looking over my shoulder—''

Jake pushed away from the window. It took only that to bring him close enough to her to take her by the shoulders. "Listen to me," he said in his softest, growliest voice. "You are not to do anything except what we tell you to do, *capish?* No poking around, no snooping, no lurking in places you shouldn't be. You'll plant the bugs *only* where it's possible to do so without arousing suspicion, and that's *all* you'll do, or no deal. You understand?''

She nodded and whispered, *"Capish."* And her eyes clung to his face as if she were mesmerized.

As for Jake, after the first sweeping search for the verification he needed, and finding it in her eyes and her nod, his gaze zeroed in on her mouth and stayed there. He watched it form the word as she whispered it, saw the first fine sheen of perspiration appear on her chin and upper lip, like diamond dust on her skin. He felt the tickle of a pulse in his fingers where they gripped her shoulders, and his own heart slamming hard against his ribs.

Her lips parted. She drew a breath in the soft, careful way of someone afraid of shattering a soap bubble…or preparing to be kissed.

He let go of her as if she'd burst into flames and spun away, holding up one hand in a vague gesture that was meant to be the "I'm sorry" he couldn't quite form into words.

Lord help us, I've lost my mind, he thought, staring morosely down at the parking lot from his safe haven by the window. It was the only explanation. As if this whole thing wasn't balanced on the razor's edge as it was…

"Jake?''

He didn't want to turn around. Didn't want to answer her. Sure as hell wasn't going to look at her.

"I've been thinking. You know, about what you said before? About how could I change my feelings so quickly? And

what I told you, about Sonny, and it being a matter of timing…well, that was true, but I think it was only part of it. I
know this is going to sound like I'm trying to justify myself
with the benefit of hindsight, but…somewhere inside, I
think…I knew.''

''Knew…?'' With great reluctance he shifted so that he
could look at her, one shoulder against the wall, arms casually folded, one ankle crossing the other. Aloof, he told himself. Completely detached.

She had pulled her knees up and wrapped her arms around
them, and above the drape of hospital bedding, her eyes were
the luminous violet of a twilight sky. ''Knew…that it was
wrong. Oh, not that I knew Sonny was a crook, I don't mean
that. Just that he was wrong…for me. That I was wrong to
marry him. Because I kept finding excuses. For God's sake,
we were in Vegas—the world capital of weddings! I could
have married him months ago—that's what he wanted. But
I said no, I wanted my family there. Then I got the bee in
my bonnet about Savannah, and I insisted on that particular
church even though there was a three-month waiting list.
What was *that?* I'm not even religious.'' She let out a breath
and looked away, and he watched a blush deepen under her
natural tan, like time-lapse photography of a ripening peach.

''What you said? About being ready to 'jump his bones'?''
She sounded ashamed but hell-bent on confession. And why
tell him? he wondered. Her relationship with Cisneros was
the last thing he wanted to have to hear about. But she was
going doggedly on, in a low, tense voice. ''It wasn't…quite
like that. I mean, that wasn't what it was about. When I
opened that bottle of champagne and went looking for Sonny,
it wasn't because I wanted him so much, I just couldn't wait
to…'' She collected another breath, a quick little in-and-out,
stalling for time, then dragged her gaze bravely back to him.
''I think…what I wanted more than anything else, was to be
convinced. I had all these butterflies. I was thinking, My God,

Evie, what are you doing? Are you *crazy?* All of a sudden I wanted to prove to myself I wasn't crazy. I wanted Sonny to make love to me—I mean really knock my socks off—so I'd know I was doing the right thing by marrying him. As if sex was enough…'' She swallowed, looked away again briefly, then came back to him with a wry smile.

Detach, he thought, silently grinding his teeth.

"See, I have this awful tendency, where emotions are concerned. I sort of go overboard in the opposite direction from what I'm really feeling, you know what I mean? Like, I cry at parties and make jokes at funerals—that sort of thing. Terrible. So…the more uncertain I was about whether I wanted Sonny, the more I… Well, you know.''

She groaned and bowed her head, resting her forehead on her drawn-up knees. He saw her shoulders begin to shake, but it was a moment before he realized that she was laughing. "Oh, God…'' She lifted her head, but covered her eyes with her hand. "I bought all this sexy lingerie. I mean, what was *that?* It sure as hell isn't *me.* That thing I was wearing—''

"You mean, the teddy?'' Jake asked, in a tone of polite interest. Complete detachment.

The hand came away from her face and something sparked in her eyes, something bright and breathtaking and too quickly gone, like a bluebird flashing across the periphery of his vision, or a fish breaking the silver surface of a lake at dawn. She cleared her throat. "Actually, I believe the technical term is merry widow.''

"Ah,'' said Jake. Detached? Sure he was. On the outside, anyway. Only problem was, somebody had forgotten to clue his vital organs in on the plan. So there was his heart pumping away like crazy and a furnace firing up in his belly, sending all that heat and blood flow to the parts of his body where he needed it the least and leaving him critically short in other vital areas—like his brain.

She made another small, throat-clearing sound. "I'm strictly into cotton and comfort myself."

"Uh-huh." Her face was so demure and still. And what did that mean, he wondered, in light of what she'd just said about always showing the opposite of what she was feeling? Did that mean that right now her heart was banging away like the Energizer Bunny and her temperature soaring and all her nerves jumping and twitching and pulses thrumming like jungle drums?

Aw, hell, he thought. Just because he was crazy, didn't mean she was. And with everything she'd had come down on her in the last twenty-four hours? No—no way.

He shook himself and straightened; oxygen starved, he found himself fighting an urge to yawn.

Which Eve was quick to pick up on. "You must be tired. You didn't get much sleep last night. Or did you sleep at all?"

He shrugged and didn't answer her; the last thing he needed was for her to be concerned about him. For her to be *nice*—on top of everything else. He frowned at his watch. "I've got some things to do. It's almost lunchtime—I need to be going before they show up with your tray. Didn't your family say they were coming back later on?" She nodded. "Okay, then. I'll see you this evening. Should have everything in place by then. We'll…ah…go over the details with you—make sure you're up to speed on the equipment, arrangements for making contact, get you familiar with the collar…. Okay?" Again he waited for her nod.

"Capish," she said with a faint smile.

So it was he who nodded. "Okay, then. See you later."

He opened the door a crack, looked through it, up and down the corridor. He threw one last look over his shoulder at the woman huddled in the middle of her hospital bed, arms hugging her drawn-up legs, forehead resting on her knees. Then he slipped out of the room and left her there.

* * *

Mirabella and Summer came out of the third-floor rest room just as the elevator doors were closing.

"What?" Mirabella demanded, as Summer checked abruptly with a small exclamation of surprise.

"Oh...nothing. I'm sure it wasn't...." But she went on frowning for a moment in the direction of the elevators, before shaking her head and turning away. "I thought I saw somebody I knew, but...I'm sure it wasn't." She shifted some of the shopping bags she was carrying in order to consult her watch. "It's past noon. I'll bet she's going to be right in the middle of eating lunch. We should have picked up something. I'm starving."

"You want a breakfast bar?" Mirabella was rummaging in her cavernous handbag. In her sixth month of pregnancy she was constantly ravenous and never beyond reach of a food source.

Summer shook her head. "Thanks, but I believe I'll wait for some real food." She leaned against the wall while Mirabella hunched over the water fountain. "I hope Evie likes the stuff we got for her. I hardly know what her taste is anymore. It's been so long since we all used to go shopping together...borrow each other's clothes..."

"*You* used to borrow each other's clothes. The only thing of Evie's that ever fit me was that poncho she brought back from Baja, remember? I think you were a freshman that year."

Summer gave soft huff of laughter. "Yeah, I remember. She and a bunch of her friends took off down there in a Volkswagen bus. Pop had a fit. Didn't he call the CHP and try to have them stopped, or something?"

Mirabella nodded, popped an antacid tablet into her mouth, drank water and swallowed before she answered. "He'd have called out the marines, if he could. He was sure something terrible was going to happen. As usual, where Evie was concerned, he was wrong. They were fine—probably had an absolute ball, too.''

Summer shifted restlessly. ''You know what? We probably are, too—wrong to worry about her, I mean. Bella, as long as I can remember, Evie's been doing crazy, wild things and driving everybody mad with worry, and it always turns out to be for nothing. She's just not like the rest of us. She doesn't know the meaning of the word *fear.*''

''That's just it—'' Mirabella interrupted herself with a soft burp; indigestion had been a major annoyance with this pregnancy. ''She's *never* afraid. That's why—''

''Who's never afraid?'' her mother asked, coming from the rest room just then, shaking her hands irritably. ''I hate those hand-dryer things.'' She gave up and wiped them on her slacks.

''Evie,'' said Summer, handing over some of her parcels.

Her mother gave a bark of surprise. ''Why would you think that about Eve?''

Summer and Mirabella looked at each other. ''Well, Mom,'' said Mirabella with exaggerated patience, ''she's always done such wild and crazy things. Skydiving, spelunking, whitewater rafting—is there anything terrifying she *hasn't* done?''

''She's never been a mother,'' said Summer dryly, and they all smiled. Then, still smiling but in a different way, their mother shook her head.

''I can't believe she managed to hoodwink the two of you all these years.''

''*Hoodwink?* What do you mean?'' the sisters said together.

''Oh, my dears, don't you know?'' Ginger Waskowitz looked at each of her daughters and laughed softly. ''Eve didn't do all those things because she *wasn't* afraid. She did them because she *was.*''

Chapter 8

Eve stared out of the limousine's darkened windows, watching the warrens of Sun City's massed rooftops and islands of outlet shopping malls give way to marshes. Not even the breathtaking flash of an egret against the seas of waving yellow-green grasses, or the glimpse of a 'gator sliding into the murky-blue waters of an inlet could prevent the blanket of loneliness from settling around her.

Heaven knew, Eve was no stranger to loneliness. Growing up in the California deserts, she'd called it the "wild lonelies," and mistaken it for wanderlust—a vague, unfulfilled yearning fed by the endless wind and vastness of sky and a land as cruel and beautiful and spellbinding as any sorcerer. I don't belong here, she'd thought then, and had spent hours gazing at the sparkling skies and empty vistas like a foundling hearing the call of some distant memory, sure that her true home must lay out *there* somewhere, just beyond the place where the sky and the desert came together. So far, she'd spent her life pushing that horizon and had yet to find her place of belonging.

But *this* loneliness was different. For the first time in her life she understood the difference between loneliness and *alone*. Never before had she known such a terrible sense of isolation and abandonment, the feeling of being cut off from anyone who could help her, and everyone who loved her.

"Hey, babe, what'sa matter? You feeling okay? You look scared. Like you seen a ghost." Sonny's voice was solicitous, full of concern. But Eve, shifting her eyes carefully sideways to look at him, couldn't help but wonder whether, if she'd been able to look more quickly, she might have caught the gleam of speculation and suspicion in his black, unreadable eyes.

His eyes are like the windows of this limo, she thought. Nobody can see what's going on inside.

She didn't even try to repress her shiver. "Don't try to hide the fact that you're scared. You've been a victim of a violent assault," Jake had reminded her during her final briefing last night. "Fear is normal. Cisneros will be warned to expect it, so don't worry about letting it show...."

And she'd murmured, "*Capish—*" at the same time he'd said it, and had laughed. He had not, but instead had looked for a long, silent moment into her eyes.

"I was just...thinking about...it," she answered Sonny now, sliding her gaze once again to the windows. "Yeah, I feel scared. I wish I didn't, but I can't help it. I keep thinking—"

"Hey—it's okay...it's okay." Sonny leaned over to give the cashmere blanket that covered her legs a reassuring pat. There was a pause...and then his hand began to stroke her leg. When it moved past her knee, she couldn't hide a reflexive stiffening.

Instantly he took his hand away, and Eve gave a sharp gasp and then groaned, "Oh, God—Sonny, I'm sorry. I didn't mean—I'm just so...jumpy—"

"It's okay...it's okay." But this time his voice was more

growl than croon. "The doc said it was gonna take some time—you know, before you're your old self again. I understand that. I'm not gonna rush you. Hey, baby, you take all the time you need—you just let me know when you're ready, okay? Come on, Evie. What's this, huh?" He leaned over to brush away a tear that was balanced, trembling, on the lower lashes of her good eye. "Aw, baby, don't do that. You know it makes me crazy...."

The tear had surprised Eve, too. She didn't know what was the matter with her. Sonny was being sweet...so gentle and kind. She was beginning to feel confused. This was the Sonny she'd fallen for, the Sonny she'd intended to marry. How had she forgotten so quickly how wonderful and charming he could be? Was it possible...could she have been mistaken somehow? What didn't seem possible was that this could be the same man she'd heard coldly regretting the fact that his men hadn't killed her sister! What if it was all a mistake? Maybe she hadn't really heard what she thought she'd heard After all, that Dumpster lid had come down on her head pretty hard....

But...there was Jake. If she was mistaken, he would have to be, too. Either that, or he was lying to her, he and the whole FBI: Jake, Dr. Shepherd, that nice teddy bear of a man, Agent Poole... And the other one, the guy in charge—what was his name? Coffee?—who'd shown her how to plant a bug in a telephone, and finally, *finally* provided her with the one thing she'd been too embarrassed after all that time to ask for: Jake's last name.

In any case, the notion that they could all be either wrong or lying was ludicrous. Which left only one alternative: they were right, and so was she, and Sonny Cisneros, no matter how wonderfully charming, how seemingly gentle and sweet, really was a powerful crime boss and possibly a cold-blooded killer.

Oh, God, how did I get myself into this mess?

The cervical collar that held her head and neck motionless seemed weighted with lead. She could feel every one of the tiny battery-operated transmitters nested in the specially designed cavity inside the collar, almost as if they were living things, each with its own pulsating heartbeat. She could almost hear the GPS tracking device sending out its silent signal to the satellite that would relay its location, and hers, back to Jake.

At least I know he's out there somewhere. Right now. He knows where I am.

"You want a drink?" Sonny waved a hand at the bar. "Whatever you want. We got Black Jack…Scotch…soda… champagne…"

"Maybe some water." Eve wiped her eyes, then asked with a pitiful sniffle, "Do we have any straws?"

"Straws?" Sonny threw her a questioning look. Then comprehension flitted across his face in a little grimace of sympathy. "Ah—got it, babe. I think so…yeah, here we are." He poured mineral water into a glass, plunked in a plastic straw and held it for her while she maneuvered it awkwardly to her lips.

"We've got to get some of those bendy kind," she said with a giggle as the straw slipped away from her and spangled water onto her chin.

"Whatever you need, baby…." And Sonny wiped away the drops with his thumb as tenderly as if she *were* a baby. "Anything in the world—you just say the word and Sonny'll get it for you. You know I love you, don't you?"

Unable to nod, she blinked and whispered, "Sonny…" Her pulse hammered against the collar.

"Hey, nothin's too good for my Evie-girl. And lemme tell you, nobody's ever gonna harm my girl again—nosir. From now on, Sonny's lookin' out for you. You don't ever have to be scared of anyone, ever again, understand?"

Capish…

In her mind she heard her own and Jake's voices saying that word in chorus, and from a tiny well of warmth somewhere deep inside a bubble of laughter rose and spilled across her lips.

"That's my girl," Sonny crooned approvingly. He leaned closer, and now it was her lips he stroked with the fleshy pad of his thumb. "Come on, baby, lemme hear you say it...."

She closed her eyes and her mind. "I love you, Sonny."

"Yeah...that's my Evie...."

As Sonny's lips brushed hers, the limousine swooped onto the bridge connecting Hilton Head to the mainland, and she felt the stomach-dropping sensation of being on a roller coaster.

Jake and his partner, Birdie Poole, watched the limo glide past the portals of the gated resort community and disappear from sight like a great white whale sinking into the sea.

Birdie breathed a toneless whistle. "Holy...shinola. Talk about your velvet cage. This place is huge. We gonna be able to get within range?"

Jake picked up a pair of binoculars from the seat beside him and surveyed the surrounding terrain. "It's doable." He glanced at, then tapped the GPS monitor mounted on the dash. "Depends how far they are from the perimeter fence. Might have to put up a booster antenna...." He laid the binoculars aside but went on frowning at the gatehouse, at the spot where the limo had disappeared, his fingers playing a restless tattoo on the steering wheel. "Won't know until she gets those bugs planted. *If* she does..." He could feel Birdie's eyes on him.

After a silence that lasted for...oh, maybe a long five count, his partner let out a breath and faced the front of the vehicle. "And...you're sure this was a good idea."

Jake lifted one shoulder. "She had to go back to him. What were we gonna do, cut her loose and send her in on her own? This way, anything goes wrong, at least we've got a shot."

Even without looking, he could feel Birdie's eyes come back to him like homing beacons. "Why do I get the feeling it isn't Cisneros you're wanting to keep tabs on?"

Jake grunted, a sound few besides Birdie would recognize as laughter. "In five years of surveillance on Cisneros, have we ever gotten anything we could take to the U.S. Attorney? You and I both know the man's too careful for that."

"Then you mind telling me what the hell's all this about?"

"A feeling." He let out a breath and muffled it in the hand he scrubbed restlessly across his mouth. "She's the key, dammit. She's important—I know she is."

"I can see that," Birdie said softly. "Question is, important to whom? And why?"

Jake threw his partner a pained look. "Come on, Bird. She's the key to nailing Cisneros. Period." He punched a tape into the deck and reached for the ignition key. "Tell me, partner, have you ever known me to give a rat's ass about anything else?"

"Nope," said Birdie, "never have."

"Uh-huh. Let's get some lunch while we've got a chance."

"Yeah…okay. Aw, man—" Birdie winced as a scratchy rendition of "St. Louis Blues" filled the van. "You're not going to make me listen to that junk *now?*"

"Whadaya mean, junk? Don't you know who that is? That's Bessie Smith. That's a classic, man."

"No, no, don't give me that—classic is Bach, maybe Beethoven, definitely not Bessie. Hey, if you gotta listen to blues, at least get rid of the scratch—is that too much to ask? Hey, compromise. Got any Ray Charles? Now—I can take ol' Ray. *'Georgia…'"*

Jake sighed and switched off the stereo.

* * *

In the week that followed, Eve experienced what she was certain must be the emotional equivalent of being buried alive. She felt completely isolated, but at the same time as if every move she made, every breath she took, every beat of her heart were being monitored...measured...judged.

She lived every waking moment with a vague and unformed sense of menace, but it was at night that the fear came to settle over her like a shroud. She kept waking every few hours in a clammy, heart-pounding panic, only to lie awake in a twilight that seemed alive with watching eyes and listening ears, haunted by vague memories of dreams in which she was being slowly suffocated.

None of which made sense, considering she couldn't have asked for more pleasant surroundings. The resort, which Sonny had told her would eventually include a five-star hotel, luxury condos, a golf course and tennis courts, bike paths, three swimming pools and miles of gently sloping white sand beaches, wasn't scheduled to open until spring, but most of the external layout and landscaping had already been completed. Sonny's private quarters, nestled in a remote corner of the hotel grounds, were like the keep within the castle, surrounded by walls of brick and wrought iron and lush tropical landscaping, so new they still smelled of fresh paint, with rooms that were airy and light and open to endless vistas of sea and sky.

Eve didn't kid herself; she knew it was only an illusion of freedom. In a way it made her think of Alcatraz, which she'd had occasion to visit while filming a piece on the federal penitentiary for a cable channel a few years back. She'd found the island an eerie, unnerving place, and one of the things that had haunted her was the fact that inmates serving life sentences could look out through barred and slitted windows and watch sailboats skimming over white-capped waves, and in the distance, the shimmering towers of San Francisco—Baghdad by the Bay—taunting, beckoning, a constant and cruel reminder of everything they'd lost and would never have again.

Not that Eve couldn't come and go as she pleased—oh, quite the contrary. She had the run of the island. She could and did go for walks, within the limitations of her supposed "injury," along the beaches or down the few remaining unspoiled avenues shaded by canopies of moss-festooned live oaks and Palmettos and Southern coastal pines. If she wanted to go shopping, a car was instantly at her beck and call.

But she was never left alone. If she ventured beyond the walls of the house, someone was always with her—Sonny, if he was home, or if he was gone, which was most of the time, then either Ricky or Sergei, which was infinitely worse. One of the two was always there, within arm's reach, silent and watchful, like vaguely menacing shadows. She no longer dismissed them as witless thugs—Sonny's "Two Stooges." Now she realized that they were, in fact, extremely good at what they did, which was, like the highly trained attack dogs they were, to follow orders without question. And like attack dogs, if the order was to kill, she imagined that they would do so unhesitatingly and efficiently, without either enjoyment or regret.

Worse even than the constant company, though—which was at least a menace she could see—was the formless and skin-crawling sense she had that she was being *watched.*

Okay, maybe it was only a bad case of paranoia fostered by the weight of her guilty conscience, not to mention a collar full of listening devices. After all, she'd never actually *seen* the cameras. But she knew Sonny, and what a stickler he was for security, and she was taking no chances. Wherever she went, indoors or out, she acted on the assumption that unseen eyes followed her every move. Not even trusting the privacy of her own bathroom, she dressed, showered and used the toilet in the dark whenever possible, and only removed her collar in order to access the cache of bugs late at night, in bed, with the covers pulled over her head.

Needless to say, her suspicion that she was being watched made planting the bugs more complicated than she'd expected. In the rooms to which she had free access, it was mostly a matter of slipping them into place during the course of some seemingly innocent activity—selecting a magazine to read, for example, or admiring a potted plant, searching for a pencil with which to work a crossword puzzle, mixing a drink.

The first one she'd installed had been in her own room. That had been Jake's request. At the time she'd found the suggestion unnerving, an unwelcome reminder of the danger she was about to plunge herself into. But during that first week in the suffocating isolation of the resort compound, that bug had come to seem almost like a friend, her one source of comfort, her only lifeline, a tiny and tenuous umbilical cord connecting her with Jake and her family. With *safety*. With a world that included work and laughter, children and family dinners and dogs and touch football on the lawn. Brothers arguing and newlyweds snuggling on the sofa, and mothers and daughters bickering, and the smells of dinner cooking in the kitchen. She thought of the bug almost as a living thing, and talked to it under the guise of reading aloud or talking to herself. She tried to imagine Jake's face as he listened, out there beyond the compound walls.

Would he smile, she wondered, if he thought no one was watching? Someday, she thought, I'm going to make him smile, and I'm going to catch him at it, too.

The thought made the loneliness seem less oppressive.

The biggest problem with the bugs was that after a week she still hadn't found an excuse to go into Sonny's private office, not without raising suspicions. He'd been gone most of the week, during which time the office was locked up tight. And when he was home he treated Eve like a convalescent princess, smothering her with attention, gourmet dinners complete with wine and candlelight, breakfast in bed. Business, he said grandly, was off-limits—taboo. He was there to spend time with his Evie, and nothing was allowed to interfere with that.

How strange it was, Eve thought, to realize that the focused attention she'd once considered a major facet of Sonny's charm she now considered the biggest pain in the neck.

Another problem was, as Jake had explained to her, that the bugs would periodically have to be replaced. They were voice activated to save battery power, but even so…

She was pondering those problems as she returned from her walk late Monday afternoon, one week to the day after she'd arrived at the Hilton Head resort, to find Sonny pacing the white marble entryway.

Her heart gave a little skip of fear. "Sonny…hi! When did you get back?" She went to him for a welcoming kiss, but drew back as he rounded on her with a scowl.

"Where the hell've you been? I've been waitin' for hours."

"I went for a walk on the beach. If I'd known—"

"Yeah? Hell, I was worried about you. You shouldn't be out there so long. Who was with you? The guys go with you?"

"Ricky was with me." Eve gestured toward the huge, bull-necked man who'd followed her like a bad smell into the house. "Sonny, what's wrong? Did I do something—"

"Come 'ere." Unsmiling, Sonny jerked his head for her to follow him.

Oh God, he knows. Eve's heart dropped into her stomach and began to pump with a jackhammer rhythm. Her chest felt constricted; she couldn't get a breath.

As she followed Sonny on wet-spaghetti legs up the long,

curving staircase, her mind, paralyzed at first, came to life and began to hurl itself frantically in all directions.

He's found the bugs! How many? One? All? *Jake—are you listening? Help me!*

Wait, dummy…if he'd found the bugs, how would Jake know what was happening? And even if he did, how far away was he? Could he possibly get here in time?

Wait a minute—time for what? Why would Sonny necessarily think *she'd* planted them? He had no reason to suspect her…unless he'd known all along! Unless he *had* seen her running away that day in the church garden, and knew from the beginning that the "mugging" was a charade. *Jake…help me.*

No—it was hopeless. This was it, she was going to die. She was never going to see her family again—Mom, Pop, Summer and Bella—not even to say goodbye. *Jake!*

In a massive, roaring silence she followed Sonny into his bedroom suite, wincing as he shut the doors behind her. Why am I going so meekly, she briefly wondered, like a lamb to the slaughter? I should at least *try* to make a run for it.

Was he going to give her a chance to explain? Could she deny it all and lie her way out…?

She came to a dead halt.

Sonny, who had stayed by the door, was pressing buttons on a remote control panel. While she stood tense and trembling, the room lights dimmed and the draperies covering the French windows that opened onto an ocean-view balcony rolled back.

Eve gasped and then went limp with relief. She couldn't say a word. She could only stare.

The balcony had been transformed into a tropical bower, lit with hundreds of tiny Christmas lights that twinkled like stars amidst the foliage. Portable patio heaters held the autumn chill at bay while the scent of flowers and the gentle whispers of tropical rain drifted into the room. In the center of this paradise, a table set for two gleamed with crystal and candlelight.

Sonny, coming close behind her, bent so that his lips just brushed her ear, and whispered hoarsely, "Happy birthday, baby...."

Another gasp escaped her, this one accompanied by the sharp sting of tears.

"Hey, what's this? What's this?" Sonny's hands were on her shoulders, gently turning her so that he could look at her face. "Don't tell me you're cryin' again. What're you cryin' for? It's your birthday—be happy!"

What's this? What's this? What *was* this? *Happy?* How could she feel happy? Her feelings were confused as hell, an overwhelming sadness mixed up with anger and even touches of regret. *Why, Sonny? How can you be so sweet, and so evil at the same time? Why can't you just be one or the other so I can make up my mind to love you or hate you and be done with it?*

Because, a voice more cynical than wise inside her head answered, people are who they are and nothing is ever black and white. And all the other clichés you ever heard of. If life was simple, it wouldn't take twenty or thirty or...hell, forty-three years to get it figured out.

"I thought you'd forgotten," she said in a quavering voice, laughing and brushing at her eyes with shaking hands. "I thought everyone had." To be honest, *she* had. For the last week she'd been so wrapped up in her situation—worrying about bugs, dealing with the isolation, thinking about the danger....

"Forget your birthday? Come on. The day after Halloween—you think I could forget something like that?" Sonny's voice was jovial as he ushered her onto the balcony and pulled back her chair. But as he was seating himself, a double take made him pause. "Whadaya mean, you thought everybody forgot? What about your family? Your mom...your sisters? Nobody called?''

Eve cleared her throat. Her mouth was dry, her heart racing. ''Ah...well, no, they couldn't, really. I didn't give them the number. I was going to call—''

''You didn't—*Jeez,* baby, why the hell not?''

''Sonny, it's your private number. I didn't think—''

''What're you talkin' about? This is *family.* Family is family—you know how I feel about that. Your family is my family. Hey—'' he reached for her hand and leaning across the table, raised it to his lips ''—right after dinner you call 'em. Talk to 'em all night if you want to. Okay? Okay. Now, try some of this champagne. I know you like champagne...and here—I didn't forget, I got you a straw, see? One of those bendy ones.''

While Eve was laughing at the prospect of drinking champagne with a bendy straw—how could she help it?—Sonny casually drew a flat velvet-covered case from under the tablecloth and handed it to her with a gruff and succinct ''Here—this is for you.''

She set her champagne down untasted and reached for the case, while her cheeks flushed hot and her insides curled with a cold that felt like shame. She knew that case, knew without looking what she'd find inside; she'd seen it before, or one just like it, the night before what was to have been her wedding day, when Sonny had given it to her—his wedding gift.

She opened the case, gazed down at the pearl choker. Her throat closed. ''Sonny, you shouldn't have....''

''Hey—'' He waved it off with a gesture. ''Like I told you. What's a pearl? Gives an oyster a bad case of indigestion. I had 'em put a rush on it so it'd be ready for your birthday. It's supposed to be an exact duplicate of the one that got stolen.''

''It's beautiful. I wish—'' Her hand fluttered involuntarily toward her collar.

"Hey, hey…" He leaned toward her, his voice low and guttural. "The day that damn thing comes off, I'm gonna take great pleasure in puttin' these on you myself. I never did get to see you wearing it." His eyes glittered in the candlelight.

Dry-mouthed, she whispered, "I know, I'm so—"

But he reached across the table to stop her with a finger touched to her lips. Then he closed the velvet case and took it from her and said with a grand wave of his hand, "Forget that—that's just a replacement." And with the air of an amateur magician producing a floppy bouquet from his sleeve, he handed her a smaller box instead. "Here ya go, babe— happy birthday."

Eve took the box, moving slowly, as if in a dream—or a nightmare. She opened it and stared down at the twin diamonds that winked back at her from their bed of indigo velvet. Earrings. Exquisite diamond and dropped-pearl earrings. They must have cost a fortune, she thought dully. She felt strange—almost numb. *Earrings.* She didn't even wear earrings, not anymore. Once upon a time she'd been the first in her circle of friends to get her ears pierced, but that had been years ago.

"I know you don't wear earrings," Sonny said, as if he'd heard her thought, and dismissed it with a shrug. "What the hell—they went with the necklace. I thought maybe someday you might wanna get your ears done, you know? And if not, hell, I'll get 'em made so you can wear 'em without." Once again he reached for her hands, closed them around the earring box and brought them to his lips. "Can't wait to see you in 'em, you know that, don't you, baby? And nothin' else…okay, maybe the choker…" Then abruptly he let go of her and leaned back in his chair, swearing under his breath. "What the hell am I doing?" he muttered. "Makin' myself crazy. Jeez, I hate that you have to be in that damn thing."

Eve's heart was pounding so hard, she couldn't speak. She

groped for her champagne, got the end of the straw between her lips and sucked greedily, draining the glass. "I won't always be wearing this collar," she said huskily. *There...that was better.*

Sonny refilled her glass, then lifted his to her in a toast. "I'll drink to that.... Reminds me," he said, wiping champagne from his lips with a napkin, "your doctor called."

Eve choked and then had to cope with champagne up her nose. Sonny had to get up and come around behind her and hold her steady while she coughed. She did have the presence of mind to say, "Ouch! Ow!" every time the spasms shook her, and Sonny, deeply concerned, said, "Jeez, don't do that, baby—you're gonna wind up in traction."

"You said...my doctor called?" Eve wheezed when she was once again capable of speech. "What...what'd he want?"

"What? Oh—just said to tell you your appointment's been changed to tomorrow afternoon. That's in Savannah, right? You're gonna need the limo—Sergei can drive you."

Fortunately for Eve, who was once again carefully sipping champagne through her bendy straw, there came a knock at the door just then, and Sonny, instead of resuming his place across the table from her, said, "Hey—that must be dinner," and went to admit the waiters. Because how on earth would she have explained the shine in her eyes, the deepening pink flush in her cheeks that could never be mistaken for anything else but joy?

Jake! I'll see him tomorrow. Tomorrow!

Jake peeled off his headphones and dropped them on the narrow countertop. "I need some air," he growled, pushing back his chair. He dove through the back doors of the van and kept going. He didn't intend to stop until he'd reached the top of the nearest dune, where maybe the wind off the Atlantic, harbinger of the first nor'easter of the season, would be strong enough and cold enough to blow the cobwebs out of his brain.

Brain? What brain? Because as far as he was able to tell, at the moment all he had between his ears was a scrambled mess of rage and frustration.... Yeah, okay, admit it—and *fear.*

"What's goin' on?" Birdie joined him on the dune, puffing a little, Jake observed. He'd have to have a talk with Margie—the woman was too good a cook for her husband's own good.

He shrugged, jerking his shoulders in the manner of someone shaking off an unwelcome burden, and punched words through his tightly clenched teeth. "Couldn't take it anymore. Had to take a break."

"Take what? You mean, Cisneros?" Jake snorted. Birdie hunched his shoulders against the chill wind and chuckled. "He is one charming son of a gun when he wants to be, isn't he?"

Jake didn't share his partner's amusement. In his opinion, Cisneros was about as charming as a rattlesnake, and his wordless reply was more snarl than chuckle.

"What?" Birdie shot him a look along his shoulder. "Come on—you're not afraid she's falling for it?"

Jake kicked at a hummock of grass with the toe of his shoe. "The way that bastard's laying it on?" He made a sibilant sound, replete with disgust. "You gotta hand it to him, he sure knows how to push the buttons. Champagne, flowers, candlelight, jewelry, pretty words... Hell, it worked once, didn't it?"

Birdie was silent for a moment, kicking at his own hunk of grass. Then he shook himself—or maybe shivered—and said, "You don't think he might have...genuine feelings for her? Hey—" he held up both hands to defend himself against Jake's snort of derision "—even wise guys fall in love...get married."

Jake swore bitterly. "If he's convinced you, what's he doing to her?"

"Come on..."

"You're forgetting. Cisneros isn't just a wise guy, the man's a classic sociopath. He doesn't have feelings for people—he uses people. That's the only value they have for him—to be used. Otherwise he cares about as much for them as you do for that weed you're stomping to death. If he's giving her the royal treatment it's because he wants something from her—period. I just hope she's smart enough to realize that, is all."

"Come on," said Birdie after a moment, sounding unhappy, "you don't really think she'd fall for it, do you? After what she heard? Knowing what she knows? What, just because he gives her some *jewelry?*"

Jake snorted, and this time the sound was meant to be laughter. "Some jewelry... That 'replacement' he was talking about? The one he said he had made like the one that got stolen? You know what that little bauble consists of? I know, because I took it off of her myself. It's a pearl necklace—the real thing. Three strands perfectly matched with a diamond clip. Had to cost more'n you and I make in a year, and now she's got two—a matched set."

"Big deal," said Birdie, "she's only got one neck." He punched his hands deep into his jacket pockets and shook his head, laughing softly. "All I can say is, I hope she doesn't ever find out we had this conversation. She didn't strike me as the type who could be bought with diamonds and pearls."

She hadn't struck Jake that way, either, and to be honest, it wasn't the jewelry he was riled up about. And it wasn't anything Cisneros had said or done—he was pretty much used to the way the man operated; nothing surprised him anymore. What had done it to him was Eve's voice, whispery with tears. *"Sonny, I wish..."* Low and husky... *"I won't always be wearing this collar."*

As for why that should be, well...he didn't want to go there himself, much less bring his partner along for the ride. In the years since his divorce, Birdie and Margie Poole had done way more than their share of matchmaking on his behalf and he'd just as soon not give them any new ideas to work with.

So he grunted cynically and said, "I thought all women were the type—yours excepted, of course—you know I firmly believe Margie's a saint. She'd have to be, to put up with you all these years." He elbowed his partner, who chuckled in companionable agreement.

But as they started back down the dune together, under the cover of darkness Jake was frowning. The fact that his partner had made a success of his marriage when so many agents' relationships failed had always been a mystery to him. Now, it seemed like one it might be important for him to solve.

"Seriously," he said when they were slogging through the sand, making their way back to the side road where they'd parked the van. "Isn't that what women want? Flowers, gifts...jewelry?"

Birdie threw him a look. "You really don't know much about women, do you?"

"That comes as a surprise to you? It's pretty obvious *I* don't know what it takes to make a woman happy. It's pretty obvious you do. So?"

Birdie hunched his shoulders and muttered uncomfortably. "Hell—don't put this on me. I'm no expert on women in general. Anyway, there's no such thing as 'women in general.' Far as I can see, they're all different. One thing I have noticed, though..."

He paused, and Jake prodded, "Yeah?" Birdie turned to face him. "Seems to me, when it comes to gifts, it's not the cost or what it is that matters, it's how she feels about the giver. Bottom line? She loves you, she'll love the gift."

"Oh, come on."

Birdie shrugged and walked on. "Okay, maybe there are some women, all they care about is money—there're men like that, so why not women? But the ones that matter? Why do you suppose mothers go ape over plaster of Paris hand-prints and cards made out of macaroni? A kid brings his mom a handful of wilted dandelions, she cries every time. Guaranteed."

"Yeah, but that's her kid. That's different. For us—"

"Same principle applies. Hey—I gave Margie a Weed-wacker for her birthday once. She was so happy, she cried."

"Yeah, but that's Margie. You got a genuine saint."

Birdie laughed. "You'll get no argument from me there."

"You ask me, I think you got the last one, partner."

"Oh, I wouldn't go *that* far." Birdie's head swiveled toward him, and Jake could feel the speculation in his eyes even if he couldn't see it. "And even if it were true, not everybody wants a saint. Ever think about that? For instance, would you?"

Jake didn't say anything. But he was thinking about a certain battered and barefoot bride reeking of garbage and drunk on champagne who could never be called a saint.

Chapter 9

Eve really hadn't known what to expect; although she didn't know much about Dr. Matthew Shepherd, she was fairly sure he wasn't really a practicing G.P., at least not in Savannah, Georgia.

But as it turned out, she'd reckoned without the resources of the Federal Bureau of Investigation. Dr. Shepherd's offices had been set up in a busy, modern medical complex not far from the hospital where she'd spent her first two nights as a Bureau undercover informant, and not even the most suspicious and critical eye could have found anything to suggest he hadn't been in residence there since the day the complex opened.

Quite a few heads turned as the white stretch limo wove its way through the parking lot and eased to a stop at the main entrance. People walking by on their way in and out of the building tried hard to look without seeming to as Sergei, six and a half feet tall and built like Arnold Schwarzenegger, emerged from the driver's seat and walked around to open the passenger door.

They must wonder who in the world I am, Eve thought as she took Sergei's gloved hand and allowed him to help her out of the car. Exiled royalty? Rock star? Or more likely, just somebody with wa…ay too much money. The possibilities didn't exactly amuse her, but they did provide distraction from her quickening pulse and the nervous knots accumulating in her stomach.

She paused in a breezeway to check the directory. "I'm not sure where it is—he just moved here recently," she explained to Sergei, waiting impassively at her shoulder. It had occurred to her that he would almost certainly report to Sonny the fact that she'd had to look up the location of her own doctor's offices. "Oops—there it is." She pointed to the letters that spelled out Matthew Shepherd, General Practice, with a suite number on the ground floor, then turned her whole body so she could look Sergei in the eye. "I'm sure I'll be okay from here on, if you need to go and park the car."

He stared back at her, unblinking. "The car will wait."

Damn. What was he going to do, follow her right into the exam room? She drew a resigned breath.

God, she felt nervous; her teeth all but chattered. Why, because somewhere in this place, only a few doors away, now, Jake would be waiting for her? Because in a few more minutes, for the first time in more than a week she'd be seeing him face-to-face? What was the matter with her? Why was she like this, scared as a virgin bride on her wedding night?

Ah—there it was, the door, like all the other doors, with a plaque like all the other plaques, identifying this as the office of Dr. Matthew Shepherd, General Practice. Eve pushed open the door and went in, Sergei trudging right behind her.

Maybe that's what it is, she thought—just the idea of the doctor's office. She hated going to the doctor—always had.

Her supposedly annual checkup was an ordeal she dreaded, and usually managed to postpone at least a few months past the due date.

This doctor's office was like any other she'd ever visited, down to the last detail—a huge lighted tank filled with tropical fish along one wall, a child-sized table littered with children's books and play blocks in one corner, tweed-covered chairs and racks filled with well-thumbed copies of *Newsweek, Woman's Day, Reader's Digest* and *Sports Illustrated.* From the other side of a counter a cheery and efficient-looking receptionist greeted her and invited her to "sign in" on a roster attached to a clipboard, then please take a seat. She then looked around Eve at Sergei and said, "May I help you?"

Sergei's cold blue eyes swept the waiting room, narrowly scrutinized its only other occupant, a burly man in a plaid wool shirt-jacket and an Atlanta Braves baseball cap who was deeply engrossed in *Sports Illustrated.* "I'll be back," he rumbled, and turned and walked out of the office.

The receptionist waited until the door had closed completely. Then, eyes sparkling with unmistakable amusement, she murmured, "Did he really say that?"

Eve let go of a breath of relieved laughter. "I'm afraid so." The man in the baseball cap lowered his magazine and winked at her, and her mouth popped open with surprise as she recognized Jake's partner, Agent Poole.

Before she could say a word, however, the receptionist pointed to a door next to the counter and said quietly, "You can come on back."

Eve's heart pounded beneath the weight of her collar as she reached for the knob and turned it. Would he be there waiting for her, she wondered, just on the other side of the door?

But when she opened the door and walked through, into the corridor beyond, it was the receptionist who met her. She identified herself as Agent Franco, then led Eve down one hallway, around a corner and into another, past several closed doors and finally ushered her into a large exam room.

"I'll take that collar," Agent Franco said in a brisk but not unfriendly tone as she followed her in and closed the door.

Numbly, Eve undid the fastenings and handed it over.

The crushing weight of her disappointment was an eye-opener. It also both appalled and humiliated her. What had she been thinking? When had she forgotten, if indeed she'd ever really realized before, the fact that it wasn't simply Jake Redfield who wanted Sonny brought to justice? This wasn't Jake's operation, it was the FBI's. What had given her the notion that it was…somehow personal?

And the worst of it was, though she didn't want to, she still had to ask. "Is Jake—I mean, Agent Redfield…?" She stopped, cheeks flaming.

Agent Franco was speaking to the pocket of her uniform. "We're clear," she murmured, then nodded at Eve. "Just have a seat." She went out, carrying the collar.

Eve muttered aloud to herself, "This is ridiculous."

With her fantasies supposedly disposed of, why on earth was she still so *nervous?* It wasn't as if it was a *real* doctor's appointment. And yet, as she gave the examination table—*not,* thank heaven, one of those short ones with the stirrups at the end—a sideways and wary glance, she felt as vulnerable as if she were perched on its slick paper covering wearing nothing but one of those tissue paper napkins. Her neck, completely bare for the first time in more than a week, felt fragile and exposed, her head too heavy for it to support. Tremors rippled through her in waves, almost as if…

But, she thought, I'm *not* afraid. Why would I be?

Why indeed, when she was surrounded here by FBI agents, in the middle of an operation so efficient, they made it look routine? They must do this sort of thing all the time. She was in absolutely no danger. She knew that. So why was her heart pounding and her breathing quick and shallow? Why were her hands so clammy and cold?

Because, her truthful soul insisted on answering, you *are* afraid. There's all kinds of fear—your body's just not programmed to know the difference. It's not your life you fear for, dummy. It's your—

No! Oh God, no. Don't even go there.

At that moment the door opened and Jake walked in. Eve's stomach flip-flopped, her mouth opened and air rushed out in a soft, helpless gasp.

See? Aha—I told you so!

Shut up. No sir, no way.

"Eve." Jake's nod was brief and impersonal, and of course unsmiling, as he moved aside to make way for Dr. Shepherd, who pushed into the room after him like a big, wet, friendly dog wallowing through a crowd.

"Hey, there, Eve—honey, how we doin' today?" The doctor loomed in front of her, his white coat and FDR grin blocking her view of Jake, who was looking unexpectedly handsome, she thought, in his FBI uniform of dark gray suit, crisp white shirt and blue-and-navy-striped tie, with jaw freshly shaven and his thick, unruly hair neatly tamed.

Okay, that's all it was, she told herself, drawing a careful, relieved breath. Just a little bit of physical attraction. Nothing you can't handle.

"Well, you're lookin' pretty good," Dr. Shepherd mused, giving her cheekbone a cursory brush with his thumb. "Little yellow here, still, but that'll be gone in a day or two, and you'll be your gorgeous self again. How you doin' with that collar? Doin' okay? Gettin' a little bit uncomfortable?"

"Nothing I can't handle," said Eve, flicking a glance at Jake, just visible beyond the doctor's shoulder, leaning against the door in his familiar brooding stance—arms folded on his chest, one ankle crossing the other.

His examination completed, Dr. Shepherd stood back, folded his arms and frowned. "Don't really like the idea of you wearin' that thing all the time, young lady, especially since we've got no way a'knowin' how long you're gonna have to keep up this charade. Tell you what—I believe it's time we started you on some physical therapy. What do you think? Three days a week? We can set it up somewhere out there on the island so you don't have to come all this way. That way we can keep those neck muscles toned. Jake—that okay with you?" He turned to ask the question as Jake straightened and pushed away from the wall.

"Long as you don't bring her along too fast," he said in his expressionless, federal agent's voice. He came, arms still folded, to stand beside the doctor. "Don't want her graduating out of that collar before she's done what she needs to do, do we?" His dark eyes studied her, heavy-lidded and surly.

"Unless…" he murmured, "you've changed your mind about staying out of your fiancé's bed?"

"No," she answered him, the word soft but emphatic. "*I* haven't changed my mind—about anything." And suddenly she found her gaze locked with his in a struggle she could neither fathom nor escape, a struggle some buried instinct evidently considered vital, because it focused on it all her physical and emotional energy, every sense and perception. Dr. Shepherd simply disappeared; the room around her faded into darkness and shadow. She saw nothing except Jake's eyes, lit from within by that strange, angry glow; heard nothing except the sound of his breath, poised to form words that he didn't utter. She felt nothing except the energy from his body that seemed to flow across the space between them like an electrical charge.

"Well, then, I'll get on it—see what I can set up for you." Dr. Shepherd's jovial voice released her from the spell.

She jerked her head toward him and answered breathlessly,

and with more than a small measure of guilt, "Yeah, okay, that'd be great. Thanks…" She returned his wave, waited until the door had closed behind him, then jerked herself half-around and took two steps away from the man who still stood gazing at her, motionless and silent.

The movement had been instinctive, an attempt to escape the attraction that still held her like the grip of some powerful magnet, but with that increased distance came, not release, but instead a jangled, off-balance feeling as if her entire being had been knocked off its axis. Her throat felt raw and raspy as she tried a careless laugh. "What the hell was that? You decided not to trust me?"

Jake made a soft, hissing sound. "It's got nothing to do with you. It's Cisneros I don't trust."

"Yeah, right," Eve muttered without turning. She lowered her voice an octave, mimicking his cynical tone. "'So, you've changed your mind about staying out of your fiancé's bed?'"

"Your fiancé can be very persuasive."

Something shivered through her, though she couldn't have said whether it was anger, hurt or fear—or perhaps a little of all three. "Please," she said, throwing him a sharp, bitter look, "give me *some* credit."

Silence thundered between them. But if she'd expected— hoped for—an apology, none came. Instead, after a long pause, he abruptly asked, "Neck bothering you?"

She realized only then that she'd been rubbing it. Still royally miffed, she waved her hand and said coldly, "A bit of a crick—it's nothing I can't—"

"—handle…yeah, I know." There was an odd thickness to his growl that perhaps should have warned her, but didn't.

So it was with a jarring sense of unreality that she felt the warm weight of his hands on her shoulders. So unexpected, it was—and so unexpected a pleasure—that her entire body responded from the top of her head to the tips of her toes with an all-over tingling that was like the hot-cold prick of sparklers on a sultry Fourth of July. And at the same time she could feel the warmth melting into her shoulders and spreading through her insides, and it was like being a little girl and drinking hot cocoa on a cold frosty morning.

"Relax, Waskowitz." His voice, raspy and soothing as a cat's purr, stirred the air near her ear.

Relax? Redfield, if I were any more relaxed, you'd have to pick me up off the floor.

But that was only her body. Her mind was sputtering like a bad electrical connection, alternating between dead blankness and shooting out useless sparks. *What's this, what's this? Oh…that feels good.… Don't react—don't make a fool of yourself! It's not personal—remember that. This is his job…his job…*

But her body wasn't listening. Jake's fingers were pressing into her cramped trapezius muscles, his thumbs stroking upward along the sides of her spinal column and pushing under her hair to probe the base of her skull…and her head dropped forward, her eyelids drooped, her knees grew weak and her nipples shivered and hardened.

"You're too high," he complained, and Eve blamed her own fuzzy-headedness for the fact that his voice seemed slurred and thickened. "I can't reach you. Here—lie down." He patted the table with one hand while he guided her to it with the other.

Oh, how she wanted to say something clever and witty, fire off some wisecrack double entendre that would show him how sophisticated and cool she was. Unfortunately, her mind was a blank; if he'd led her to a bed of fire ants and poison ivy, she'd have laid herself sweetly down. She thought, *And he's worried about Sonny's powers of persuasion?*

The paper-covered table was cool under her cheek. But her body felt trembly and hot, and her heart was beating so hard, she could feel it pushing against the table's resilient surface. He must feel that, she thought, panic-stricken. *He must!*

She couldn't let the silence go on. She had to think of something to say, something that wouldn't humiliate her....

So she groaned, laughing a little, and said, "Oh, that does feel good." That seemed safe enough. Anyone would say it. Wouldn't they?

There was no answer from Jake—not in words. But his fingers played over her back as if he were a musician and she his instrument, lightly stroking the delicate cords of her neck, pressing deep into the thicker muscle along her spine, gentling the thin, ticklish places over her ribs and finding with unerring precision the sensitive pressure spots hidden among the complex bones of her shoulders.

Her mind wandered.... She remembered the music she'd heard playing in Jake's apartment that first crazy night, and thought of the old blues guitar man she'd interviewed for the music piece...rheumy-eyed and toothless, he'd been, wasted by a life of booze and poverty. But it had been his hands the camera had homed in on, and it was his hands she saw now in her mind's eye, caressing the strings of that old acoustic guitar as if they were the body of a beautiful woman....

"Where'd you learn to do that?" she asked weakly.

Jake grunted. "Doesn't take a rocket scientist."

No, she thought, just an extraordinarily *gentle* man. She'd been given massages before, by men who thought they were being gentle. Probably they'd thought they were being seductive, too, but invariably they'd be too rough, press too hard, and instead of relaxing, she'd feel the reflexive urge to tense her muscles to protect her tender places. Usually she'd been relieved when they'd abandoned the attempt at subtle seduction and switched to the more direct approach. But never before in her life could she remember feeling like this in a man's hands—so relaxed, so pampered, so utterly and completely *safe*. And at the same time—ridiculous, for a woman just turned forty-three—so dreadfully, terrifyingly vulnerable. It was a contradiction she couldn't begin to unravel.

"By the way..." It was his quiet, even-toned cop voice, as his hands, stroking lightly up and down her back, signaled an end to the massage. "A day late, but...happy birthday."

And pleasure burst inside her as if he'd switched on a floodlight, pouring warmth and light and happiness into every corner of her being. She felt warm-cheeked and lightheaded, as if she'd been gulping champagne.

She sucked in air, and as she rolled over and into a sitting position, tugging her blouse back into place, gave it back, sparked with laughter. "How did you...? Oh, right—I guess you heard us last night—Sonny and me." And was puzzled by the shadow of annoyance—and could it have been disappointment?—that flashed across his face as she said those words.

What now? she wondered, indefinably frustrated, sorry without knowing why she should be. What an enigma he was, this man from the FBI. Like a river of contradictions: deep dark pools and sweet, sunny shallows and just when you least expected, treacherous, nonnegotiable rapids.

"Thank you," she rushed on, trying with her smile to tell him the secret she'd never reveal with words—that *his* words, just the acknowledgment, had given her more joy than all Sonny's diamonds and pearls. "And thanks for the massage—best present I ever got." She said it lightly, jokingly, safe in the knowledge that he wouldn't believe it.

He grunted and muttered, "The massage is on the house." Then he reached into his inside jacket pocket, giving her glimpses of a holster harness, and pulled out a plastic audiotape case. "I did get you something, though," he said as he handed it to her. "Just a bunch of stuff I pulled off my albums that I thought you might like. There's a pretty good mix—Leadbelly, Bessie Smith, Ma Rainey... Billie Holiday, of course. B.B. King. I think there's even some blues harmonica…'' He gave a quick, almost negligent shrug. ''You said you hadn't had time to listen to music before. I thought maybe now you might.''

For perhaps the first time in her life, Eve fully understood the word *speechless*. There were feelings inside her—tremendous, enormous feelings—but no words at all. There were no words even in her mind, like the ones that formed sometimes but which she couldn't quite bring herself to say. Without them she felt strangely defenseless…unarmed and exposed. She stared down at the cassette in her hand and waited for words to come to her rescue, and when they didn't, finally lifted her eyes to Jake's. His dark eyes gazed back at her with that inexplicable melancholy, and she felt her cheeks warm with a schoolgirl's flush.…

A breath sighed between her lips and she heard herself say, ''Thank you…this is nice of you.'' Thank God for habits and conventions, for the saving grace of manners. ''I will play it.''

''I'll know if you do.'' One corner of his mouth lifted, in what *might* have been a smile. *Yes!* It was…definitely a smile.

Once, in Brazil, she'd caught a glimpse, just the smallest glimpse of a jaguar as it slipped away into the shadows of the rain forest. And her breath had stilled then and her chest had tightened in just this way, in homage and in awe of something miraculous and rare. Something wonderful.

Laughter hovered, balanced on her lips, the effervescence of pure joy. But at that moment the door opened, and instead of letting the joy flow forth, she swallowed it in a guilty gulp as Dr. Shepherd bounded into the room, carrying the collar over one arm. He looked them over from one to the other and back again and lifted one eyebrow, but if he'd felt any unusual tensions or undercurrents he wisely—in view of Jake's black and forbidding glare—did not comment.

"There you go—all recharged, restocked and ready to go," he said as he handed the collar over to Jake, who gave its cargo of listening devices a cursory inspection before he passed it on to Eve. "Now, this here—" and the doctor took a sheaf of papers from his lab coat pocket "—is all your documentation. Here's your bill, with copies for your insurance company, and this here's the order for your physical therapy. Now, there's several different ways we can do this, but in the interest of keeping curiosity and medical community gossip to a minimum, you're going to in effect be assigned a personal therapist who'll have regular appointments with you at a local health club out there on the island. The therapist is gonna be one of our agents, and since this isn't going to be happening at a medical facility, nobody else needs to be brought in on what's going on. That okay with you?" He looked at Jake, who nodded. "So, if you need to get in touch with her, you'll find a way to do it during her sessions." Jake nodded again.

"All right, then, young lady, it looks like you're good to go," said Dr. Shepherd, turning his toothy smile back to Eve. "Shall I tell Agent Franco to have your driver bring the car around?"

"Give us a minute," said Jake softly.

Dr. Shepherd nodded, gave Eve a jaunty little half wave, half salute and went out.

As the door clicked shut, Jake said abruptly, "Here, let me help you on with that." He took the collar from her and hefted it impatiently while she slid down off the table, then helped settle it into place around her neck, all the while frowning with that curious combination of edginess and melancholy she'd come to accept as normal for him.

There was no need for anyone to say anything, and she was glad for that. Speech would have felt awkward and artificial just then, and silence without the activity to fill it infinitely worse. But she knew without being told the moment it was time to turn and give him access to the Velcro fasteners at the sides of the collar, and he seemed to know without asking whether it was too tight or too loose, instead gauging its adjustment with fingers slipped between the collar and her neck while she tried without success to still her own pulse.

When the collar was in place she turned again to face him, and found that his hands were on her shoulders still, and those grave and speculative eyes so close to hers, she couldn't focus on them both at once.

For her, the world seemed to stand still and the moment stretch and swell and take on a stature far beyond a casual leave-taking. Because, for her, at least, it *wasn't* just a casual leave-taking. Suddenly she knew that something had happened in that tiny room, between the moment of Jake's walking in and now, this moment, the moment of his going. Something had happened to *her,* something had changed, and she was not the same person she'd been when she'd entered this room. *It's what's between us that's changed. It's what I feel…what I know.*

"Thank you," she murmured, searching his eyes.

He returned the look, measure for measure, then said with unexpected harshness, "Don't take chances. Screw the bugs."

"But I thought—"

He shook his head with controlled violence, started to say something, then stopped. He closed his eyes briefly and drew in a breath and then, giving her shoulders a little shake to emphasize each word, growled, "Just…don't…get…caught—*capish?*"

"I won't." Her heart hammered against her breastbone.

For a moment longer she felt the scorching weight of his eyes, and then he was gone.

Alone in the silence, Eve heard a faint sound, and looking down, discovered that the audiocassette he'd given her was rattling in her shaking hands.

Chapter 10

Returning from that evening's pizza run, Jake found his partner hunched over the recorder with one hand pressed to his earphones and a rapt expression on his face. He slid the pizza onto the narrow countertop and said, "What's goin' on?"

Birdie pushed back his chair and peeled off his earphones. "You gotta hear this." He reached over to switch on the speaker.

"...*sure that thing's waterproof?*"

Soft laughter...

"*I sure hope so. Not that I intend to get in that deep. Ummm...this is far enough. Oooh, that feels good.*"

"*Yeah? Move over, baby... Oops—here's your wine, complete with straw. Got it? Aaah, man.*"

"What the hell's that swishing noise?" Jake asked. His skin was crawling and his heart rate had quickened to a brisk walk. "Where in the hell are they—the *shower?*"

Grinning in admiration, Birdie shook his head. "She

bugged the Jacuzzi—you believe that? Nervy little rascal, isn't she?''

''That's one word,'' Jake muttered.

''...wish you didn't have to wear this thing.''

''Mmm...me, too.''

''Or this. What're you wearing this for? Hey, come on, it's just you and me, babe....''

''Sonny...'' The voice carried an undercurrent of distress.

Jake realized he was making a growling sound low in his throat when his partner turned to give him a startled look. He muttered, ''Bastard...'' under his breath and shrugged off the look, but there wasn't any way he could shrug off the images that were fogging up his mind: Purple shadows swirled with golden steam...a tropical soup of flowers and humidity and sweat permeated with the music of water in all its variations—a minute and subtle symphony. And Eve, languid and supine, her long, lush body rocking gently in the water's undulations, a sheen of moisture on her cheeks and lips and brow...breasts just visible, firm and round beneath a frothy lace of bubbles...and Sonny's hands—

''What the hell's that noise?'' Birdie asked.

''How should I know?'' said Jake. ''Shut up so I can listen.'' But he made a mental note to stop grinding his teeth.

''...enough I'm not allowed to touch, now I can't even look?''

''Sonny...it's not like we've got any privacy. Not with Sergei and Ricky popping in all the time.'' And she was laughing, a sound almost indistinguishable from the gurgle of the water.

''Aagh...I know, baby. I'm sorry about that. I'm not crazy about it, either, but you gotta understand, this isn't like at home in Vegas. Security's not in place yet. What, they bothering you? They get on your nerves, tell 'em take a hike, okay? Yeah...just want you to be happy, babe, you know that.''

"I know, Sonny...I want us both to be happy."

How could she say that with a straight face? Jake wondered. And sound so damn sincere? He didn't know why she'd worried about being a good enough actor. Far as he could see, women were all natural-born actors.

"Sheesh..." Birdie was swearing under his breath.

"What?"

"Didn't you hear that? She sounds about as sincere as a used-car salesman. No way Cisneros is gonna buy that. No way."

Jake coughed. "Guess guys hear what they want to hear."

"Yeah." Birdie sighed. "I hope so."

"So, you saw the doc today? How'd that go? He say when you're gonna be getting outa that neck thing?"

"Nuh-uh...but—oh! I almost forgot to tell you. The good news is, I'm going to be starting physical therapy. Three times a week. They're setting it up so I don't have to go to Savannah every time. I'm going to be having it at that health club downtown—the one next to the Hilton—what's it called? The Body Shop? The therapist is going to meet me there."

"Yeah? So, what's this...physical therapy supposed to do?"

"Oh, well...I'm not sure, really. I guess right now it's mostly heat treatments, massage, whirlpool...stuff like that."

"What the hell you gotta go to some...health club for? What's wrong with the therapist comin' right here?"

"Uh-oh," said Jake. Birdie uttered an obscenity, sibilant and succinct.

"Sure, why not? Hell, we got the hot tub already, anything else you need, you just tell me what it is and you got it. No need you havin' to go... Wha-at? So...what's with this face?"

"Careful..." murmured Jake. "Don't push it...don't push it..."

"C'mon…spit it out. I'm just tryin' to make a nice suggestion, here."

"I know you're trying to help. But…dammit, did you ever stop to think maybe I might want *to get away from this place once in a while? I'm not used to being cooped up, you know."*

"Hey, hey… Come on…"

"What's she doing?" Birdie whispered. "Is she crying? That's good…that's good. Sounded like she really meant that."

"I'm used to working, being around people! I mean—Jeez, I'm used to slogging through jungles, climbing around in ancient ruins, stuff like that. If I don't have something to do I'm going to go stir-crazy!"

"Hey, baby, don't do that. Don't get upset. Okay? Look, you want to go somewhere, you just gotta tell me. If I'm not here, get the boys to take you. Here—come 'ere, now—you okay? Is that better? That make you happy?"

Whatever her reply was, it got swallowed up in the music of the water, and then for a few minutes nobody said anything, while the tension in the van grew thick…then brittle. Jake and Birdie looked at each other. Birdie fiddled with the controls. Jake looked at the floor and counted silently, keeping time with the beating of his own heart and trying without success to block out the pictures in his mind. When the words came again he let out his breath in a low, slow hiss of relief.

"Reminds me…your sister called—what's'er name? Bella?"

"Mirabella? Really? What did she want?"

"Like she's gonna chat with me? No—she said she wants to talk to you about Thanksgiving. How come you told her we're not coming to her place for dinner?"

"Oh, God, Sonny, it's just such a hassle—my family…"

"Come on, one minute you're tellin' me how you're goin' crazy bein' all cooped up here—"

"Uh-oh," said Birdie. Jake breathed a one-word prayer.

"...and now you're tellin' me you don't want to go see your folks on Thanksgiving? What the hell's this? You lyin' to me?"

"Be careful," Jake pleaded. "Be careful."

"I was just trying to spare you—"

"What the hell you talkin' about? Didn't we have this conversation already? They're your family. That makes 'em my family, too. You love somebody, you take the bad with the good."

In a futile attempt to ease the tension, Birdie joked, "You got that right. You ever meet Margie's brother Melvin?"

"Anyway, what could be so terrible about Thanksgiving dinner at your sister's place? Where's she live? Someplace up in Georgia, right? Hey—if you think the drive's too much for you, we can take the plane—no problem."

Birdie turned around and comically arched his eyebrows at Jake. "No problem." Jake lifted a hand and hissed at him to shut up, which Birdie didn't take personally. "Relax," he said, "looks like she's pulled it out okay."

"Yeah," said Jake, "like she's tiptoeing through a damn minefield."

"Sonny, you have no idea. It's at Bella's—that means her husband's whole family is gonna be there. Kids everywhere—a dozen, at least. A bunch of guys playing football on the front lawn. Granny Calhoun'll probably put a curse on you."

"What're you talkin' about? Sounds like a blast."

"Oh, God...Sonny, are you sure?"

"Hey, baby...like I said. It's Thanksgiving—you should be with family. Y tu familia es mi familia. *Right, baby? Yeah..."*

Again they listened to the water music. Jake stared at the floor and folded his arms across his chest to hold himself still. God, how he hated the silences. Without words to set the scene for him, his mind insisted on painting its own pictures. How could it not? If *he* were in that hot tub, with that woman, he knew what *he'd* be doing.

"So, tell me more about this therapy. Massage, you said?"

"Sonny…" And suddenly her voice had gone breathless and panicky. The hair on the back of Jake's neck stood up; tension stiffened his legs and straightened his back.

"Wha-at? You used to love it when I gave you a back rub. Now you don't even want me to touch you?"

Heat exploded in the pit of Jake's belly and raced through his entire body. He could feel it burning in his face, in the backs of his eyeballs, in the palms of his hands. He discovered that he was alternately rubbing his palms with his fingers, then curling them into fists…remembering the feel of Eve's tender muscle, smooth and springy beneath his fingertips…imagining the fleshy parts of Cisneros's face bursting beneath his knuckles…

"It's not that…at least—"

"What, then? I gotta tell you, Evie, I'm startin' to wonder if that damn mugger did something more to you than just hit you on the head."

"Wha-what do you mean?"

"Jeez, baby, it's not like he raped you or anything…."

Birdie made a disgusted noise. "Mr. Sensitivity."

"No! Of course not. But…oh, I don't know, it's hard to explain. It's still a violation, and it's hard to get my…confidence back. It just takes time, I guess."

"So, in the meantime, I'm supposed to be like, what—your brother? Hell, I'd just like to sleep in the same bed with you—what's wrong with that? You won't even let me do that."

Jake reined himself in with the sheer force of his willpower. He had to force himself to listen. He wasn't sure how much more of this he could take. Every second, every word was torture. He couldn't remember ever feeling like this before—one minute wired and burning, twitchy with the urge to punch the hell out of something, or someone, the next minute cold and clammy and feeling like he was one deep breath away from puking. And weirdest of all, underlying both of those, there was this pressure behind his temples and in his belly....

What had he done? What had he been thinking of, to send the woman into a situation like this?

"Sonny, what do you think, I'm made of stone? If you touch me it's just going to make us both crazy, don't you see that?"

Her voice was rapid and breathless. Too eager, Jake thought. Too desperate. How could Cisneros help but hear it?

"I think it's easier if we just...you, know, keep our distance. Just...don't think about it."

"Easy for you to say...."

"If we keep busy, the time is going to go by.... Sonny? What's the matter? Where are you going?"

"Cold shower, that's where I'm going...gonna make me crazy..."

As the grumbling voice faded into the gurgle and chuckle of the water, Jake let go of the breath he'd been holding for what seemed like a week and began to swear.

His partner, on the other hand, was laughing. Birdie wiped a hand across his brow and said, "Hoo boy, is it hot in here, or is it just me?"

Jake drove a hand through his hair and turned away, muttering, "This isn't funny. I've gotta get her out of there. It's too damn dangerous...gotta get her out of there *now*."

Birdie, reaching for the pizza box, looked at him in surprise. "Why? She handled herself like a pro."

"He's suspicious as hell."

"You don't know that. Sounded like normal reactions to me. Hell, I'd be upset if my bride-to-be was all of a sudden off-limits. Damn, if it was anybody but Cisneros, I'd almost have to feel sorry for the guy.''

Jake swore. "You heard her—he's trying to isolate her.''

"What, you mean the therapy? That's also a pretty normal response. Guy's got more money than God, he could outfit his own health club if he wanted to.''

"If he gets her where we can't get at her—''

"Hey, she nipped it in the bud, didn't she? Sounds to me like she knows how to handle the guy pretty well. We just have to back off and give her some time. You said yourself— he wants something from her. Okay, so sooner or later he's gonna tip his hand. And he's not going to do anything before then. Until he gets what he wants—''

"Family…" Jake growled the word, straightening slowly, stretching to ease the tension out of his neck and back muscles. "Her family—that's what he wants from her. More specifically, her sister—Summer, the ex Mrs. Hal Robey. He still thinks she's got 'em—the files Robey stole from him. He's using Eve to get close enough to her sister to find those files—remember? He said so himself, in that conversation she overheard.''

Birdie rocked back in his chair. "Then what's she doing—?''

Jake interrupted him, swearing with quiet fury. "She's trying to protect them. She's trying to keep Cisneros away from her family. Probably thinks she can get something on him without getting them involved again. *Damn.*''

His partner shrugged. "Maybe she can.''

Jake was trying to pace in the confined space of the van. "Cisneros isn't stupid. Sooner or later he's gonna figure it out—hell, probably already has. He's just biding his time. Look—we've gotta get her out of there. It's too big a risk. I think we should bring her in while we still can.''

"We can run it by Coffee, I guess.'' Birdie paused in the middle of a stretch to shake his head doubtfully. "But I think you're being premature. Man, I don't get this. I don't get *you*. You've been trying to nail this guy for how long? Five years? Six? You say this Waskowitz woman is the key, the break you've been waiting for. You set this up. Now you want to call it off before you've even given it a chance? If I didn't know better—'' He broke off, and both men stared at the microphone.

"What in the hell is that?" Birdie looked sideways at Jake, who for some reason couldn't think of anything to say. "That isn't...tell me that's not Bessie Smith."

Jake cleared his throat. "I, uh...gave her a tape. For her...you know, for her, uh...birthday."

"Oh, Lord...Lord Almighty." Birdie rocked back in his chair and stared at Jake as if he were indeed the Second Coming. "I'm beginning to see—yes, I'm beginning to understand now." His tone was awed, but his eyes were positively gleeful. Jake had to resist the temptation to tip him over backward. "You are starting to *care* for this woman! Don't tell me you're not."

"Sure I care," Jake said reasonably. "She's a nice lady."

"Uh-uh—don't give me that. Long as I've known you you've cared about one thing—bringing down Cisneros. At any cost. You are as a brother to me, you know that, and I know you'll forgive me when I say this, but you are a little nutty where this man is concerned. This is the first time I've ever known you to put something—or someone—else ahead of that priority."

Jake waved that angrily away, like taking a swipe at a fly. "Yeah, well this is the first time I've been responsible for sending a civilian into harm's way, too."

Birdie, who could be every bit as annoying as a fly when he wanted to be, just smiled. "Jake...Jake. I wouldn't go so far as to say you'd send your own mother undercover if you thought it would get you Cisneros's head on a pike, but I imagine just about anybody else would be fair game. No, son…no. That's not what's going on here. Hot damn—'' he rubbed his hands together briskly, then helped himself to a slice of tepid pizza ''—I do believe it's finally happened. Wait'll I tell Margie.'' He bit into the pizza while offering the box to Jake. ''Not bad. Care for some?''

Jake shook his head; for some reason he'd lost his appetite. He was staring at the microphone, transfixed by a new voice, an unexpectedly full and throaty voice—not Bessie's—which was at that moment crooning a familiar blues standard. He thought, She can sing. I'll be damned.

''Kidding aside…'' Birdie's voice came to him softly, and with a steely edge of warning. ''My friend, happy as I am that this has happened to you, your timing's way off. This is bound to affect your judgment. Already has. If you can't see that…''

Jake rubbed at his burning eyes and nodded. He *could* see that. He could see a lot of things. That was the problem. He could see Eve with Sonny Cisneros's hands all over her…caressing that creamy skin as he fastened a pearl choker around her slender throat. And he could see those same hands on that same throat, choking the life out of it. Not that it would happen that way. Cisneros wouldn't soil his own hands with murder. He'd have his men do it. And maybe, since he supposedly cared about this woman, this one time he'd tell them to do it *quick*.

''I need to talk to her,'' he growled. ''Tell her she's got to quit fooling around, quit trying to keep Sonny away from her sister. I want this *over. Capish?*''

''Yeah,'' said his partner gently, ''I believe I do.''

Eve's first appointment with her ''physical therapist'' had been set for Friday. As the day approached, she felt like a six-year-old counting the days until her birthday party. Who would be there? Her hair was a mess. What should she wear?

She had Sergei drive her to town so she could buy workout clothes.

"Whadaya need those for? It's not like *you're* gonna be doing anything physical," Sonny pointed out. He'd been noticeably cranky since the Jacuzzi episode.

"I want to fit in," Eve calmly explained. "Plus, I *like* them. I think they look sexy."

"Yeah, they do," Sonny grumbled, "for all the good that does anybody."

While she was at it, she went to a salon and had her hair trimmed. She got hair clippings all down inside the collar, which itched like fire until she was able to get home and take it off. Then she had them in her bed instead.

"What're you so excited about this physical therapy stuff for?" Sonny wanted to know.

"One step closer to getting my life back," Eve answered fervently, and watched with satisfaction as the lines of suspicion in Sonny's face softened into sympathy.

The key to undercover work, she'd discovered, was to tell the truth whenever possible.

Even so—and whether out of suspicion or genuine interest she couldn't be certain—Sonny insisted on accompanying her to her first therapy session. At least, thanks to the bugs, she knew Sonny's presence wouldn't come as a surprise to anyone.

She did her best to throttle back her anticipation. After all, she told herself, Jake might not even be there. To avert suspicion, the therapy sessions were scheduled for three times a week, because that was what would be expected for her type of "injury," not because there was any real need for her to check in that often. Would Jake come himself unless there was something he needed to talk to her about? And it had only been a few days since she'd seen him. She told herself he wouldn't be there. Of course he wouldn't. She'd gotten all worked up—not to mention prettied up—for nothing.

So it came as something of a shock to her when she walked into the Body Shop and there was Jake in sweatpants and tank top, pounding the daylights out of a punching bag.

Not like it was anything that obvious. She was checking in at the lobby desk, which was situated behind a curving counter in front of a wall of glass overlooking the main work-out room, the purpose of which, she assumed, was to give visitors a view of the club's sumptuous facilities so that they'd be enticed to join. While the beefy young man on duty at the desk was on the phone, Eve watched an interesting assortment of sweaty people of varying ages, genders and degrees of fitness pumping away on stationary bicycles, stair-climbers, rowing machines and Nautilus equipment.

The area in the back of the room was devoted to free weights. These were serious bodybuilders, she assumed from the look of them—brawny guys with bulging biceps, massive deltoids and necks with a greater circumference than their heads. Most of them wore headbands to keep the sweat out of their eyes, and some wore hand protectors and heavy support belts. All of them wore looks of grim concentration, if not intense pain.

"Serious stuff," Eve said to Sonny, nodding toward the weight lifters. Sonny, who had declined the attendant's invitation to pay the fee and join the fun, merely grunted and resumed his pacing. Not that Sonny was in terrible shape, but as far as he was concerned, that physical stuff was for the Rickys and Sergeis of this world. He preferred more subtle methods of power and control.

So, since the attendant was still occupied, Eve went back to watching the club's patrons. Through large glass windows on one side of the main exercise room, she could see aerobics classes in progress. In one, a dozen or so senior citizens in sweats gamely flapped and stretched and marched and swiveled at the exhortations of a fiftyish woman wearing a fuchsia leotard and purple tights. In the room next door, a younger group wriggled and pounded energetically on and off stair-steps to the beat of a dance tune only they could hear. And farther back along that same wall, partially obscured by the huffing puffing weight lifters, a tall, lean man in gray sweats and a white tank-style undershirt was attacking a massive punching bag with the single-minded fury of an enraged bull.

"My goodness," Eve murmured under her breath. She wasn't even into boxing; she hated violence—she'd seen too much of its end product. But for some reason she couldn't take her eyes off the man at the bag, and watching him, unaccountably felt her heartbeat quicken and her breath grow thick in her chest. This was violence, yes, but it seemed more like an imperative of nature than a product of mankind's folly—like a grizzly bear pummeling a tree trunk, or a bull elk's charge; primitive and exciting; a bit frightening, but in a way, soul stirring, too.

The man paused, steadying the bag with a glove while he wiped sweat with a forearm. Then he lifted his head and looked straight at her; even from that distance she could see his eyes glowing black as coals beneath the furrowed brow. Her breath gushed from her as if one of those gloved hands had just made contact with her solar plexus. She thought, *My God—it's Jake.*

"Miss? Uh, ma'am?" The attendant was talking to her. "Okay, if you want to go on back, your therapist is gonna meet you. Go through there—that's the ladies' locker room, you can change in there—then go on through. You'll go past the pool and you'll see the doors marked Steam Room, Whirlpool, and so on. She says she'll meet you there—at the whirlpool."

Eve nodded. She was still trying to recover her breath. She started for the door the attendant had indicated, to the right of a large arrow and the sign Ladies.

"Wait," Sonny blustered. "I wanna meet this therapist."

The attendant said, "Sir, if you'd care to wait till she's

done, if you could just have a seat... Or else you can come back for her—whichever you prefer. Should be 'bout half an hour.''

"How about if I bring—?" She looked at the attendant.

"Name's Marcie," he supplied.

"Okay, I'll have her come out afterward so you can meet her. Is that all right?"

"Just want to make sure she knows what she's doing," Sonny said gruffly. "Don't want some quack messing around with my girl." He stroked her arm, then leaned over and kissed her forehead. "Go on—get it over with. I'll be waiting."

Eve whispered, "Okay," breathless as a child. She picked up her bag and walked through the swinging door, and instantly was slapped in the face by the humidity and swamped by the unmistakable smells of the gym—sweat and steam and disinfectant and oil of wintergreen. Her knees felt weak, as though she'd just had a bad fright, or narrowly avoided an accident.

She placed her bag on a bench in front of an empty locker and undressed quickly, putting on the one-piece bathing suit she'd just bought, and her new warm-ups over that. And all the while her heart was pounding, and her mind kept replaying the words, *Oh my God...my God—it's Jake.*

Chapter 11

He came in while she was in the whirlpool bath, still sweating from his workout, with a towel looped around his neck and his hair standing out from his head in a bristle of wet spikes. He spoke in an undertone to the FBI agent posing as Marcie the physical therapist, who nodded and left the room.

Eve observed this from under cover of her lashes as she lay in the tub, half-reclining in the warm, churning water with her head back and her neck supported by a specially designed cushion, pretending drowsy indifference while her heart mocked her with its thundering tattoo. She watched him approach the tub with a rocking, unhurried gait, his eyes pinioning her, studying her with a curious combination of self-confidence and wariness, like a seasoned fighter taking a new opponent's measure. And even though she knew most of her body would be invisible to him in the swirling water, under that dark, unyielding gaze she felt utterly and completely naked.

With her pulse throbbing at the base of her throat, she

waited, hoping to let him speak first. But when it became apparent that he wasn't going to, and when she couldn't stand the terrible feeling of vulnerability another minute, she curved her lips into a languid smile, forced her voice low in her throat and purred, "I wasn't sure you were coming."

He made a short, ambiguous sound. "You knew I'd be here." And he moved closer, towering over her so that in order to see him she had no choice but to open her eyes.

Oh, but her eyelids felt heavy…and the rest of her body, too, weighed down by a strange lassitude that had nothing to do with the warmth and the water.

Strange, too, that in the midst of all that water and humidity her throat felt dry as dust; and when she swallowed, the thirst was carried deep into her belly and from there to every part of her. When she stared at Jake's chest, hair shadowed and glistening with sweat, she felt as if she were beholding the only source of relief for that thirst in a cruel and barren desert. When she gazed at his hands, even knowing that moments ago those same hands had been engaged in brutally pounding a bag of sawdust, her body felt the water's gentle caress only as a taunting, teasing simulation of *their* touch. She felt heavy and ripe at her core, like a fruit ready to fall of its own weight; and at the same time as if she would shiver into a million pieces and blow away if he touched her.

"Weird…" she murmured, closing her eyes.

"What is?"

His voice is like…molasses, she thought. Blackstrap molasses…rich and thick and not too sweet…kind of a bite to it.

"This…the water…it feels weird."

Jake growled, "I thought you liked hot tubs." And he couldn't look at her a moment longer, lying there spread out before him like a banquet, and he the beggar standing outside the hall with his face pressed up against the window.

Turning one shoulder to her, he leaned his backside against

the tub and buried his face in the towel he'd thrown around his neck after his workout. But it did no good. He could still see her—almost more vivid in his mind's eye than the lush reality—the outlines of her body undulating beneath the swirling water, moisture beading on her chest and throat, face dewy and pink from the heat, lips parted, breath suspended…as if, he thought, in the very next moment she expected to be kissed.…

"I'm curious." He cleared his throat. "How in the hell did you manage to bug a Jacuzzi?"

She laughed—a blood-stirring chuckle. "That was easy, actually. I put it in the boom box. Had it sitting there on the deck beside me. I played your tape."

"I heard. Heard you singing, too." He said it harshly, and she looked momentarily startled. Then her face hardened almost imperceptibly, as if she'd donned a transparent mask.

"Heard about your Thanksgiving plans," he said, and she shifted as if the water had suddenly become uncomfortable to her. "So, you're going to your sister's?"

She shrugged and said without expression, "I tried to get out of it, but…Sonny wants to go."

For a moment Jake didn't trust himself to speak. Then, very quietly, he said, "What the hell were you thinking?"

Her head snapped toward him, too quickly for muscles that had been immobilized for most of the past several weeks. He saw her wince and grab at the back of her neck, then gingerly rotate her head as she flashed at him, "Look, I don't want him anywhere near Summer and her kids, okay? Not after what he tried to do to them. I don't want him anywhere near any of my family."

A dozen angry replies to that zapped through his mind. He squelched them, and instead found himself moving around to the head of the tub, slipping his hands under her head. He began to massage the muscles of her neck with his fingertips, and heard her give a gasp, then a sigh…saw her lashes settle onto sweat-spangled cheeks…felt her head grow heavy in his hands.

He found that there was something relaxing about it for him, too. Something about the touching…as if her warmth and weight and textures measured on the nerve endings of his fingers had opened doors and allowed those messages of pleasure and contentment to pour into the corners of his body, soul and mind.

After a while, without altering the rhythm and pressure of his fingers, he said quietly, ''You know it's what has to happen. We have to allow Cisneros to play his hand. It's the only way we're ever going to end this. The *only* way.''

Her voice was soft and slurred. ''I thought—if I can get something on him, or if you get something from the bugs—''

''Never happen. The man's too careful—and too smart. Lady, we've got state-of-the art equipment at our disposal— hell, some of it sounds like science fiction even to me. If it was possible to nail Cisneros with electronic surveillance, we'd have had him put away years ago.''

Her lashes flew upward. He felt her neck muscles tighten in his hands, but instead of pulling away from him she tilted her head back in order to look at him. ''Then why did you have me do this? The…collar. The bugs. What's the point, if it's not—''

Jake was shaking his head. ''Unless you wanted to reveal the fact of what you heard, which would make your life not worth…doo-doo, you had no choice but to go back to him. That being the case, we figured we'd keep an eye on him through you, he'd eventually make his play to go after those records Hal Robey stole from him, and that's when we'd be there to nail him.'' He let out a breath. ''You know what the collar's for.''

''And the bugs?'' Her upside-down gaze was unflinching. Her pulse hammered against the pads of his fingers.

He cleared his throat, but the words came in a growl anyway. "We couldn't let you go in there unprotected. Had to have some way to keep an eye on you—or ear, rather."

"All this time I've been bugging *myself*?" She jerked in his hands, and he braced himself. Then he realized she was laughing. "Oh, man. And I was really getting into it, too. Little Miss Espionage." She sighed.

Her eyes had started to close when he rasped, "Don't sell yourself short, Waskowitz." And they flew open again, and her head jerked back and he found that instead of massaging her neck muscles, his fingers were stroking the taut arch of her throat, the wet-velvet undercurve of her chin. "For this to work, we need you there, and we need you safe. You've got to quit doing things to arouse his suspicions. *Capish?*" Her head moved slowly in the cradle of his hands. Her lips parted.

And suddenly he couldn't feel his own feet. He felt like one gigantic throbbing pulse. "If he doesn't want you to go to a health club, if he wants to set you up with a private therapist, don't worry about it." His voice seemed to come from a great, echoing distance. His jaws felt rigid as wire. "We're flexible, we'll find another way to contact you. Let us do our job. Yours is to go along with him. Play his game. Keep him happy."

Her rueful laughter bumped against his fingers. Electric charges ran up his arms and into his chest. "I don't think he's very happy right now. I just wish..." The laughter ended, and then she whispered, "I just want it to be over."

He held her still, her face framed upside down in his hands, and stared down...down into her eyes. She gazed steadily back at him for a long, unmeasurable time...just time enough, it seemed, for him to play back over all the moments of his life from the very first until this one...the very moment when it seemed almost inevitable that he would kiss her.

Time enough to relive all the missteps and wrong turns he'd taken, all the blind alleys and deep waters he'd stumbled into. Time to review his failures and broken dreams and the reasons for them. To remember who he was, and why for him, some things, no matter how much he wanted them, simply were not possible.

"You're a civilian. You don't have to do this if you don't want to," he said in that cracked and gravelly voice he was learning to accept as his own. "If you want to call it off—"

"No! No…" Her lashes drifted down as if she felt utterly exhausted, and she said in a soft, dead voice, "This is the only way. I know that. I want to finish it."

"All right then." Exhaling through his nose, Jake pulled his hands away from her neck and straightened slowly. He felt stiff and achy in every joint. "You'll go to your sister's for Thanksgiving?" He waited for her nod. "Okay. Unless something comes up in the meantime, that'll be our next meeting."

She lifted her head and her eyes followed him as he came around to the front of the tub. "You'll be there?"

He almost smiled, but in the end just snorted again instead. "Do you seriously think we're gonna let Cisneros anywhere near your sister unless we're within shouting distance? Of course we'll be there."

"But how—it's clear out in the country, there's going to be people all over the place—"

"Waskowitz—" he squinted up his eyes in an exasperated grimace "—let us worry about that, okay? That's our job." He walked to the door and paused with his hand on the knob. "We'll think of something. Or you will. If you do, just…talk into a bug. We'll hear you. And if we come up with a plan, we'll give you the signal. Which is…?"

She bobbed her head impatiently. "The appointment's been changed. I know, I know." She suddenly looked overheated and cross. "Okay, so…I guess I'll see you on Thanksgiving.

"Oh—do me a favor, will you?" She stopped him as he

was going out the door. "If you see Marcie out there, ask her to come get me out of this…blinkin' tub? I'm starting to prune."

"Will do," said Jake solemnly. He closed the door and leaned against it for a moment, eyes closed, breathing hard. If he hadn't been in so much pain, he probably would have laughed.

Somehow the weeks passed. Not that there was any lack of things for Eve to do—as Sonny had pointed out to her more than once, and with exasperation, Hilton Head was a veritable playground, at least for the privileged. But golf and tennis, two of the island's principal attractions, were obviously not available to her, and if the truth were told, wouldn't have appealed to her even if she hadn't been wearing a neck brace.

It was also true that the recent surge of development had produced a plethora of shopping and dining pleasures, ranging from touristy T-shirt and souvenir shops and every kind of fast food known to mankind, to the finest champagne, candlelight and caviar restaurants and upscale malls anchored by the likes of Saks Fifth Avenue. Plus, just across the bridge on the mainland were the new factory outlet malls—small cities of stores that could swallow up shopping enthusiasts for days at a time. But Eve had never considered either food or shopping to be forms of recreation; she shopped when she needed something and ate when she was hungry. These days, thanks to Sonny's attentiveness to her every need, she seldom fell into either of those categories, and as a result, was losing weight at a rate that would have alarmed her, had she not been too miserable to notice.

She spent her days walking the beaches in search of shells and sand dollars, strolling the miles of equestrian and bicycle trails through resorts and golf courses, staking out man-made ponds and lagoons in hopes of spotting one of the alligators

that gave a whole new meaning to the term ''water hazard.''
Sometimes she wandered into one of the few remaining pockets of undeveloped land, where modest and ramshackle frame
houses squatted stubbornly beneath century-old live oaks on
real estate grown valuable almost beyond the comprehension
of the people who lived there—for these were people who
did not measure the worth of their land in money.

Once in a while Eve caught a glimpse of one of the few
black people left on the island, descendants of the Gullah
people who had been Hilton Head's original owners, working
in a yard or walking down a shaded back road. They didn't
return her waves, and who could blame them? To them she
was just another of the mainlanders who'd invaded their island, bought them out, fenced them off and made them unwelcome in their own land.

They couldn't know that Eve understood them. That she
knew what it was that made them cling to their land so ob-
stinately, in spite of pressure and hostility, skyrocketing taxes
and offers of money beyond their wildest imaginings. She
knew that, simply put, this was *home*. Their place of belonging.

She envied those people, and when she passed their
homely little houses she sent up silent cheers of encourage-
ment, and vowed that if ever she did find her own place she
would hold on to it as tenaciously.

Sometimes she stopped at the edge of the marshes to watch
the sun go down in a red blaze of glory, and alerted by distant
honkings she would catch the breathtaking descent of geese
as they settled into their night's refuge. It was at times like
that that she felt the familiar wave of longing that was almost
like grief. Why? she would cry out in silent anguish and
bewilderment. *Why?*

As always, she reminded herself that she was the luckiest
of women. She had been privileged to see so much of the
world, and so much that was wondrous and beautiful. But

why was it that the more fascinating, awe-inspiring or poignantly lovely something was, the sadder it made her feel? Watching a glacier calve or finding a hermit crab in a tide pool, she would gasp first with the wonder of it, the bright, sharp stab of joy. And then, as she looked in vain for someone to share the joy and wonder with, feel instead the creeping ache of loneliness.

With Thanksgiving approaching, she felt more guilty than ever for feeling sad. As she had that day in the church garden in Savannah, the last day, it seemed to her now, of innocence, she thought of all her many blessings with a fervent, almost superstitious thankfulness. She *was* the luckiest of women. And if her place of belonging had thus far eluded her, and if beauty made her sad because she had no one to share it with, she could at least give thanks for the beauty. And she did—oh, she did.

She did wonder, sometimes, if there might be a connection between those two things—the search for her place, the longing for someone to share her soul's secrets—but when she tried to pin down exactly what the connection was, it eluded her; it was like trying to remember the details of a dream. Though lately she'd had the feeling that she was coming closer to the answer, that it was hovering out there, just beyond her reach.

So intent was she on trying to grasp it, that she failed to notice the refrain that played constantly now in the background of her mind. Or perhaps she'd grown so accustomed to it that, like music in a shopping mall, she hardly heard it most of the time. *Oh my God...* it went. *My God...it's Jake...it's Jake.*

It was Thanksgiving Day. Dinner had been served and consumed, and in its aftermath, on her way back to the kitchen with her hands full of dirty plates, Mirabella nudged Summer in the ribs with her elbow. "He's making himself right at home, isn't he?" she muttered, sotto voce.

Summer looked lost for a moment, then, following the jerking movement of Mirabella's head toward the living room, where an assortment of male bodies in varying degrees of somnolence and gastric distress were sprawled in front of the television set, said, "Oh, you mean…"

"Sonny. Our sister's fiancé, Mr. Cheesy Las Vegas himself, making like one of 'the guys.' And did you notice the way he oiled himself through dinner, complimenting every mouthful and oozing charm from every pore? Just about ruined my appetite."

"Oh, Bella." Summer sighed. "Don't be so judgmental. Maybe he really *is* nice. Did you ever think of that? He does seem genuinely crazy about Evie. Isn't that what counts? It doesn't really matter what *we* think."

"It wouldn't," Mirabella huffed in a fierce undertone meant only for Summer, as the sisters unloaded their burdens into the already crowded sink, "if I thought for one moment she felt the same way about him. If I thought she was *happy*."

Summer cast a troubled glance over her shoulder at the bustling, noisy trio of Starrs—Jimmy Joe's mother, Betty, his sister, Jess, and Granny Calhoun—discussing the disposition of heaps of leftovers on the kitchen table. She lowered her voice to a barely audible murmur. "You don't think she's happy?"

"Do you?"

"Well, I—"

"Did you see how *thin* she is?"

"Yes, but don't you think it could just be…you know, the injury, the neck brace…"

Mirabella said derisively, "Oh yeah, right—if I couldn't exercise, couldn't do anything except lay around all day and eat, I'd certainly lose weight, wouldn't you? No—something's not right. I can feel it. She does not look like a woman in love—at least not with…'' Her voice trailed off as a new and appalling thought crossed her mind. She pushed it aside.

"She doesn't have that…that *glow*,'' she said to Summer, who was gazing distractedly through the window above the sink, watching the children romp and play in the piles of leaves on the lawn. Their shouts and laughter and the sound of crackling leaves made a staccato counterpoint to the mellower murmurs and chuckles of the three women behind them, and to the rush and roar of the football game and the occasional accent marks of exclamation from its audience in the living room next door. "When she's around him, you know what I mean? She doesn't look like *you* do when you're anywhere near Riley, that's for sure.''

Summer threw her a look, as a beautiful, rosy flush spread over her cheeks. *"There,''* said Mirabella, "that's what I mean. The glow. Have you seen Evie *glow?''*

"You know, actually,'' said Summer, "I haven't seen Evie at all, for quite a while. Have you?''

Mirabella made a wry face. "And you won't. It's clean-up time. Eve always was a magician when it came to doing the disappearing act when there was work to be done, remember?''

Summer smiled. "That's right. That always used to bug you so bad. Still—'' she cast a futile look around her "—I wonder where in the world she is. She's not in there with the guys. Do you suppose she could be upstairs with Charly, taking a nap?''

"Who? Your sister?'' Jess, Jimmy Joe's sister, had come to the sink with a load of serving platters in time to hear the last question. "She was in here just a little while ago, dishing up a plate.''

"Dishing up…?'' Summer and Bella looked at each other.

"Yeah, you know—like she was fixin' to carry it to some-body? Heaped it high. Covered it all up with aluminum foil…

Oh—and she took along a couple bottles of Corona, too. Last I saw of her, she was headin' across the lawn. I figured she was taking it out to the limo driver, or something.''

Summer's eyes widened and a pleat of distress formed between her eyes. Mirabella could see that they shared the same thought—a mental image of their sister tiptoeing across the church garden in her wedding gown with a bottle of vino and two crystal glasses in her hands.

Eve stood contemplating the row of behemoths in the grassy field behind her sister's house. When she'd come up with the brilliant idea for Jake to meet her in Jimmy Joe's eighteen-wheeler, which she knew would be parked, as it always was when he was at home, in the field next to the house, it hadn't occurred to her that there'd be more than one. Much less a whole fleet. Who knew that sweet brother-in-law of hers would make sure every last one of his drivers was home for the holiday? Because here, arrayed before her like a congregation of huge, curious beasts, were not one, but six tractor-trailer rigs, plus another two extra reefer trailers besides.

So, what next? Which one was the right one? Mirabella had once confided to Eve that Jimmy Joe didn't always lock up his truck when it was parked in his own yard. Eve had passed that information on to Jake, who had assured her a locked door wouldn't present a problem anyway. So, the bottom line was, he could be in any one of these royal-blue monsters. What was she supposed to do, go down the line trying every door? Carrying a couple of cold ones and a plateful of turkey and trimmings?

Oddly, Eve found the little problem almost comforting. It was an annoying inconvenience, a small obstacle to overcome. And there was something about the mental exercise that seemed to help calm her jitters and steady her rapidly beating heart. Even so, as she approached the trucks she noticed that her legs felt weak and her insides wired and shivery, as if she'd been plugged into a low-voltage electrical current.

Suddenly she saw the truck on the end of the row, the one farthest from the house, flash its headlights—once on and off, then once more. Her head went light with relief, and at the same time, confusingly, apprehension made a shivery starburst in her belly. She moved quickly to the far truck and around to the passenger side, and was contemplating the step up to the cab, debating the best way to tackle it, when the door swung open and a hand reached down to her.

"Come on, give me that," said a familiar masculine growl, and Eve's heart gave a leap of pure, unadulterated joy.

"Which do you want?" she asked mildly, squinting up at him against the reflected glare of a late-afternoon sun. "The plate or the bottles?"

Jake grunted as he relieved her of both. "Hurry up—get in here. You want somebody to see us? What *is* this?" He was sniffing the foil-covered plate like a suspicious bloodhound.

"I brought you some dinner. Happy Thanksgiving."

She was already hauling herself awkwardly up the steps and into the cab when Jake transferred the plate and bottles to the driver's seat and reached down to help her. His hands, one warm and dry, the other cold and wet from the condensation on the beer bottles, grasped one of hers and enfolded it, and she felt a lurch in her middle.

"You sure nobody saw you?" Jake asked in his grave and gravelly voice once they were inside the truck and the door shut firmly behind them.

Eve rolled her eyes. "I can't guarantee nobody saw me leave the house, but I know for sure nobody followed me out here. The guys are all sacked out in front of the TV set—"

"Cisneros?" He looked as if he found that hard to believe.

"Oh, yeah." Her smile was off center. "He's very busy

being 'one of the boys.' Anyway, the women are, of course, cleaning up in the kitchen, Charly and the babies are napping upstairs, and the bigger kids have some sort of tag game going on the lawn, clear on the other side of the house.'' She stopped, out of breath, to sweep her hair back from her face with both hands. It helped to quell her jitters somehow. "So—I'm pretty sure we're in the clear. How 'bout you? Have any trouble finding the place? Was the truck unlocked?''

"No problems…'' Jake's mumble was distracted as he scowled through the windshield, as intently as if he expected hostiles to pop up any minute out of the landscape of grassy hummocks and fire ant mounds.

"Where's your backup?''

"Parked on a logging road on the other side of that stand of pines.'' He threw her a look as he moved back between the seats. "If necessary, they can be here in three minutes.''

"Three?'' Eve murmured, her tone faintly mocking. Had he timed it? she wondered. And she thought that a lot could happen in three minutes….

"We can talk in here,'' Jake said tersely. He was poised in the entrance to the sleeper compartment, one knee on the bunk, one hand on the sliding curtain. "Doors are locked. If we pull this curtain, no one'll ever be able to tell anyone's inside.''

Eve scooped up the plate and bottles from the driver's seat, then paused. "Oh, look,'' she said, "this must be Jimmy Joe's truck.'' Clipped to the dashboard were two photographs—a school portrait of Jimmy Joe's son, J.J., and a snapshot of Mirabella holding her baby, Amy Jo.

"Come on, hurry up.'' Jake was gesturing urgently.

She nodded and eased herself between the seats to join him in the sleeper, at the same time looking around her, overcome by an unexpected sense of awe. She was thinking that this must be the very same truck, the very same sleeper in which Mirabella had given birth, with Jimmy Joe's help, to a beautiful baby girl on a snowbound Texas interstate. On Christmas Day, that had been—almost two years ago.

Jake, watching her, asked as he pulled the curtain across the opening, "Never been in one of these before?"

"Nope," she murmured, scooting herself backward onto the bed and pulling her legs up under her, Indian-style, "it's a first." She wanted to tell him about Mirabella's Christmas miracle; it was part of her family's folklore, a tale told and retold around dinner tables and at family gatherings. But for some reason it seemed too intimate a thing to share in these circumstances, the two of them closed in together in this tiny, womblike space. Instead, she said casually, "Nice digs. Are we bugged?" It had come to seem almost natural to her.

But Jake looked at her for a long, somber moment, then shook his head. "Not today." He pulled the foil-covered plate toward him.

"You didn't have to do this," he mumbled as he peeled back the foil. He felt twinges of guilt when he thought about Birdie and Franco out there in the van, dining on fast-food burgers and fries, but then the smells of roasted turkey, sage stuffing, giblet gravy and candied sweet potatoes assailed him, and he went light-headed with pleasure. He'd read somewhere that the sense of smell was the most evocative of the senses. Right now he understood what that meant, because for one achingly poignant moment he was a child again, and back in his mother's kitchen, cracking walnuts on the warped linoleum floor. He swallowed saliva along with the unexpected lump in his throat and said in a dazed voice, "I haven't had a feast like this since…"

Eve was digging in the pockets of her jacket. She glanced at him as she drew out a set of silverware wrapped in a white linen napkin, another napkin bundle containing home-baked rolls, and a triangular-shaped, foil-wrapped package Jake devoutly hoped was pumpkin pie. "Go on, you can say it—

since your divorce. Last time I looked, that's not a four-letter word.''

He made a sound as he reached for the silverware, one she probably wouldn't recognize as a chuckle. It was, though— he was profoundly glad for the distraction; sentimental at his core, the prospect of revealing such feelings dismayed him.

"How come?" Having taken his response for agreement, she was watching him with glittery-bright eyes and flushed cheeks above the rim of her collar, reminding him not so much of a titmouse now, but of the furred variety, peeking out of its hole, nose all aquiver with curiosity. ''Don't you have other family? What about your parents? Are they alive?''

''Yeah, they are. They live in Pittsburgh....'' Fork poised above the heaped plate, he pondered the delicious choices.

''Really? *Pittsburgh?*''

''Yeah. And I have a sister who lives in Philly.'' He stabbed the side of the mashed potato crater, allowing the pool of gravy to pour into the stuffing, then scooped up a huge forkful of all three and put it in his mouth. The combination of flavors almost sent him into ecstasy. He closed his eyes as he chewed, and made soft, guttural sounds of pleasure.

He opened his eyes and found her watching him hungrily. ''You want some of this?'' he offered, nudging the plate slightly toward her. ''There's plenty—more'n I can eat.'' Which was an out-and-out lie, and he was relieved when she shook her head.

''No, thanks—I'm stuffed.'' But she belied that as soon as she'd spoken, claiming one of the rolls.

He watched her as she broke it open, slathered it liberally with cranberry sauce, closed it up again and took a generous bite that left a small blob of sauce clinging to her upper lip. Instantly, without thinking, he reached over to wipe it away with a corner of the white linen napkin.

Her tiny, almost inaudible gasp woke him to himself and what he'd done. For a few moments he stared at her over the napkin, frozen…half in embarrassment, half in fearful anticipation, like someone who'd stepped on a squeaky stair tread and now waited to see if he'd given himself away.

Chapter 12

Jake cleared his throat and searched his mind frantically for the thread of the conversation. What *had* they been talking about? Oh yes—his parents. And Pittsburgh.

"They like it there," he said. She was dabbing self-consciously at her lips now. He averted his eyes like a polite stranger. Staring down at the plate before him, he felt again that peculiar sensation of mouthwatering hunger he knew no amount of food would ever assuage. "Actually, you know, Pittsburgh is a very elder-friendly town. Plus, they'd lived there pretty much all their lives, except for a brief stint in the service before I was born. So when they retired—"

Eve interrupted with a small, interested sound. "So, you grew up in Pittsburgh?"

His mouth full, Jake nodded. "Yeah, I did. My dad was a cop, the first in his family to escape the mines and the mills."

"Really? No kidding? My pop was a cop, too!"

"Yeah?" He didn't tell her he was already privy to that information, as well as quite a few other tidbits about her she'd probably rather he didn't know.

Unable to nod, she bobbed eagerly. "Chief of police of Desert Palms, California. How 'bout your mom?"

"Strictly a homemaker—like every other mom I knew." He shrugged without looking up. "That's the way it was then. I didn't know anybody whose mother worked outside the home."

"Yeah," said Eve, "me, too." She paused, and when he glanced at her he saw that she was looking into space, smiling and remembering. "It seemed like she was always busy, though. And I don't mean housework. She was into so many things—our schools, community organizations, charities and churches—I don't know what all. And when she was home, she was always into something—gardening, redecorating, remodeling, you name it. Didn't leave much time for us kids. And since Pop's job had him gone most of the time, we were on our own most of the time. I guess that's why we were so close...." Her voice trailed off. Jake, glancing up, just caught her fleeting look of wistfulness.

He said gruffly, "My dad was gone most of the time, too, but to tell you the truth, I didn't really notice. It was sort of like...that was the way things were supposed to be. You know what I mean? A clear division of labor and responsibility. I think my mom must have raised us to expect it. My sister and I always just took it for granted that Dad was working out *there,* and Mom was *here,* with us. I never once heard my mom ask anything more, or utter a word of complaint. I took her for granted," he muttered, staring at his plate.

But he was thinking, not of his mother, but of the woman he'd married, and how unhappy he'd made her. Thinking that his mother wasn't the only person he'd taken for granted.

Eve picked up one of the bottles of beer and unscrewed the top, bringing him out of the mire of past regrets. She offered it to him, but he shook his head and gestured at his half-empty plate. "Maybe later. Don't want to ruin a good thing."

So she tipped the bottle to her own lips, and with the notion of taking people for granted fresh on his conscience, it occurred to him how awkward it must be for her, wearing that collar, to do a simple thing like that—tilt her head back and swallow. He motioned toward her with his head, and thinking that she wouldn't even be able to do that much, said in a voice made gruff with guilt, "Why don't you take that thing off? If somebody catches us together, we're busted anyway. Might as well be comfortable while you can."

She gave a funny little feline growl as she anchored the beer bottle between her crisscrossed legs, a sound that reminded him of the actress—he couldn't think of her name now—who used to play Catwoman on the old *Batman* television series. He wondered if she had any idea how sexy it was, as she laughed softly and murmured, "You make it sound like an assignation."

She lifted her hands to the straps that fastened the collar together. Already in the act of reaching out to help, Jake paused, then decided to ignore the warning bells and claxons of every pitch and tone that were sounding inside his head. She moved her hands out of the way, giving over the task to him. The fastenings were simple—why were his fingers so clumsy?

"Tell me, Jake," she said softly, watching him across the narrow chasm between them, her eyes full of laughter and a strange, dark glow. "What does it take to make you laugh?"

He hesitated for a long time, vibrating like a high-tension wire and fighting to hang on to his self-control, before he replied solemnly, "You make me laugh."

"Oh, yeah..." Her voice was husky. "I can see that."

"I'm laughing on the inside," he said, absolutely deadpan. Mercifully, at that moment, the two halves of the collar separated in his hands. He eased them and himself gently away from her, leaned back and laid them aside.

But if he'd expected the retreat to a safer distance to ease the strain on his willpower, he was out of luck. If anything, the wider perspective only made things worse. He was struck, for example, by the naked vulnerability of her bared neck, like the stalk of some delicate flower—a buttercup, maybe, or a wild primrose. He thought it seemed too fragile to support her head and the jaunty, childlike tousle of her straw-colored hair. Yet he knew there was nothing fragile about her body. He remembered the graceful arrangement of muscles in her back...the silky-firm resilience of her flesh beneath his fingertips...

"So," she said on an exhalation that was both a celebration of freedom and a sigh of pleasure, raking supple fingers through her hair, "you don't go home to your parents' for Thanksgiving?"

"Haven't for a while," said Jake gloomily. He was staring down at the plate in his lap, thinking that he was rapidly losing interest in its contents. He heaved a small and, he hoped, inaudible sigh. "When I was married we did. My wife saw to that. Family was important to her—probably because she didn't have any to speak of. Only child...parents were both dead."

"So," said Eve, as she had once before, "she only had you."

He snorted, utterly without mirth. "*Did* she?"

"Stop that." She shook her head and leaned toward him, forearms resting on her knees, both hands encircling the bottle of beer. In a tense voice, she said, "You're not being fair."

He said nothing, but waited in wary silence for her to explain. After a moment, not looking at him, she lifted the bottle and took a sip. Her movements were quick and jerky—almost, he would have said, angry. She swallowed, still looking past him, then muttered under her breath, "Or she wasn't."

"Oh?" he said very quietly, for it was a subject, and they were feelings, he seldom if ever allowed himself to touch upon. "How do you figure that?"

She made a hissing sound, impatient and angry. He could feel himself shoring up his defenses even before she drilled him with a look and fired. "Look—this guilt trip you're on— didn't it ever occur to you that your wife wasn't being fair when she put the entire responsibility for her own fulfillment on to you?"

"That's not—" he began, withdrawing behind his bulwarks.

"Any of my business...I know," she finished for him in a gentler tone. "And you're thinking I don't exactly qualify as an expert on marriage and divorce. But I have been in a lot of relationships, and I'm a terrific observer of other people's, and I do know that human beings are so complex, and their needs are so different, that it's just not possible for one person to provide everything another person needs. A woman in the happiest of marriages still needs her girlfriends. Still needs challenges, goals, mental stimulation, spiritual nourishment. No man could possibly fill all those needs, even if he devoted all his time and energy to the job. It's just not possible."

"*All* his time and energy?" Jake said bitterly. "How about *none?* I was gone all the time. And when I was home, I was wrapped up in my work—especially the last few years. Are you saying I bear no responsibility for making my wife happy?"

"Of course not." Eve gestured impatiently with the beer bottle. "Obviously you can't mistreat or neglect somebody and expect them to be happy in spite of it. I don't know how to explain. It's...complicated." She subsided, momentarily defeated, then drew breath and blurted out, "All I'm saying is, your wife needed to get a life. If she'd had one, maybe she'd have been able to share and understand yours.''

In the silence that followed her unpardonable outburst, Eve sipped beer and listened to the echoes of her own words. *Get a life.* I used to have a life, she thought, and was suddenly as lonely and wretched there with Jake in that cozy little space as she'd been out on the edge of the marshes, hearing the call of the wild geese at sunset. *I want my life back.*

"I'm sorry." She mumbled the words, not looking at Jake's face. "I had no right to say that." She tried for a lighter tone. "In my own defense, I think it's because…I miss—"

Jake's soft-gruff voice interrupted her. "You'll get your life back—I promise you. You will."

Her gaze snapped back to him, and his eyes were waiting for her, black and impenetrable, but at the same time familiar and somehow welcoming, like a well-known and well-loved room in the dark. How had he known? she wondered. It was as if he'd heard her heart talking.

And when had that long, unsmiling face with that patrician nose and those melancholy eyes, the unruly hair and five-o'clock shadow, become so pleasing to her eyes? Gazing at him, she felt her heart twist inside her, and a terrible longing all but overwhelm her.

What would it be like, she suddenly wondered, to turn to him as he came to their bed late at night, to feel his arms around her as she snuggled close to him and whispered, "Guess what I saw today? The most amazing thing…" Or to walk with him through an autumn woods, on a day when the sky was the crystal blue of sapphires and the scent of wood smoke filled the air, and breezes swirled leaves like confetti. And finding herself too overcome by the sheer loveliness of it for words, to just look at him and reach for his hand… What would it be like? Would he understand? And would she ever have the chance to know?

"I wish…" she whispered, then stopped.

"What?" Jake prodded.

But she shook her head, smiling a little the way people must when they ache inside. Because she couldn't tell him what she'd just at that moment realized, which was that getting her own life back wasn't going to be enough. That it was never going to be enough for her again. Because she wanted Jake's life back, too.

Oh, it was complicated. He had such issues! She wanted him free and unencumbered. Unencumbered by guilt over the failure of his marriage, free to love again. Unencumbered by his quest to bring Sonny Cisneros to justice, free…to love *her*.

"Come on, tell me what you wish," Jake urged her, and again his eyes seemed to darken and glow. As if he already knew.

"No—it's nothing." But her breath caught and a terrible fear seized her. What if it never happened? What if he never did manage to shake off his emotional baggage? What if she never got a chance to find out if he was the one—the *right* one—for her? Or…what if she found out he *was*, but that he didn't feel the same? That would be the very worst thing, she thought. Far, far worse than never finding the person you were meant to share your life with—to find that person, and after waiting and searching for so long, to have it be only on one side.

"Waskowitz—" he was regarding her with a teasing glint in his eyes "—I'd never have thought you'd be one to mince words."

"I'm not," she said stubbornly, grabbing a sip of beer more out of a need for distraction than thirst. "But I'm not going to tell you this. It's too—" she waved the bottle "—complicated."

"And I'd never have taken you for a coward."

Coward. Her eyes jerked back to him, collided with his

with a jolt she felt clear through to her soul. No, she'd never been a coward. Afraid, yes. Terrified out of her wits. And always, the more frightened she was, the more determined and reckless she became, just to prove to herself that she was brave.

So now, when she looked into Jake's eyes and they stared back at her, gleaming with challenge, in the face of that, and her own fear, what else could she do? She leaned across her folded legs and his drawn-up knee and the plate full of the remains of Thanksgiving dinner, and kissed him.

In her lifetime she'd ridden camels, shot rapids, jumped out of airplanes, plunged in a submersible to the bottom of an inky sea. But *this*... this was surely the bravest and most reckless thing she had ever done. Her heart leapt into her throat and stayed there; her hands felt frozen, her breath came in shivery sips, or not at all. She heard a rushing in her head as if she were in freefall, and the wind whistling past her ears as she plummeted down...down...down toward a distant unseen earth.

Not that he didn't give her plenty of help; she knew she'd never have survived the humiliation if he hadn't. With all the time in the world to see what was coming, he must have leaned toward her, met her halfway; she never knew for certain. But there was his mouth, sooner than expected...vibrant and warm.

Her breath caught; trembling, she swayed slightly, breaking the contact for a moment. He altered the angle of his mouth and found hers again. And this time he leaned into the kiss with deepening pressure, and his lips opened under hers. Startled, she retreated just a little. There was time for one quick breath before her body rocked forward again almost of its own volition, seemingly governed by hungers beyond her control. Her lips parted, their mouths met, and this time clung...melded...merged. As if it had always been intended that they should.

Except for the pounding of her heart, her world went still and silent. As if at that moment she had entered a place of perfect peace and safety...after a long and difficult journey, at last found her harbor, her home.

She would have wished for such a moment never to end, but of course it had to end, and did. Jake pulled away from her and the world rushed in on a wave of sound and sensation, leaving her shocked and reeling, conscious of the ache in her throat, the burn of tears behind her eyelids. She opened her mouth, searching for words, and when she couldn't find them, pressed her fingertips to her lips in mute apology, though he wasn't even looking at her. She supposed she should be glad of that.

Then she realized what he was doing. Realized that he'd taken the beer bottle from her nerveless fingers and the plate from his lap and swiveled around to place them on the shelf that ran across the side of the sleeping compartment behind him. That he was gathering up the silverware and napkin, the pie and the rolls and placing them on the shelf, as well. And that the shelf formed the head of the bed they were sitting on. And that they were sitting on a bed.

What had she been thinking of, to suggest as a meeting place, of all places...a *bed?*

With the decks cleared, Jake turned back to her, his face grave and eyes as dark and opaque as molasses. Wordlessly he reached out, and with his thumb, touched the faint scar on the bridge of her nose that was all that remained of her facial injuries. She closed her eyes as she felt his fingers fan over her cheek and temple and burrow into her hair. He had big hands, powerful hands, with long, strong fingers. Hands that had been trained to kill—perhaps had killed. But oh, how gentle they were.... She remembered how he'd touched her, how skillfully he'd massaged her neck and how gently, when moments before he'd been mercilessly pounding a leather dummy with his fists.

She heard a sound, an inarticulate murmur. Opening her eyes, she saw Jake's searching hers, bright with unspoken questions. Not knowing what to say to him, instead she put her hand over his and guiding the palm to her mouth, pressed her lips into it. As silent as she, he lifted his other hand to touch her cheek and finger the short tendrils of hair past her ear, and she covered that hand, too, and held it cradled against her head. It was a strange and unbearably tender embrace.

So tender, she could only stand it for a few moments. Then the swelling ache inside her became shudders, a gust of released breath...and in that instant before it could become a sob, he swooped down, caught her open mouth and pulled her to him. And in so doing, it seemed, let go the leash...opened the floodgates. He kissed her with a hunger so intense, it shocked her. It robbed her of her breath, all thought, reason and will.

In the beginning, she'd only meant to kiss him—she'd have sworn it. But now it seemed to her that there'd never been a question where that first kiss would lead. Now she knew that she wanted him—had been wanting him—and that was all that mattered. Wanted him so desperately, she wondered how she'd ever survived so long without him. Wanted him—*needed* him—as much as she needed her heart to keep beating, and her lungs to draw their next breath. To her it was as simple, fundamental and inevitable as that.

They came together and surged upward like two waves, two irresistible forces meeting, and kneeling upright, mouths hungrily exploring, tore frantically at each other's clothes. Eve's coat was easiest, and went first, followed immediately by her short, button-front cotton knit top. Jake's casual plaid shirt and pullover sweater—probably chosen because he'd hoped they'd be less conspicuous in that rural neighborhood on a Thanksgiving Day than his customary FBI uniform of suit, white shirt and tie, not knowing they made him look like a walking ad for L.L. Bean—proved more difficult, if only because neither of them wanted to let go of the other or stop kissing long enough to pull it over his head. Somehow, though, they managed to divest him not only of his clothes, but of his inevitable agent's accessories. His gun and its holster, his beeper and badge went on the shelf beside the abandoned dinner plate.

Then it was just Jake in his undershirt and Eve in her bra, and that quickly those barriers, too, were disposed of.

Kneeling face-to-face, both naked to the waist, they paused…but only for a moment. It wasn't a time for lingering explorations, for feasting the eyes, for stimulating the senses. Those senses had been stimulated quite enough as it was.

Eve felt sick with desire—dizzy and light-headed. When Jake reached for her and dragged her to him, she whimpered. His body was a furnace; she clung to him desperately, straining to get closer, dug her fingers into the muscles of his back, raked his shoulders with her teeth. He did the same, trying, it seemed, to touch every part of her at once. Forgetting to be gentle, but who cared? And there were no words. The only sounds they made were gasps and pants and whimpers of pleasure.

As if he'd reached the limits of his endurance, he suddenly captured her head between his hands, held it still while he first gazed with smoldering intensity into her eyes, then swooped down like a raider and took her mouth and plundered it without mercy, until she tore away from him sobbing, and cried out in panic and fear—not of him, but for her own sanity.

She couldn't fight this. Instinctively she knew that her only relief lay in surrender. With eyes closed she tipped her head back and gave herself up to the waves of desire. Rocked on the rhythms of her own body, utterly lost, like one cast adrift on a stormy sea, she trusted *him* to be her anchor. Weightless, she had no grounding, no point of reference save for the burning heat of his mouth. And it was everywhere—a searing brand on her throat, a pounding pressure where her pulses leapt and jumped beneath the skin…gently laving the soft hollows of her neck, then fiercely raking the taut and quivering cords. It was an overwhelmingly sensual and exquisite torture. She felt it in every part of her, every corner of her being.

"Please…" she whimpered, not knowing how to articulate what it was she wanted. Just… *"Please…Jake…"*

While his hands held her hips pressed tightly against his body so that she felt its heat and hardness, its rocklike strength and powerful desire, his mouth continued its journey of conquest, as inevitable and devastating an assault on her senses as a wildfire. His lips whispered over her breasts like promises. His teeth raked a rigid nipple, his tongue bathed it with cooling moisture. His mouth encircled it, drew it deep into a melting, tugging warmth, and she thought she would explode, break apart in his hands…shatter into a million tiny pieces.

Her hands found his belt buckle, the waistband of his trousers. And as if it was the signal he'd been waiting for, his found hers, as well. She felt the scrape of fabric on sensitized nerve endings, the cool kiss of air, and then the warm embrace of his hands…and pleasure so intense, she wept. With his head cradled against her breasts, she buried her hands and her face in the thicket of his hair, and the sobs rippled through her like seismic waves.

He whispered something she couldn't quite hear, and his arms came around her, encircling her in comforting warmth and reassuring strength. She pressed her face into the hollow of his neck and shoulder, reveling in the rasp of his beard on her cheeks, tasting the saltiness of his skin, drinking in the familiar spicy smell of him—oh yes, she remembered that smell. Had she known even then, somewhere deep inside, what it would come to mean to her? Now it seemed as if she had always known, as if she'd been born with his scent programmed into her genes.

Dimly she felt him drag her legs across his lap and shuck away her jeans and panties. She gave him no help. She was far beyond that. And then he laid her down, oh, so gently, and moments later followed her, having sloughed away his clothing like an old skin. She opened her arms to him with a welcoming chuckle and felt his body slide over hers…smooth and warm and silky hard. Ecstasy settled over her like a gossamer blanket woven of star bursts and sunbeams.

Nowhere in her consciousness was there even a glimmer of doubt, or the faintest echo of suggestion that there might be things she should attend to, reasons why she ought not to be doing this—here, at least, and now. Her world, her existence was Jake. His arms were her foundation, his body her fortress, his face her sun, moon and stars. He was the air she breathed; his heartbeat was her heartbeat; his mouth was her nourishment. When she closed her eyes she felt as if she'd ceased to exist as a separate entity entirely; she existed only as part of him.

So when he pulled away from her and, kneeling between her parted legs, began to blaze a new trail of kisses and love bites over her body, she cried out and clutched at him in panic, writhing and whimpering in inarticulate protest.

And with a low growl of understanding—as incapable of words as she—he straightened, and stroking and gentling her with his hands, reached under her thighs and drew them even farther apart…positioned himself and then at last, with excruciating care and quivering self-restraint, drove himself home.

Breath rushed from her lungs in a gasp of shock, relief and pleasure. She arched her back and opened to him in delighted welcome, half lifting her body to meet him. He scooped his arms under her and raised her to him so that she found herself again more upright than reclining, sitting astride his thighs and clinging to him in joyous abandon. The strength in his body both awed and exhilarated her; she felt the trembling of self-control deep within his muscles and from somewhere found the words, and the sanity, to whisper, "It's okay...it's *okay.*"

Then it was he who gasped, and with one hand supporting her head and the other pressing her lower body hard against him, took her mouth and plunged his tongue deep, while at the same time he surged into her with all power and passion unleashed.

She lost all sense of time and space. She knew only wave after wave of unimaginable pleasure alternating with mind-less panic...tension that seemed to build and build, higher and higher until she wanted to scream with it. And fi-nally...the deliciously terrifying, heart-stopping plunge from the highest point of the roller coaster, a cry torn from the depths of her soul, the absolute certainty that she could not survive this....

And then the trembling, pulsating quiet. The wondering joy at finding herself alive. The overwhelming sense of awe, humility, and...love? *Oh, yes! That's surely what it was. Love...*

She was laughing, shaking with laughter while tears ran down from the corners of her eyes and into her hair. And Jake was kissing her mouth, her wet cheeks, her eyes, fram-ing her face with his hands and rubbing the tears away with his thumbs. She could feel his body shaking. Staring up into his face, she blinked away the tear shimmer...and suddenly her heart was swelling, bursting inside her. She lifted her hands and touched his face, holding it as if it were something rare and wondrous—as indeed it was.

"Well," she said in a voice soft with laughter and awe, "I guess I know now what it takes to make you laugh...."

Chapter 13

Unable to find the words, Jake gave up and kissed her.

Eve whispered, "I guess we'll have to do this more often," as she traced the curve of his mouth with a fingertip.

He heard her words, and his heart leapt beneath his ribs— a primitive cognizance of danger. *What had they done?*

He lay back with a careful exhalation, bringing her with him, wrapped in his arms. Even now, with the return of full awareness and, he hoped, a measure of sanity, he still couldn't bear to separate from her. But, oh, what had *he* done?

He couldn't imagine what had possessed him to do such a thing. It was against all his training, his professional ethics, not to mention common sense. And yet...and yet. The tousled head tucked under his chin felt so *good* there. Her body, thinner than he remembered, seemed to fit the planes and hollows of his own as if it were meant to be a part of it— like the yin to his yang, or the missing piece of a puzzle he'd been looking for all his life. Had he ever felt like this before? If he had, he'd surely have remembered it. What did it mean?

That question he had no answer to.

One thing he did know: the thought of sending this woman back to Cisneros made him sick to his stomach.

"Jake?" Eve raised herself on one elbow to look down at him. Her eyes had a misty, worried look, and he remembered belatedly the postcoital vulnerability of women. "You're already regretting this, aren't you?"

He reached up to touch her face with what he hoped was reassurance. "Yes…and no." He looked at her for a long time, thinking how complicated it was, wondering if he'd ever be able to explain so she'd understand. He was filled with regrets, he ached with regrets…about all the years he'd spent without knowing her, what his life might have been like if he'd met her twenty years ago, the fact that he couldn't wrap her up and take her home with him and keep her safe, make love with her every night and wake to her laughter every morning. How lonely that apartment of his was going to seem, how empty his bed, after this.

He sighed and closed his eyes, and wrapping his arms around her, pulled her down onto his chest. "I'm still having trouble believing I actually let it happen."

She tensed in protest. "What do you mean, *you* let it happen? I kissed you first."

"I met you halfway." He let several beats go by before he said quietly, "We took no precautions."

He felt the quick intake of her breath, the shivery tickle of her fingers stirring in the hair on his torso, then the warm flow of an exhalation. "I know. But I thought…since you're in the FBI you probably have to be tested regularly, and I just had blood tests for the marriage license…." Her voice trailed off.

Jake lifted his head and pulled in his chin so he could look at her. "You thought of all that, did you?"

Her eyes danced up to meet his. "Well, no… It was maybe more like…instinct."

"Instinct..." He lay back, jerking with silent laughter. A few more seconds ticked by, and then he said, "You know, that's not the only consideration. I did tell you it was my wife who couldn't have children." He paused, surprised by the rasp of emotion in his voice, then added wryly, "I've been thoroughly tested, believe me, so I know. There's nothing wrong with me."

For a long moment she said nothing. Then she cleared her throat and murmured, "It's okay, I'm on the Pill."

She pulled away from him and sat up, keeping her back turned toward him as she searched awkwardly for her clothes. He could see only the curve of a flushed cheek, the sweep of lowered lashes, the childlike nape of her neck, but something about her seemed fragile, suddenly, and off-limits to him, as if she'd put away an essential part of herself behind glass walls.

"I have to get back," she said huskily, hurrying. "They must be wondering where in the world I am."

"Eve..." He reached out his hand and unable to resist touching her one more time, brushed his fingers lightly downward over the delicate bumps of her spine, the twin indentations just above the place where her buttocks began. He felt her breathing catch, and a shiver ripple through her body. Felt her hesitate... Then she stabbed her arms through the straps of her bra and pulled it around her and into position. The tiny *click* of the front catch was like a punctuation mark. A period. A closing.

Jake sat up and reached for his pants. He was suddenly thinking what he wouldn't give for a shower, some cologne, a wet washcloth—at the very least, some of those little moist towelettes they give you at fried chicken places. As it was, he was going to have to crawl back into that damn van with Birdie Poole and Agent Franco, reeking of sex. And Eve...my God. He was sending her back to a houseful of people and a murderous fiancé, with his scent and the scarlet burn of his beard on her skin!

As if she'd heard his thoughts, she pressed her hands to her cheeks. "My face feels so hot," she murmured, turning to him. "I have a whisker burn, don't I?"

He took her by the shoulders, touched her chin and turned her face to the light. "Yeah," he said gruffly, "you sure do. How are you going to explain it?"

Her eyes clung to his, jewel bright. "I went for a walk. A long one. I was trying to work off the calories. I got flushed…sunburned…poison ivy. I'll explain it, okay? Don't worry about me." Breathless, she picked up her collar and thrust it at him. "Help me with this, will you? Please?"

He took it from her and held it for a moment in his hands while he gazed at her. Then he lifted it slowly and settled the two halves into place, one in front, one in back, once again entombing her neck—that lovely neck, with its vulnerable nape and elegant throat, vibrant pulses and petal-soft skin—in cushioned plastic. He felt as if he were strapping her in irons, or the guillotine.

"I don't want you to go back," he heard himself say. It was his voice, but not his voice. When had his voice scored his throat like shards of ground-up glass?

She was wriggling into her panties—not a dignified moment—but she froze and stared at him in confusion. "What are you talking about? Of course I have to go back. Considering what happened the last time I disappeared, they'd probably call the cops. Maybe have already."

"No." And his voice was firmer now—more his normal, confident, federal agent's tone. "I mean, I don't want you going back with Cisneros. It's too dangerous. I'm pulling you out. Bringing you in. Whatever you want to call it. You're no longer working for the Bureau—undercover or otherwise."

At his first words her jaw dropped and her mouth opened.

Unable to break in with her protest, she held it until he'd finished, then let go an outraged "Sez you!"

It wasn't easy to look and sound authoritative with his pants unzipped and his undershirt caught in a stubborn roll around his pecs, but Jake did his best. "Now look," he began, "I don't think you—"

"No—*you* look. I don't think *you* understand." She was breathing rapidly, groping for her socks and shoes. Thinking what a funny thing it was to be doing in the middle of an argument, Jake found them and handed them to her. She muttered a breathless "Thank you" then rushed on, her words coming in jerks and gasps as she struggled into her footwear. "It's like...I told you before. I want...my life back. The only way I'm going to get it back...is if Sonny is put away—for good. *Capish?*"

An incongruous bubble of laughter bumped against Jake's sternum. "He will be," he growled. "It might take a little longer, but we *will* get him. It's just a matter of time."

"Time..." She finished tying her shoe and lowered that foot over the side of the bed before she lifted her head and leveled a look at him—a strange, dark look full of messages he couldn't read, challenges he didn't understand. "How much time?" she said quietly. "Weeks...months...years? A lifetime? I don't have that kind of time, Jake." She reached for the other shoe.

"What's time got to do with it?" He waved one hand in impatience and frustration; the other was caught in the sleeve of his henley. "You go in there, break it off with him—tell him you've changed your mind—hell, women do that all the time, don't they? Tell him you don't want to marry him. Then you leave, and let us take care of the rest. What's so difficult about that? You get your life back—"

"Do you really think so, Jake?" She skewered him with a look. "Do you really think I, or anyone in my family, will ever be safe as long as Sonny's out there? As long as he thinks we have information that could destroy him? 'A ticking time bomb'—that's what he called it. He knows it's there, just waiting to be found. Do you think he's going to just hang around and wait for that to happen? And we don't know if he really bought it that I didn't hear anything that day in the rectory—what if he's just pretending to go along with this charade?'' She tapped the collar angrily. ''I have to go back. I have to see this through. You know that. We've been over this. What's changed?''

He stared at her in furious silence. What's changed? He wanted to shout, What's changed is the way I feel about *you.* That changes everything. Perspective…priorities… *everything.*

For what seemed like minutes her eyes searched his face. Then she lifted her hand and laid it along his jaw, and her fingers were a warm and gentle reminder of the heat and passion with which they'd touched only a short time ago…like a breath of a soft, sweet wind when summer is long over. ''Nothing's changed,'' she whispered.

She drew back the sleeper's partitioning curtain a few inches and looked out, then opened it wide and stood stiffly upright between the seats. Turning to gather up her jacket, she paused. ''You can't stop me from going back, Jake. You can pull your surveillance and all that if you want to—that's up to you.''

''Don't be ridiculous,'' he snapped.

Unable to shrug, she smiled crookedly. ''I *am* going back. And I'm staying until the end—whatever that may be. *Capish?*'' Her eyes seemed to brighten and shimmer, and then she quickly turned away.

''Hey,'' Jake said in the raw and scratchy voice he was coming to know well as she slipped between the front seats, ''don't you want to take the plate back?''

She gave a little wave of her hand without turning. ''How on earth would I explain it?'' Her voice sounded breathless…almost panicky. "You can take the pie and stuff to your partner…what's his name? Agent Poole? I have to go. So, I guess I'll see you…." The passenger door opened and she was gone, as completely as if she'd tumbled off the edge of a precipice.

Left alone in the sleeper, Jake sat and stared at the plate in his hands. *Capish?* Hell no, he didn't *capish*. He didn't understand anything. Somehow, without his noticing it or being able to do a thing to stop it, his world had turned upside down.

Mirabella and Summer were the only ones left in the kitchen when they heard the bang of the screen door and footsteps coming across the back porch. Summer, who had just that second finished wiping and putting away the last piece of silverware, laughed and said, "That's Eve—right on time."

Mirabella, who was suffering from indigestion and less inclined to be forgiving, fixed the delinquent with a fishy stare as she came through the door. "Where've you been?"

Eve closed the door carefully behind her, and her eyes darted to each of her sisters with a quick, guilty look. But before she could answer, Mirabella felt a nudge in her ribs, and Summer said, "Evie? What's wrong?" That was when Mirabella noticed Eve's scarlet cheeks and too-bright eyes.

"What have you—?" she began, but stopped when Summer gave her arm a warning squeeze.

"Wrong? Nothing's wrong." Eve was brightly smiling, but the smile looked as brittle and ephemeral as the leaves that scuttled across the lawn outside, as if it would crumble at a touch. "I went for a walk—farther than I meant to. I'm pooped. Where are the guys? Sacked out in the den? God, I hope so—I'm all sweaty—is it okay if I take a shower?"

"Uh…yeah, sure, go ahead," said Mirabella with a questioning look at Summer, who returned it with an almost undetectable shrug. "Use ours—leave the other one free. Extra towels are in—"

"Thanks—you're a doll." She slipped past them and danced sideways through the door—not a joyful dance, but urgent—and a moment later they heard the thump of footsteps on the stairs.

"Not one word of apology for skipping out on the dishes!" Mirabella exclaimed on a gusty breath of sheer exasperation.

Summer threw her a troubled look. "Didn't you hear how fragile her voice was? She sounded like she was going to cry any minute. And her face—Bella, she really looked upset. If I didn't know better..." She pressed her fingertips against her lips as a pleat of worry formed between her eyebrows.

"Something is definitely wrong." Mirabella gave the countertop a slap. "I knew it. Didn't I tell you? There's something fishy about that guy. She's not happy with him."

"But—" Summer cast a look over her shoulder in the direction of the living room and dropped her voice to a husky whisper "—how could this have anything to do with *him?* He's been in *there* all afternoon. Wherever she's been, whoever's upset her, it couldn't have been Sonny."

Mirabella sucked in air and put a hand over her mouth. *"What?"*

"Oh no—it's too impossible. Even for Evie. She wouldn't..."

"For God's sake, *what?"*

Mirabella's voice was hushed and horrified. "You don't think...she's cheating on Sonny?"

Summer let out a gusty breath. "What? Cheating—no!" Then she gave it up and closed her eyes. "Oh God..."

Now it was Mirabella's turn to say, *"What?"*

As Summer hesitated, a distraught hand pressed to her forehead, a muted roar went up from the other room. The football game had just ended; in another moment the kitchen

was going to be full of menfolk foraging for pie and leftovers, coffee and beer, it having been all of two hours since
they'd finished stuffing themselves beyond all good sense.

"What?" Mirabella persisted, nudging up next to Summer.

"I was just going to say, I think you may be right," Summer urgently whispered back. "Because you know that flush
on her face? When I saw it, the first thing that went through
my mind was that if I didn't know better...I'd say she had
one hell of a whisker burn."

"Oh...God."

An hour later, Mirabella and Summer stood on the front
porch watching Riley, Helen and David as they loaded up
the Mercedes. Or rather, the children were doing the loading
while Riley supervised, and that ridiculous little Chihuahua
of theirs—Beatle—frisked and danced between their feet.

Everyone else had gone home—Eve and Sonny were on
their way back to Hilton Head in the limo, Troy and Charly
to Atlanta with Bubba drooling in the back seat of the Jeep
Cherokee. Jimmy Joe had driven his mom, Granny Calhoun,
Jess and Sammi June home, and J.J. and Amy Jo had gone
along for the ride. He'd probably stay an hour or so at least,
visiting and talking business with his brothers.

The sun was going down in a rosy-gold blaze behind the
leafless woods. A chill was in the air—there would be frost,
the weatherman said, by morning. Which meant no more
fresh tomatoes, Mirabella thought, and felt a pang of sadness
for the passing of the season and the coming of winter.

"She's probably not—" she started to say, just as Summer
did the same. They both broke off, laughing. Summer recov-
ered first and finished it quickly, "I'm sure she's not...you
know. Cheating on Sonny. That would be too much, even
for Evie."

"Sonny does strike me as a dangerous person to cross,"
Mirabella conceded. Then, suddenly angry, "But since when

has Evie ever balked at danger? You know how reckless and impulsive she is. She just…does things. Sometimes I think she does things just *because* they're dangerous.''

''You know what Mom said.'' Summer's murmur was placating. A troubled frown puckered her forehead. ''That Evie does those things because she *is* afraid.''

Mirabella waved that impatiently aside. ''I know, and I find it hard to believe. What's she ever had to be afraid of? Everything's always come so damned easy for her.''

''Oh, well—I wouldn't say that. Evie's worked hard to get where she is. Filmmaking is a tough field.''

''Okay, but the point is, she's made it—how many people can say that? Don't tell me it's all hard work—a lot of it is pure luck. Even she will tell you that. And think back when we were kids. She always got good grades without even trying, won every contest she ever entered, always had boys crazy about her. Everything she wanted she got.''

''How do you know? You don't know what she wants. She hasn't got what we've got.'' Mirabella had no answer for that. After a moment, Summer said thoughtfully, ''I don't think it's that things come easier for her. Things come to everybody. Evie knows how to grab on to them when they come her way.''

''That's it,'' Mirabella said, still angry. ''She *grabs*. Evie's greedy, that's what she is. Greedy for…I don't know…''

''Life,'' said her sister, nodding. ''Evie's greedy for *life*. That's what makes her so special. She *is* special, Bella.''

Mirabella didn't say anything for a moment or two, because she had a lump in her throat; she hadn't the faintest idea why.

Riley, the children and the Beatle-dog were coming toward them across the lawn. She cleared her throat. ''Well, this time I think she's bitten off more than she can chew.''

''I'm worried about her, too,'' Summer said in a catching

voice, turning abruptly to hug her. "But until she's ready to ask for our help, I don't think there's anything we can do."

Mirabella sniffed and whispered miserably, "I know."

There was a flurry of leave-taking while everyone paid one last visit to the bathroom, traded hugs and goodbyes and promises to call, and then the Mercedes crunched away down the driveway and turned left onto the paved road. Mirabella watched, rubbing her arms against the chill, until she could no longer see the big car's taillights in the dusk. Then she turned and went back inside.

She walked through the house, turning on a light here, turning one off there, tidying...setting things to rights. It was always a relief to have her home back to normal again. As much as she loved her family, and had come to love Jimmy Joe's, Mirabella did cherish her space and her privacy. And *order*. Yes, she did like things to be orderly—organized, planned, everything in its place.

Maybe, she thought with a rare flash of insight, that was what she found hard to take about her oldest sister. Eve— and her life—were so *disorderly*. Chaotic, tempestuous, impulsive, spontaneous, uninhibited—qualities many found charming, Mirabella knew, but she found them discomfiting. Even alarming.

Feeling indefinably better, she was heading upstairs to check on the condition of the bathrooms when the doorbell rang. Back down the stairs she went, utterly mystified. Peepholes being all but unheard of in her part of the world, Mirabella called through the door, "Who is it?"

There was a pause, and then... "FBI, ma'am," said a voice—a man's voice, and strangely familiar. "Jake Redfield—we've spoken on the phone."

Mirabella threw open the door and stared at the man who stood there on her front porch. She was unable to utter a single word, her heart was pounding so hard.

The first thing she thought was that he didn't look like an

FBI agent. Not at all the way she'd pictured him. He was wearing casual clothes—didn't all FBI agents wear suits and ties?—and his hair was unruly, with a tendency to stick out in spikes, as if he'd slept on it wrong. He had a long, melancholy face and grave, deep-set eyes and a bad case of five o'clock shadow.

But he was holding his ID up in front of his chest, holding it into the light where she could see it. She stared at it intently, then back at his face.

"Sorry to bother you, Mrs. Starr," he said in his grave voice. "May I come inside? I'd like to talk to you. It's about your sister."

Mirabella's heart lurched. "Summer? But I thought that was over."

"No, ma'am. This is about your other sister. Eve."

"Evie?" said Mirabella faintly. She thought, I was right. *I was right.*

"If you'll let me come in," said Agent Redfield, "I'll explain everything."

"You want to do *what?*" Don Coffee shouted. "Are the two of you completely out of your minds?"

Birdie raised his eyebrows in a look that said plainly, *Hey, don't look at me.*

Thanks, buddy, Jake thought as he shuffled gamely into the breech. "We believe there'd be a minimum of risk—"

"Have you forgotten," his supervisor interrupted in a derisive tone, "what happened the last time I authorized an operation involving the use of a private residence? This *particular* residence? The only thing that saved us from civilian casualties, as I recall, was some quick thinking on the part of a couple of household pets."

Jake threw up his hands and muttered, "Aw, for Pete's sake—"

But before he could say more and maybe get himself in

real hot water, Birdie interceded, saying diplomatically, "Sir, the difficulties encountered on that operation involved a hurricane. The odds against that happening a second time have got to be…way up there." Coffee snorted. Birdie glanced at Jake and cleared his throat. "If I'm not mistaken, sir, hurricane season officially ends on the thirtieth of November."

Coffee muttered something sarcastic about December and blizzards, and Birdie argued that Charleston, South Carolina, didn't really have all that many blizzards, but by that time Jake had regained control of his temper.

He said patiently, "The difference here is that we have a definite time frame, and we will be on the premises the whole time. We'll go in there in advance, have the place wired before anybody else gets there. This is a surveillance operation, nothing more. Every move Cisneros makes will be on camera. If he finds what he's looking for, we wait until he's clear of the premises before we make a move. If he doesn't find it, no harm, no foul." He glared at his supervisor, arms outstretched and eyebrows raised to add an unspoken *"Well?"*

Coffee glared back at him. Then exhaled and growled, "Redfield, I can think of a dozen things that could go wrong."

So could Jake, but there was no way in hell he was going to admit it. "We're going to be there to make sure it doesn't."

"There will be children there."

"Yes, sir. We've factored that in. We intend to make every possible provision to ensure their safety."

Coffee rose and disgustedly sailed a file folder onto his desk. "Ah, damn," he muttered with a sigh, "I miss the old Mafia. At least they had rules about involving families— wives and kids. These newcomers—the Russians, Asians, Colombians, freelancers—they're capable of anything. All bets are off."

Jake and his partner looked at each other. Jake cleared his throat. "Does that mean—"

"Yeah, yeah, you've got your authorization. But Redfield, hear this—" and he leaned forward on his hands and drilled him with his patented cold-steel stare "—you'd better make damn sure nothing happens to make me regret it. I don't intend for my career in federal law enforcement to end with this operation. Do you understand?"

"Yes, sir," Jake and Birdie chorused.

"Okay. You've got...what is it, three weeks? I'll expect the full details of the operation on my desk by tomorrow morning. I assume you've talked to all the parties involved? You have their full cooperation?"

"Yes, sir," said Jake staunchly, "full and wholehearted." Which was an understatement—the Waskowitz sisters had expressed delight and enthusiasm for the plan.

With one notable exception. Jake wasn't afraid of very many things, but when he thought about how Eve was going to take to the idea of using her family's Christmas gathering to set a trap for her fiancé, he got a bad case of the cold-and-clammies....

Chapter 14

If Eve had found the pace of her days monotonous before the Thanksgiving holiday, afterward they seemed to crawl by with a soul-sapping tedium she imagined must be akin to doing hard time in a maximum-security prison.

Sonny left the Saturday after Thanksgiving to go back to Las Vegas to tend to business, which was an immense relief to her for more reasons than one. He'd been in a mood ever since the blowup in the Jacuzzi, still sulking over his enforced celibacy, so being around him was already a strain. Add to that her feelings of guilt over what had happened between her and Jake in the sleeper of Jimmy Joe's eighteen-wheeler....

No, not guilt, exactly. It wasn't guilt she felt when she thought of that. Longing...hunger...craving...desire—yes, all of those. But not guilt. She felt certain that if ever in her life she had done something *right*, making love with Jake was it. It was regret at not being able to repeat the occasion that was hard to abide and to hide from those around her, and a sense of impatience at time being wasted, a deep and constant yearning to be with someone, and to be someplace, other than where she was.

To make matters worse, the lovely autumn days had finally come to an end. Although winter would not officially arrive for weeks, the weather had already declared its intent. Chilly drizzle alternated with a dreary overcast. Everything was wet, a cold dampness that penetrated clear to the bone, and stayed that way for days on end. California desert-raised, Eve longed for even a glimpse of the sun.

Somehow the days did pass. She went, trembling inside, to her first scheduled physical therapy session after the holiday, but Jake didn't show, and she was too proud to ask the FBI's therapist about him. After that she called and made excuses not to go, claiming she had a cold and didn't feel up to it.

Then, after stubbornly refusing to give up her daily walks along the fog-shrouded marshes, she actually did come down with a cold, her first in years and one of the worst she'd ever suffered. She spent her days in front of the television, sniffling into soggy tissues over the likes of *Casablanca* and *An Affair To Remember,* as the pounds that had slipped away unnoticed a few weeks before came gleefully home, and brought friends. The calendar rolled over into December, and she still had not given a thought to Christmas.

On Saturday morning, the week after Thanksgiving, Sergei interrupted the death scene in *A Farewell To Arms* to inform her, with sneering deference, that she had a telephone call.

"Who is it?" Eve asked soggily and without much interest, blowing her nose. Surely not Sonny; it wasn't even seven o'clock in the morning in Las Vegas—practically the middle of the night to a night owl like him.

"She said she is your sister," said Sergei stiffly. He handed her a cordless phone and went out.

Eve sniffed and punched the button. "H'lo? Bella...?"

"It's me, Summer. Evie? Are you crying?"

"What? Oh, doh—well, yeah, but...dot really. I was watching this ridiculous movie. Plus I have a cold. What's up? *You* sound upset. Is everything—"

"Oh, Evie. It's Bella. She's gone into early labor! She might lose the baby. I'm going up there now—can you come?"

It was afternoon when Eve pushed through the Augusta hospital's slow-to-open automatic doors with two beefy and edgy-looking men close on her heels. A lavender-haired lady in a pink smock at the information desk in the main lobby directed her to Maternity on the fourth floor.

"You *could* wait for me in the car," she suggested to Sergei and Ricky with mild sarcasm when the elevator arrived. The door opened; they followed her on in stony silence, one on each side.

On the fourth floor Eve found a nurses' station manned—and that was the word—by a very large woman who looked like a cross between somebody's mama and an M.P. "Family only in the patient's room," she announced, sizing up Eve's companions with an implacable eye. "You two can wait in the waiting room, if you want to—down there to your left." She pointed the way. Neither Sergei nor Ricky were stupid .enough to give her any lip.

To Eve, she said kindly, "Miz Starr's room's right down there—number 412." She pointed in a direction opposite the one to which she'd dispatched Sergei and Ricky. "Her sister and her husband are with her, but you can go on in."

Eve said, "Thank you," and hurried down the corridor, past doors standing open to reveal weary but happy-looking women propped up and surrounded by clusters of relatives. Some of them cradled tiny pink- or blue-wrapped bundles in their arms. All of them wore ecstatically happy, bemused or besotted expressions on their faces.

Oh, God, Eve prayed as she glanced enviously at them, *please let Bella and her baby be all right....* Her own troubles suddenly seemed ridiculously small.

The door to 412 was closed. She paused in front of it to blow her nose and take a deep breath, then, resolutely smiling, heart pounding, she turned the knob and went in.

The first thing she saw was Mirabella, cranked up in the hospital bed almost to a sitting position, obviously still pregnant, also rosy-cheeked and smiling—no, *laughing*—at something Summer had said. Summer stood beside the bed, and the two of them had turned their heads to look at her, both bright-eyed and breathless, as if they shared some delicious joke.

Eve halted. What was wrong with this picture? Suddenly wary and suspicious—the exact same feeling she'd occasionally had right before someone jumped out at her and yelled, ''Surprise!''—she ventured a cautious ''Hi, what's going on?''

''False alarm,'' sang Mirabella gaily. ''They think it must have been muscle spasms. Guess I overdid it, raking leaves yesterday.'' She and Summer exchanged that secretive look. ''Anyway, the baby—*John William*—and I both check out fine.''

''Thank—'' Eve did a double take. ''John—does that mean...?''

Mirabella looked ready to burst with delight. ''Ultrasound confirms it—we're having a boy.''

''You *know* that child is going to wind up being called John Willie,'' said Summer in mock disgust. ''Or worse.''

''Over my dead body,'' promised Mirabella blithely. ''Anyway, they gave me some stuff for muscle pain, and now I feel just peachy. Sorry you had to come all this way for nothing.''

''That's okay....'' Weak in the knees, Eve sat on the edge

of the hospital bed. She looked around. "Where's Jimmy Joe?"

"Who? Oh—" Mirabella waved a hand "—somewhere between here and Houston, I imagine. Why?"

"I just assumed... The nurse said your husband was here." Eve looked at Summer. "Riley came with you?"

Summer shook her head; she seemed to be holding her breath. But before she could say anything, the curtain surrounding the bed next to Mirabella's was drawn back. A voice, gravelly and solemn, said, "I believe she meant me."

To Eve it felt as if her heart exploded. A powerful electrical surge shot through her body; her scalp prickled, her hair lifted and her hands and feet tingled with it. *"Jake..."*

"Evie, are you all right?" That was Summer.

"Don't faint," said Mirabella tartly. "And don't get mad. This was my idea. We had to think of some way to get you away from You-Know-Who so we could make our plans."

"P-p-plans?" Eve sputtered, recovering fast. *"Our plans?"* She rounded on Jake, who was watching her from under lowered brows, a look of appeal in his eyes. Which she ignored. She felt cold; her scalp prickled now with fury. "You *told* them?"

"Yes, he did," Mirabella answered for him, "and I'm sure glad he did. I knew something was wrong about that guy— I *knew* it." She glared at them all in happy triumph; there was nothing Bella enjoyed more than being right.

"I wanted them kept out of it. You knew how I felt." Eve's voice was pitched low and for Jake alone. She was trembling with shock, stunned by what she saw then only as a terrible betrayal. "You *knew*. You had no *right*. Not without—"

"Yes, he did." This time it was Summer who broke in, and her voice was so uncharacteristically sharp that Eve turned to stare at her. *"We* had a right to know. How could you even *think* about keeping this from us? We're your *sis-

ters. And what about me? This was my fight a long time before it became yours.''

Eve had to look away from her sister's tear-filled eyes before she could speak. ''All right, maybe I should have told you what was going on. But—'' and she threw Jake a glaring glance ''—I do *not* want you guys involved in this. I will deal with it. *We*—Jake and I—will deal with it. You stay *out* of it.''

''Oh, no,'' said both of her sisters together. And Mirabella continued, ''Don't even *think* about going it alone. The Sisters Waskowitz, remember? Nobody can beat us if we stick together.''

''Don't forget,'' Summer added softly, ''I tried it. It doesn't work. Trust me.''

''It's too dangerous,'' Eve whispered, already knowing it was futile. ''You both have families...children to protect.''

Summer nodded. ''That's exactly why you can't shut us out. That's why we're doing this—to protect our families. Sonny's a danger to all of us, Evie, not just you. If there's one thing we can do to help put him away, of *course* we're going to do it.''

''Yeah...okay.'' Ignoring Jake, Eve reached for the box of tissues on the bedside stand. But his presence was a drumbeat inside her chest, a silent scream in her ears, a bomb burst inside her head. She blew her nose, cleared her throat. ''Fine—I understand that. But there isn't anything you can do. So—''

''But,'' said Mirabella gleefully, ''that's where you're wrong. We already have a plan.''

''Plan?'' Eve stared over her wad of tissues with a feeling of foreboding. ''What plan?''

''Well...it involves Christmas—''

''—which we're going to have at my house,'' Summer continued, firing the words with machine-gun speed, hoping to get it all in in one burst before Eve could object. ''We'll all be there—except Mom and Pop—we'll send them off on a cruise, or something. Troy and Charly will be there, too. Troy's an ex-SEAL, which should come in handy in case something goes wrong.''

"Which it *won't,*" Jake growled.

Summer glanced at him and smiled tranquilly. "Of course not. Anyway, apparently, Sonny thinks Hal hid something there that can incriminate him, right? So—we'll let him look for it. Jake's going to have the whole house wired for surveillance.''

"No," Eve choked out. *"No."* She bolted for the bathroom.

Summer and Mirabella looked at each other. After a moment, Summer said, "That went well.''

Jake muttered, "Excuse me," and went to knock on the bathroom door. There was no answer. He glanced at the two sisters, who both gave him a nod. He opened the door a crack, then pushed it the rest of the way and went in, shutting it behind him.

She hadn't turned the light on, so he did. Then for a few moments he stood where he was, not knowing what to do or what to say to her. His heart felt as if it would pound a hole in his chest. He didn't know when he'd felt so unsure. So exposed.

She stood with her back to him, hands braced on the sink. For some reason she'd taken the collar off; the pieces sat askew in the basin in front of her. Her head was bowed and her shoulders hunched, and her nape looked unprotected and vulnerable as a child's. Seeing it like that, he thought about what she'd had to endure these last few weeks, what she must be feeling now, and anger burned in his belly like acid.

"Eve," he began in a cracking voice, reaching toward her.

About as vulnerable as a cougar kitten, she rounded on him, eyes spitting dark fire. "How could you do this? How could you go to them without even telling me? You knew how much I wanted to keep them out of this. Couldn't you at least have *told* me?''

"You didn't give me a chance," he said stonily. "You haven't been going to your therapy sessions lately."

Her mouth twisted, and she looked away. "I went to the first one after…the holiday. You weren't there."

"I was in a meeting with Coffee—getting authorization for all this." But he'd talked with her sister by that time, and that knowledge was heavy in his belly. He took a breath, but it didn't ease it much—or the pounding of his heart, either.

"Eve—" he said, and her name was thick and scratchy in his throat. But she interrupted him before he could say what he wanted to say, gazing at him and slowly shaking her head.

"I don't understand, Jake. I mean, I know how important it is to you to bring Sonny down—I know you've been working on it for years, I know you feel that it's at least partly to blame for the breakup of your marriage. But just a week ago you wanted me out of it completely. You were going to 'bring me in.'" She raised two sets of fingers, setting that off in quotes. "You wanted me to break up with Sonny and call the whole thing off. *I'm* the one that wanted to keep on with it. And then you turn right around and get my whole family involved? I don't understand, Jake. What's going on? What's changed?"

"What's changed…" He released a breath that was like a pressure valve letting go. She'd asked him that before, and he hadn't had the courage to answer her. "What's *changed?* For starters, we—" And he stopped, suddenly terrified, like a man walking on thin ice, hearing it crack under his feet.

"For starters…?" All at once she was breathlessly alert, as if she'd heard that *cra-ack,* too. "You mean…because we…"

The tension inside him was unbelievable. "Because of what happened in the truck…*yes.*" There was so much emotion in him, his jaws had locked tight, so the rest was a thickened mumble. ''We've never…addressed that.''

''Addressed what?'' In the glaring bathroom light, her eyes seemed to shine and shimmer like sapphires. ''We made love. That's it. What's there to talk about? You think just because we made love, that automatically changes everything? That it gives you the right—'' And suddenly her jewel-like eyes had turned to liquid; tears sparkled like tiny pearls on her cheeks.

That was it. He felt it like a gunshot inside his head—the ice cracking under him, the tension snapping, his self-control giving way. With a groan of anguish he reached for her, felt her flesh beneath his fingers, felt her mouth, her lips warm and wet and salty from her tears. Sinking…drowning…he moved his mouth over hers, felt the moisture slick on his lips, and the salt-taste sweet on his tongue. He felt her mouth open under his, and heard—no, *felt*—her sigh.

He made a sound, then, deep in his throat, an animal sound of hunger and need that stunned him, shocked him to the depths of his soul. Helpless to stop himself, no longer even wanting to, he drove his tongue deep into her mouth. And when he felt her give way, yet whimper and open to him, hungry for more, he brought his hand up to the back of her head to steady it. With her head cradled in his hand, he drew back just long enough to nip at her lips and glaze them with his own moisture, until she gave a tiny, gasping cry and lifted to him, blind and trembling.

Her response and her helplessness touched him unbelievably, and when he plunged his tongue between her lips again, it was no longer a plundering, but a giving. He took nothing from her, exerted no dominance, extracted no surrender, but instead poured into her all the hunger and need he'd stored away deep inside himself during the years of his self-denial, and the loneliness and vulnerability he hadn't even known was there inside him, too. He let it flow from the depths of his soul in trembling, shuddering waves of emotion that should have appalled him, but instead came as unbelievably sweet relief.

At last, drained and fragile, he tore his mouth from hers and with his arms around her, held her as though she were the only thing keeping him upright and anchored to the ground. "Not because I made love with you," he whispered with his cheek against her hair. "Because I'm probably *in* love with you."

He wrenched himself from her, suddenly high on the overdose of his own emotions and finding it impossible to keep still. Unable to pace in that tiny room, he turned jerkily, driving a hand through the wreckage of his hair. "Which is without *any* doubt the most *insane* thing I have ever done." He whirled back to her. "Do you have any idea how insane this is? *Do you?* You're involved in a case I'm working on—not just any case, probably the most important of my career. So all of a sudden my judgment is impaired, my objectivity shot to hell—do you have any idea what my superiors would say about this if they knew? I'd be off this case so fast, it'd make your head swim."

"Would that be so bad?" she whispered, so faintly he almost didn't hear her. Then she closed her eyes and touched her lips with her fingertips, gave her head a quick, hard shake and mumbled, "I know…I know. I'm sorry. I just wish…"

"You wish…what?" But she looked away and didn't answer. "You said that once before," he reminded her as he laid his hand along the side of her face and touched her lips with his thumb. "This time…I think you're gonna have to tell me."

Her eyes drifted closed and her breath flowed warmly over his hand. "Maybe…my judgment's not all that great, either," she finally said in a low and shaken whisper. "It's so complicated…all mixed-up together—this case, how we feel. I think…you'd be happy if you could just somehow separate me and my family from the case completely—put us away someplace safe and out of the way so you could go on and do your job the way you've always done it. But—'' and she quickly put her fingers against his lips to forestall any possible interruption ''—what *I* want, is for the case to be *over.* Not just for me and my family, but for you, for everybody.'' She was gazing at him now, and her eyes were the somber slate-blue of winter. ''Because until it is, I don't think it matters much what we feel. The case is always going to get in the way. Do you understand?''

Jake said nothing, because he was afraid he did understand. Heartsick and cold, he stared at her, while she searched his face, then sadly closed her eyes.

''You're thinking it's like your wife all over again. That's not what it is—I don't know how to explain it, or what I can say to convince you, but it's not. It's not your job, it's not even the case itself—not really. It's like…somehow over the years you've let this case get all tangled up with who you *are,* how you think of yourself. Everything—the breakup of your marriage, your past, your present, your future—it's all about this case. It's all about getting Sonny. It's like a cancer. It's taken over your life. Call me selfish—everybody does— but I want you whole and healthy, Jake. I have too much to give. I don't want it wasted.'' A tear spilled over and trickled down her cheek, and his fingers moved automatically to wipe it away.

Standing close, almost touching him, she sniffed and then whispered, ''That's why I won't pull out of this—not until it's finished. One way or the other.'' She closed her eyes and gave a watery and distressed laugh. ''Like I said, maybe my judgment's not so hot, either.''

Jake cleared his throat, to absolutely no effect. After a while he said, ''So, I guess we all know where we stand. Right? You want this over with. God knows I do, especially since it doesn't look like I'm going to get you out of it any other way.'' He paused, holding her by both arms, realizing that he'd begun to gently stroke them. His heartbeat thundered in his chest, and he felt its distant echo in his loins. ''This Christmas operation at your sister's looks like it may be the best hope for accomplishing both our goals.'' He took one more breath, and with his lips close to her ear, softly growled, ''Come on, Waskowitz. Are you with me on this?''

This time, when he lowered his mouth over hers, it wasn't emotions that governed him. Heat boiled through his veins; he felt pumped full to bursting with life force and energy. With the emotional battle won, more or less, and he the triumphant, if slightly bloodied victor, the surge of desire that followed felt completely natural to him—almost a biological imperative.

This time, his arms held her tightly, not for his own need and comfort, but with deliberate masculine assertiveness, to make her feel the heat and power of his body, and to brace her to receive the force of his thrusts. This time, when her lips opened under the demand of his mouth and his tongue drove deep into hers, it was a claiming pure and simple, and as graphic and unmistakable as any in nature.

And she knew the difference. Rocked by his primal rhythms, within seconds he felt her panting and gasping, raking at his clothes in a passion as compelling as his own, oblivious to surroundings and circumstances, and to the impossibilities....

But he wasn't oblivious—not quite. Somewhere, in a miniscule corner of his mind, he knew that they were standing in a hospital bathroom, that he had Eve pressed against the sink, and that her legs had wrapped themselves around his hips. And that, no matter how much he wanted to, they could not—*must not*—continue with what they were doing. Not here, not now.

The adolescent male part of him wanted to argue. *We*

*could! I could take her here—standing up...sitting down....
I want to!*

But the forty-something-year-old federal law officer part
knew that there were other considerations. People—sisters—
just beyond that door. And plans to be made, a bad guy to
catch.

"We...can't—" he gasped. It took every ounce of willpower and strength he possessed to tear himself from her and
hold her at half an arm's length. There they stood, gripping
each other's arms for reassurance and support, shaking and
panting like marathon runners, trying to regain their footing
in a universe that had just come within an eyelash of spinning
out of control.

"Are you okay?" Jake asked in a croaking whisper.

Staring at the middle of his chest, Eve replied in the same
voice, "Yes, fine." Silently and ruefully she began to laugh.

So he gathered her once more into his arms and held her,
rocking her as they laughed together in the giddy, shaken
way people do when they've just managed to escape disaster.

Presently, feeling stronger, he kissed the top of her head
and murmured, "Ready? Need another minute?"

She shook her head, pulled back from him and combed
her fingers through her hair. "I'm as ready as I'll ever be, I
guess." A residual bubble of laughter burst from her like a
hiccup. "What do you suppose they're thinking?"

"Those two?" Jake snorted and reached for the doorknob
as Eve gathered up the two halves of her collar. "I've got
news for you, Waskowitz. They don't think. They already
know."

Early on Christmas Eve, Summer Grogan stood in the middle of her beautiful formal living room and gazed critically
at the tree that soared almost to the top of the twelve-foot
ceiling.

"Not bad," she murmured in glorious understatement.

Though not as large as the one in Rockefeller Center, her tree, she was sure, was every bit as magnificent. Festooned with tiny twinkling lights, silver garlands, red bows, glass balls and dozens of ornaments ranging from those the children had made from bread dough and macaroni and popcorn to the most elegant handblown crystal, then topped with a gauzy white angel, it shimmered and sparkled from every view. Evergreen garlands looped across every mantelpiece, window and doorway in the house and twined around the banister of the curving staircase. Candles and holly adorned every tabletop; red poinsettias flanked the stairs and brightened every corner. Outside, thousands of tiny white lights winked in the trees and shrubbery and cascaded from the eaves. No house, she was sure, had ever looked more beautiful, more warm and welcoming.

She thought how incredible it was that she should be here on this Christmas Eve, in so lovely a place. What an amazing year it had been. How could anyone have forseen, in the gloom of last January, when she had first faced Riley Grogan in the humiliating courtroom debacle that had brought her already-precarious financial world crumbling down, that she would end the year in this gracious and happy home with a man she utterly adored, her precious children, Helen and David, safe and happy, and all the animals, too—although for their own immediate safety, Beatle the Chihuahua, Peggy Sue the ancient and cranky Persian cat, and Cleo the African Gray parrot had been banished to their various and separate quarters until after the holiday.

Yes, thought Summer, everything was ready—for Christmas, and for whatever else might happen this night....

The week before, Jake and an army of FBI surveillance experts in brown coveralls, under the pretext of putting in a new sound system, had installed hidden cameras and microphones in every room of the house, and throughout most of the grounds, as well. With the exception of the children, and

Sonny and his two henchmen, everyone had been shown how to cover the camera lenses and turn off the microphones, although they'd been asked not to do so unless there was a serious need for privacy. A command post had been set up in the house, in a cubicle of a room in the unused attic. In addition, a van containing a second surveillance unit lay hidden in the woods not far from the estate's front gate, and teams of armed agents had been posted, well camouflaged, all around the perimeter of the grounds.

Everything that could be done, had been done. Every eventuality had been considered and prepared for. They were ready. Summer just prayed it wasn't all for nothing.

The elements were in place for a final showdown. Eve and Sonny had arrived this morning; they and the two "bodyguards" had been assigned three of the six spare bedrooms. Two of those remaining had been taken over by Mirabella and Jimmy Joe and their children, who had come earlier in the week to help with the preparations.

The last one had, until a couple of hours ago, been reserved for Troy and Charly. Unfortunately, around noon today, Charly had begun experiencing what was at first thought to be acute indigestion. By midafternoon it was apparent that she was in the early stages of labor, and given her difficult and troublesome pregnancy, Troy had decided to take no chances. Rather than trying to drive back to Atlanta, especially with the weather forecast predicting freezing rain, he had taken Charly to the hospital there in Charleston. He had called a little while ago to report that they were settled in and things were proceeding slowly, and had offered to come back if he was needed. In spite of the fact that they'd been counting on Troy's training and experience as a SEAL in the event of an emergency, Riley had told him to stay where he was.

So far, other than the weather, that had been the only glitch in the well-laid plans, and even that had its upside. At least having Charly in labor provided an excuse for the tension that permeated the house like an electronic squeal…a hum of sound just off the register of human hearing.

As the antique clock on the mantelpiece launched into the Westminster chimes, Summer automatically checked her watch. Soon it would be time to set out the Christmas Eve buffet, but before that there were still a few last-minute things she had to do. A few more presents to be pulled from their hiding places and wrapped and put under the tree—which was already in danger of being buried beneath the mound of packages heaped around it. All day long people had been tiptoeing and scurrying, scuttling in and out of rooms, giggling behind closed doors, the children whispering in each other's ears, beckoning for help from the adults while sneaking stealthy sideways looks at each other.

Which was, Summer thought with a sigh, just as it should be on Christmas Eve. Like almost every other in the country that night, theirs was a house full of secrets.

Chapter 15

From their command post, Jake and Birdie followed Summer's progress through the beautifully decorated house. They watched her enter the bedroom where her sister Mirabella was wrapping packages, listened, with the volume turned low, to the faint background murmur of their voices.

It was quiet in the attic room, and a little too warm even though outside the dusty dormer window the long and early dusk brought on by the approaching storm had finally given way to full darkness. The volume on all the mikes had been turned off, with the exception of the rooms occupied by Sonny and his thugs, and there was very little sound even from those. One of the bodyguards—Ricky—sat hunched on the foot of a twin bed staring intently at a NASCAR recap on television. The other, the Russian, Sergei, was sprawled on his back on his own bed with headphones on. His eyes were closed; whether asleep or absorbed in what he was listening to was impossible to tell. The room next door—Cisneros's room—was empty; Sonny, at the moment, was in the library enjoying a brandy with his host.

Eve was in her host and hostess's bedroom, doing something mysterious with a dual-deck VCR. Everyone else, Jake noted after a cursory check of the monitors, appeared to be engaged in last-minute preparations for the holiday—wrapping presents, tiptoeing in and out of rooms like characters in a French farce.

He pushed back his chair, reaching for the thermos Summer had thoughtfully left for them that morning. He poured the last few teaspoons of coffee into his cup, screwed the cap on the bottle and sighed. "Helluva way to spend Christmas."

"Yeah..." Birdie rocked back his chair for a bone-cracking stretch. "'Course, Margie being Jewish, our really big celebration was a while ago."

Jake grunted a reply. He was wondering how he could have been partners—and friends—with a man for almost five years and not know his wife was Jewish. He wondered how many other things he didn't know about Birdie—or Don Coffee, or Agent Franco, or any of the other people he worked with, for that matter. That made him think again about what Eve had said to him that day in the hospital in Augusta, about this case being like a cancer in his life. He'd thought about that a lot during the last couple of weeks. That, and a whole lot more.

He drained the last of the coffee and gave his head a brief shake. "Partner, I've got to tell you, I am impressed."

Birdie looked at him in surprise. "What for?"

"You and Margie. I mean, you've got a great marriage. That's hard enough to manage in this line of work, you've got to know that. Okay, so on top of that, you've got the problem of two different religions to deal with?"

Birdie twisted uncomfortably in his chair. "Well," he mumbled, "I guess we don't really see it as a problem. It's just...you know, part of who we are. No big deal."

Jake didn't say anything for a minute; personal conversations didn't come easy for him, and he already knew this one was probably going to give away more about himself than he wanted it to. Then he decided there were questions he wanted the answers to badly enough to risk it, so he laced his fingers together behind his head and hauled in a breath. "It really isn't difficult for you, is it? Marriage, I mean. You and Margie—you make it look so easy."

"Oh, Lord, I wouldn't say that." Birdie's bark of laughter brought his chair upright with a thump. "It's never easy, partner. Don't kid yourself. You've always got to work at it."

"Okay, so how do you make it work?"

"Aw, hell." Birdie was squirming again. "I don't know. Why're you asking me? I'm no expert."

"When it comes to marriage you are. Especially in this business. Cops have a lousy record when it comes to marriage—it's a known fact. You guys are known far and wide as the exception that proves the rule."

Birdie looked pained. "What the hell does that mean? 'The exception that proves the rule...' There *is* no rule."

"Then," Jake persisted, "tell me how you do it."

His partner leveled a long, thoughtful look at him. "You're really serious about this, aren't you?"

"Yeah," said Jake, returning the look, "I really am."

"Yeah...okay, well." Birdie cleared his throat; obviously, personal conversations weren't all that easy for him, either. He leaned back and folded his arms above his expanding middle. "It helps if you marry the right person. For the right reasons."

"The right reasons...love, you mean."

Again Birdie grimaced as if he'd felt a sharp pain. "Well...see, now, the trouble with love is, everybody's got a different idea what that means. Who even *knows* what it means? And some people are always gonna mistake it for something else."

"Sex, you mean."

Birdie gave a grunt of laughter. "Trust me, one thing you do *not* want to do is marry somebody because the sex is great."

Well, hell, even Jake knew that. He nodded wisely. "Yeah, I guess that never lasts."

Birdie smiled and looked away, kind of a smug and secretive look. "Well...let's just say...it changes."

After a vibrant pause, Jake cleared his throat and said impatiently, "Okay, so if not love, what *do* you consider the right reason to marry somebody?"

Birdie shifted around to face him and leaned forward, like someone about to impart a great truth. "Turn it around. Say you marry somebody who's married you because she wants—or needs—something she thinks you can give her. Money, say. Security. Kids. Whatever. At the same time, she's got no idea in the world about what *you* need, or giving anything back to you. Think you'd be happy?"

Jake gave a distracted snort. He was thinking that the scenario had all too familiar a ring.

"Not that you shouldn't do for your partner—try to make her happy. I don't mean that. I just mean, there's got to be a give and take. You've got to take care of *each other*." Birdie chuckled. "Margie, now—she's always worrying about me...harping at me to take my vitamins, wear my vest, keep my feet warm, eat breakfast...yada yada yada. Drives me crazy. But I'll tell you this—not a day goes by I don't know she loves me. Not a day goes by I don't think about how glad I am to be married to her. She's my mate, my partner, my best friend, and I can't even imagine not having her around, having her there when I wake up in the morning, crawling into bed beside her at night." He stopped, gave his nose a quick back-and-forth swipe with his hand and finished gruffly, "As far as I'm concerned, that's the only reason for marrying somebody. The only good reason, anyway."

Jake didn't say anything; he was experiencing some emotions he knew were going to embarrass him and Birdie both if they got out. In need of distraction, he turned back to the monitors.

A moment later he was reaching for the volume control and muttering, "What's she doing? What the hell's she got?"

"What is that?" Mirabella asked. "What did you find?"

Summer, on her knees beside the bed, didn't answer. She stared at the objects in her hands—three smallish shrink-wrapped boxes in a nest of brightly colored wrapping paper.

"You put 'em away and forgot, I'll bet," said Mirabella, coming to her own conclusions. "I've done that. Who's it for?"

Summer rose slowly and sat on the edge of the bed, ignoring paper and scissors and tape dispensers. Discarding the gift wrappings, she held up one of the shrink-wrapped boxes, turned it over so she could read the back. "I did forget," she said in a shaking voice. "I must have put them under here last summer—this was my room then. Hal brought it just before he…died. It was a present for the children. Computer games, see? I put them away because I didn't think they were appropriate for kids their age. *Damn* Hal—he never did have any sense. *Way* too violent…I don't know what he was thinking!"

"Let me see that." Mirabella snatched the box out of her hands, quickly examined it, then reached for another. "Don't you know what this is?" she whispered excitedly. "It's what they've been looking for. Whatever Hal had, he probably hid it in one of these!"

Summer wiped her eyes with her hands. "I know that's what Jake thought, at first. But I don't see how they could be. They obviously haven't been opened. They're all shrink-wrapped…"

"Oh, for heaven's sake," said Mirabella impatiently, "anybody can shrink-wrap. You can do it in your kitchen.

Here, take one...." She tossed one of the boxes into Summer's lap and attacked the other with her teeth.

"Shouldn't we take them to Jake?" Summer was reaching for the scissors.

"What if we're wrong? Let's see if there's anything in here, first." Mirabella tore away the transparent wrappings.

They both froze as the door suddenly opened.

"Hi, guys, am I missing anything?" Eve chirped, grinning like the Cheshire cat.

Her sisters both slumped with relief. "Shh...get in here," Mirabella hissed, grabbing her arm and pulling her into the room. She checked abruptly to gape at Eve's wrist. "Nice watch."

Eve shook herself free and said with a grimace, "It's my Christmas present from Sonny."

Summer and Mirabella exchanged droll looks. Summer murmured, "A diamond Rolex—must be tough..."

"Look, he insisted I wear it. What was I supposed to do, refuse?" She shook off the whole subject impatiently and put the smile back on. The traditions of Christmas were among Eve's favorites in all the world, and she was determined not to let Sonny and his thugs, hidden evidence, a houseful of video cameras and listening devices and federal agents, not to mention the unnerving presence of Jake up in the attic watching and listening to everything that was said, spoil it for her. "What're you two up to in here? Can I play?"

"You're just in time actually." Summer picked up the third computer game that had been lying in her lap and tossed it to her. "Here—open it."

Eve arched her eyebrows. "At this point, aren't we supposed to be wrapping?"

"Not in here," said Mirabella, sounding disappointed and at the same time breathless with excitement. She tossed the gaudy box onto the bed. "Sumz?"

Summer passed the scissors to Eve. Her hands trembled

as she tore the box open and dumped its contents into her lap. "Here, either." She looked at Mirabella. "It wouldn't be a CD, would it?"

"More likely a floppy. Evie, get a move on—open yours."

"Okay, guys...what's going on?"

"Maybe nothing," said Mirabella briskly. "We'll know in a minute. Will...you...hurry...*up?*"

"This is the present Hal brought for the kids," Summer explained. "Last summer, you know, just before he died? If he did have that evidence—whatever it is Sonny was after him for—when he came, it almost has to be in one of these."

"Oh...my God." Eve's heart was suddenly pounding, her hands shaking. She stabbed at the box's wrappings with the scissors, then tossed them on the bed and tore at it with her hands. A moment later, she and her sisters stood with their heads together, staring at the flat, black, three-and-a-half-inch square of plastic in her hands. "Oh, God," she whispered.

Just above their heads, in the attic command post, Jake and Birdie were standing, too, their eyes riveted on the monitor.

"Is that what I think it is?" asked Birdie softly.

"Mmm-hmm...looks like it." Jake's calm was all on the surface; inside he was a typhoon.

"Show's over," Birdie exhaled through his nose. "That's all we needed...right?"

Jake looked over at him. "We don't know what's on that disk. Suppose it's a dud? I still think it'd be better if we let Cisneros find it—that way, if nothing else, at least we've got a shot at getting some kind of admission on tape."

"Yeah...guess you're right." But Birdie was shaking his head. "You're not actually thinking of letting Cisneros get his hands on that disk, are you? What if he—" A flurry of movement drew their eyes back to the monitor screen.

Jake felt a shock go through his body, almost as if he'd been hit by a bullet. Through the roaring in his ears he heard his partner mutter, in a voice heavy with foreboding, "Houston, I think we've got a problem...."

"*Sonny...*" The name burst from Eve on a gust of breath, as if she'd been punched in the stomach. She turned to face him, her body a shield between him and her sisters, and the small black disk they held in their hands.

"Hey, babe." He moved into the room with confidence, smiling his charming, Vegas-strip smile. "Whatcha up to?"

"What? Me? Nothing..." But her voice was breathless and afraid—a dead giveaway.

Sonny jerked in mock surprise. "Keeping secrets from me?"

Behind her, Mirabella said with a brave attempt at scorn, "Duh, it's Christmas—what do you think?"

"Is that what you got there?" Sonny threw back his head and laughed; a stone in one of his rings caught the light and winked at them as he placed his hand on his chest. "My Christmas present. No kiddin'." He came a few steps closer, still smiling. "Maybe I'd like to have my present early. Why don't you give it to me right now?"

Eve edged backward, shaking her head. His hand snaked out and caught her wrist, the one wearing the diamond Rolex. "Come on, baby—it's only fair." And though the voice was soft, the smile was no longer even remotely charming. "I gave you yours early, didn't I? Now...it's only fair you do the same for me." He barely seemed to move, but Eve gave a gasp of pain. "Come on—hand it over."

Jake was heading for the door when Birdie caught at his sleeve. "Hey—where do you think you're going? You can't—"

"The hell I—" Birdie's hiss of warning cut him off as he jerked him back to the monitor.

"Don't...give it to him," Eve gasped. Above the collar, her face was bone-white.

Summer took a step back; Mirabella moved with her, for

once in her life with nothing to say. "It's mine," Summer said in a shaking voice. "It belonged to my husband. You can't...have it."

But her gaze had slid past Eve, past Sonny, and was riveted now on the two men who had just stepped into the room. Both of them held guns, pointed straight at her and at Mirabella. Their faces wore no expression at all.

"Oh, I think you're going to give it to me," Sonny drawled. He reached out a hand and plucked the disk from her nerveless fingers. "There now...see how easy that was?" He tucked it into his shirt pocket, laughing softly.

"How did you know?" Eve whispered.

"How'd I know?" Pleased with himself, he held up her captive wrist. "Your Christmas present, baby. Had it custom-made, just for you—with a little something extra. You've been wearin' a wire—that's a little idea I borrowed from the feds." He gazed fondly at the Rolex. "A little flashy, I admit, but then...nothin's too good for my Evie-girl. Right?"

"It was you." Summer was still staring at the men with the guns. "Last summer. It was you...." The two men silently returned her gaze, one stone-faced, the other baring his teeth in a chilling smile. "Oh, God...this is all my fault," she whispered. "If I hadn't been such a... If I'd just let David have the stupid games, none of this would have happened. Evie, I'm so sorry...."

"For Pete's sake," Mirabella snapped, "don't be an idiot."

Sonny chuckled. "She's right, Mrs. Robey. You want to blame somebody, blame your ex-husband. Hal doesn't stick his nose where it doesn't belong, nobody gets hurt. Hey—nobody has to get hurt anyway, right? Your sister and me, we're gonna take a little trip, is all. Sorry we won't be staying around for the festivities. It's a shame, too. Everything looks so pretty and nice, all dolled up for Christmas...."

"We have to take 'em," Jake muttered through wire-tense

jaws. "We have to take 'em *now*." His eyes burned; the image on the monitor screen seared on his retinas. Eve's eyes, like black holes, staring into the camera's lens…into his soul. He heard Birdie's words… *"I can't even imagine not having her around…."*

His partner's voice came as a distant rumble. "We can't. Not until he's cleared the premises. Not with the children—"

"He's going to kill her."

"He won't hurt her until he's sure he's home-free. By that time…"

"What about those two?" Ricky's heavy voice boomed through the mike. "You ain't gonna just leave 'em here, are you? You want me to…" He waved his gun hopefully.

The look Sonny gave him was one of extreme pain. "Idiot. What're you gonna do, off somebody with the whole FBI as eyewitnesses? Place is probably crawlin' with feds. They're probably listening to us right now." He put his arm around Eve's shoulders and snugged her to his side as he snarled disgustedly, "Let's get outa here."

"They're witnesses." Ricky was disappointed.

"What difference does it make? Once we're out of the country, who the hell cares? Come on, come on—let's *go*." He pushed past the two thugs and headed for the doorway, yanking Eve with him. He paused there to murmur something in her ear, and the sensitive microphone picked up the words. "About time you and me had our honeymoon, don't you think so, baby?"

They were in the doorway, then gone from the screen; an instant later the hallway monitor picked them up, making for the stairs. From the room they'd just left came the sounds of muted sobbing.

Jake let out a breath like a pressure valve exploding and bolted for the attic stairs. Behind him Birdie was speaking into his wire. "All units…subjects are leaving the house. We have a hostage situation. Do not attempt to apprehend. Repeat—do *not* apprehend!''

They met Summer and Mirabella in the hallway, stunned and clinging to each other. Jimmy Joe was emerging from another room where he'd been supervising the children's Christmas preparations. Riley, drawn from his study by the commotion, fortunately just late enough to avoid a confrontation with the fleeing suspects, was charging up the stairs two at a time.

''Stay here,'' Jake said tersely as he brushed past them all, ''we've got it under control.''

Behind him Birdie muttered, ''Look after them,'' as the arriving menfolk prepared to gather their respective spouses into their arms and head off the curious children.

From outside the house came the muted roar of a powerful engine, followed by the shriek of abused tires. Jake burst through the mudroom and out the back door just in time to see the rear end of the white limousine disappearing down the curving drive, its taillights a red glow in the freezing mist.

Right behind him came Birdie, breathing hard. Jake dashed out onto the wet walk. The next thing he knew, he was gyrating wildly, flapping his arms and grabbing at air, anything to stay upright. He figured it had to be only the grace of God that kept him from going down hard, flat on his butt.

Behind him, he could hear Birdie cussing and muttering. Jake's heart and his hopes both plummeted, as he groaned from the depths of his despair, *''Ice.''*

Eve huddled in the limo with Sonny's arm like a steel band around her shoulders, while a dark world flashed by outside the windows. She felt nothing. *No*—she felt cold. Colder than she'd ever been in her life. Cold to the very depths of her being.

It was strangely quiet. What sounds there were came from a great distance: the squeal of tires…Sonny yelling at someone to "Be careful, you'll get us all killed"…the wail of sirens.

Even her mind was silent. She didn't think about being afraid, or about the fact that she was going to die. She didn't think about Jake and the life they weren't going to have together after all, or the sisters she'd just found again after so many years, or the parents she loved, or her children that now would never be born. But though silent, her mind was not still. It flashed random images and impressions from her life—thousands of them, each one there for an instant and then gone, too quickly to think about at all. Her life, over it seemed, in the blink of an eye.

From a vast distance she heard shouts. And suddenly forces were being exerted on her body that wrenched it from her control. The burden of Sonny's arm disappeared from her shoulders, and for one strange and magical moment she felt buoyant…weightless…free.

Then she was flying through the air, arms and legs all going in different directions, like a rag doll, and her head was filled with sounds…a cacophony of sounds, hideous sounds. Sounds from the depths of hell itself. Ear-splitting cra-acks and sickening crunches, screams and groans—not of human agony, but of tearing metal and twisting steel.

And then there was silence….

"Ah, Jeez," said Birdie. "Ah…Jeez."

"Sonuvabitch." Jake went on saying it, over and over as he braked carefully and pulled onto the grassy verge.

They were in Riley's Mercedes. Riley had offered it, since the keys were handy, it was equipped with all-weather tires, and Jake's vehicle had been parked too far away to be accessible. He pulled it to a stop just short of where the turf had been torn and slashed by the tires of the careening limousine, wrenched open the door and dove into the fine, spitting sleet. He left Birdie talking to his wire, calling for an ambulance, while he plunged heedlessly over the side of the embankment.

In the faint light of the Mercedes' headlights reflected in the freezing drizzle, he could just make out the wreckage of the limo, upside down among the trees. Slipping and sliding, he made his way to it, his heart cold and hard as iron in his chest. He could not—would not—allow himself to think about what he might find when he got there.

She would not be dead. *She couldn't be dead.* Please God, he prayed, don't let her be dead. Anything you want me to do, I'll do, just…don't let her be dead.

He was down on his knees in the ice and brambles and broken glass trying to get his head and shoulders through a window opening when Birdie came crashing down the slope to join him. He'd found a flashlight somewhere. "Driver's DOA," Jake told him tersely. "Eve's in here. I've got a pulse."

"Thank God…" Birdie was picking his way around to the other side of the wreckage.

Up on the icy road, backup was arriving. Sirens bleeped and went silent, brakes chirped, doors slammed. Jake heard the muffled thump of at least one fender-bender.

"This guy's breathing," Birdie called from the front passenger side. The flashlight stabbed through the windows of the wreck, randomly searching. "Where the hell's Cisneros? Hey—we got a door punched out over here. You don't suppose that rat-bastard got away?"

"To *hell* with Cisneros," Jake grated through jaws rigid with fear and hope and steadfast resolve. His hand was clasped firmly around Eve's wrist, and her pulse was slow and steady against his fingers. That was all that mattered.

"Anyway," said Mirabella, "the doctors say it was probably the neck collar that saved her life. Isn't that incredible?"

She was sitting on the edge of Charly's hospital bed, with

Summer beside her. On the other side of the bed, Troy sat with his arms around his wife. Riley and Jimmy Joe had been there earlier, but just moments ago had gone off on some mysterious errand, leaving the children in the competent hands of Troy's mama, Betty, who had driven down from northeast Georgia as soon as the roads were clear that morning to see her new granddaughter. Mary Christine, seven pounds, two ounces and all of twelve hours old, slept soundly in her mother's arms, swaddled in a red Christmas stocking.

Mirabella said, "Isn't it weird, the way things turn out?"

Too exhausted for speech, Charly could only smile as she gazed in bemusement at her daughter's head. It was Troy who murmured softly, "Yeah, it sure is. Looks like we've all got a lot to be thankful for, this Christmas."

Mirabella, suddenly beyond words herself, reached over to touch with a wondering finger a wisp of the silky black hair just showing beneath the edges of the baby's stocking cap. She was thinking about another baby girl, another Christmas...

"Poor little thing," she said, laughing shakily. "Another Christmas birthday. For the rest of her life she's going to have to share her big day with the Baby Jesus."

Charly looked up at her. "And her cousin Amy Jo."

"Yeah," said Troy, "let's don't forget who started this whole thing."

They all laughed. Then Summer, who had been strangely quiet up to now, frowned and said, "Where are the guys, anyway? I thought they'd be back by now."

Mirabella opened her mouth, then looked at Troy. He shrugged and said, "Aw, hell, I don't think it's any big secret."

"Right," said Mirabella firmly. "No more secrets in this family. Right Sumz?"

"They're playin' Santa Claus," Troy said, grinning. "They went to get the presents. They're bringing everything back here so we can all have Christmas together, right here. I think the nurses are going to make an exception and let the little ones in, as long as the baby's in the nursery.''

But Mirabella wasn't listening. She was gazing at Summer, who was glowing a bright rosy pink, and for some reason looking guilty as sin. ''Sumz...?'' she said on a rising note of accusation. ''You do—you have a secret, I can tell. Come on—what are you keeping from us now?''

Her flush deepening, Summer threw up her hands. ''Oh, for heaven's sake, I was just going to wait for Riley. We were going to tell everybody today anyway....''

''Summer!'' cried Mirabella, her hand going to her own burgeoning belly. ''Are you going to tell us you're *pregnant?*''

''Oh, Lordy,'' said Troy, ''here we go again.''

In the midst of the laughter and hugs and congratulations, a nurse came in and had to knock on the door to get their attention. ''I thought you'd want to know,'' she said with a smile. ''I just got a call from upstairs. Your sister's awake. You can go see her now, if you want to.''

Mirabella was heading for the door before the nurse had even finished, but Summer stopped her with a firm but gentle hand on her arm. ''Jake's been waiting all night—he wouldn't even leave her to go get something to eat. I think we should let him have some time with her first. Don't you?''

''Yeah, okay, you're right.'' Mirabella sighed. But it was a happy sigh, and after a moment she turned and put her arms around her tall, slender sister, and hugged her.

Eve opened her eyes in the hospital's perpetual twilight and knew at once that she wasn't alone....

''We have to stop meeting like this,'' she said in a slurred voice to the man who sat beside her on the bed, with her hand gently sandwiched in his. His answering chuckle was like music, the sweetest she'd ever heard.

"How are you feeling?" His voice was cracked and gut-tural, and in a way, that was sweet music, too.

She drew a careful breath. "I don't know. How *am* I feel-ing? Glad to be alive, I guess. Glad you're here. Otherwise I feel bloody awful, if you wanna know the truth." She licked her lips. "This was a whole lot more fun when it was make-believe."

Jake leaned over to pick up a plastic water cup from the bedside stand. "That make-believe probably saved your life," he said gruffly as he guided the straw—and it was the bendy kind—to her lips. "I guess if you're going to be in a car wreck, it doesn't hurt to be wearing a cervical collar."

She started to laugh, then winced. "*Ooh!* Is that ironic, or what?"

"Ironic…" said Jake. "Yeah." He shifted his gaze to the heavy blue contraption that encased her right leg from her hip to her toes. "Broken legs mend."

"Broken leg…is that what I have?"

"Uh-huh…and some bruised ribs, a few scrapes. Oh—and a concussion—a real one, this time. But not too bad."

"What about…?" Her voice was soft, and not too steady.

And it was Jake's turn to draw a careful breath. "Rick's dead. Sergei wasn't hurt too badly. They patched him up, and he's in jail where he belongs."

"And…Sonny? Did you get him?"

His laugh was the old kind, a breathy snort. "Talk about irony—the guy crawled out of the wreck and walked away without a scratch. They found him this morning, about a mile from the crash. He'd ditched the disk…"

"Oh, no!"

He reached for her hand and gathered it once more into both of his. Above them his eyes were obsidian, bright and hard. "Don't worry, we'll find it. And even if we don't, Sergei's decided he'd like to avoid his friends in the Russian Mafia, if at all possible. He's singing like a bird. Probably end up in Witness Protection. Cisneros will die in prison—guaranteed.''

"So," Eve whispered after a moment, "it really is...over?"

"Yeah, it's really over."

"I mean, is it over...for *you?*"

He leaned over and gently, carefully kissed her lips. His breath warmed them as he said in a shaken growl, "I'm on my way to being whole and healthy...if you still want me."

"I want you." She sounded fragile, almost childlike. "Any way."

"Are you sure? God knows, I'm no saint."

"Who in the world wants a saint?" And the rasp of his whiskers on her cheek was the sweetest caress she'd ever known.

After a few minutes, though, she drew back from him, wiping her eyes. "It's Christmas, isn't it? Is everyone—"

"They're all here. Oh, Lord—" and he snapped his fingers and closed his eyes in chagrin "—I forgot to tell you. Charly had her baby—a little girl. Your sisters are probably with her right now, but they'll be in here as soon as they know you're awake. Your family's bringing Christmas here, to you and Charly. Riley and Jimmy Joe were heading back to get all the presents."

Eve closed her eyes and gave a prolonged sniff. "Your present..." she whispered after a pause. "I guess I'm not going to get to give it to you. I was working on it when...everything happened. I didn't get a chance to finish it."

"Oh, hell..."

"No, it was kind of special, actually. I'd had my boss send copies of the master tapes to Summer—you know, of that piece on blues musicians? I was making a special cut for you...."

"You can give it to me later," he whispered, both touched and stricken. Because he had nothing at all to give her.

He'd thought about it—what to give Eve for Christmas. Thought about it so hard, it had kept him awake nights. First, he'd think about that pearl choker Cisneros had given her, and then he'd think about what Birdie had told him about the gift not being important as long as it came from the right person. Then he'd wonder what in the world made him think he *was* the right person...for her?

The truth was, they were day and night—she was brightness, sunshine, warmth, laughter, gaiety, fresh air; he was dark and moody a lot of the time. Often he worked in an atmosphere of secrecy and danger. He didn't smile nearly enough—all his friends said so. What made him think someone as rare and beautiful as Eve Waskowitz could ever be happy...with him? He'd tried and tried to think of just the right gift to give her, just to prove he *could* make her happy. But each idea he'd come up with, he'd discarded.

Now here it was, Christmas morning. Heartsick, he opened his mouth to tell her the truth—that he had nothing whatsoever to give her. But before he could say a word, she gasped, *"Jake—"*

Thinking she was in pain, he bent over her, heart pounding. Her face was turned toward the window, where the sun, breaking through clouds, had just touched the frozen land with gold.

"Oh, Jake...*look.*" There, outside the window, a spider's web left from summer sparkled and shimmered in the sunlight...a web woven of diamonds. "Did you ever see anything so beautiful?"

But his throat had closed. How could he answer her? He needed just one more miracle.

And he got it. He laughed out loud, and in a voice vibrant with unheralded joy and sudden understanding, said, "Hey,

Waskowitz, what do you think? I ordered it just for you. Merry Christmas…''

She stared at him, eyes bright with tears and dawning wonder. And then she smiled with such radiance, it all but stopped his breath, as she murmured, ''Oh Jake, it's perfect, the most wonderful gift you could possibly have given me.''

He kissed her tear-wet and trembling lips, and with infinite care, stretched himself alongside her in her hospital bed. They lay together, holding hands and watching the jeweled spider's web dance and sparkle in the morning breeze, until Mirabella and Summer and the rest of the family came to join them.

Epilogue

Eve's second wedding took place in early spring, in the gardens on the estate of her sister and brother-in-law, Summer and Riley Grogan. It was a most untraditional wedding, in many ways.

For one thing, the bride was on crutches, and wore a bulky blue cast on her right leg.

"But that's tradition," Mirabella pointed out. "It's something blue."

Yes, and her dress *was* borrowed—from her sister Summer—Eve having declared that she'd spent enough on her first wedding gown to finance the economy of a small Third World country. And yes, she did wear something old—a pearl necklace, not a three-strand choker of perfectly matched pearls with a diamond clasp, but a modest single strand Jake's father had given to his mother on their thirtieth wedding anniversary.

As for something new…

Well, there was her new family, of course—Jake's mother

and father, his sister Rhonda and her fireman husband, Ted, and their two well-behaved little boys, who had escaped a late-March snowstorm in the northeast to come and tell her with their smiles and hugs how happy they were to welcome her as a part of Jake's family. And there were new friends, too—Birdie Poole and his wife, Margie, and their kids, as proud and pleased as if they'd engineered the whole thing.

And the tiny being growing deep inside her was new, but for the time being it was her secret...hers and Jake's. It would be the last secret in the Waskowitz family, Eve vowed.

The Sisters Waskowitz. Eve was certain no bride had ever had a more unconventional trio of bridesmaids: Bella and Charly, both juggling babies, burp cloths spread over their shoulders, and Summer visibly pregnant. And then there was Helen the flower girl, in her Marvin the Martian sneakers, and the Chihuahua, Beatle, dancing like a pixie around their feet.

And here was Jake, his somber dark eyes gazing into hers with so much love, it almost took her breath away. As a blues harmonica played hauntingly, they pledged to each other from their hearts the vows they'd written together, based in part on something Jake had told her that Birdie had once said to him.

"...To always take care of each other...to be to each other a mate, a partner and best friend...and to never let a day go by without letting you know how much I love you..."

Could any wedding, Eve wondered, be more perfect? More *right*...for her? This was her family, the people she loved more than life, and who loved her, as she was, with all her faults.

It was a day filled with sunshine and flowers and bursting with new life and promise, a day so lovely, it made her heart ache and tears spring to her eyes. For a moment, just a moment, she felt a twinge of the old sadness.

But then Jake looked into her eyes and squeezed her hand

and smiled his rare and wonderful smile, and she knew that now *he* would be there to share it with her. That the "wild lonelies" were gone forever.

And that at last, after a lifetime of searching, she had found in him her Place of Belonging.

* * * * *